THE AUTHOR

Don Llewellyn has been described as a natural story-teller but the truth is he has honed his skills over many years. As a film editor he achieved recognition for his work in some of the hardest areas of competition gaining prizes at various European Film Festivals including Cannes, Milan, Trento and Budapest. His later successes as a director included a gold medal at the New York International TV and Film Festival for *Survival of the Fittest* and a BAFTA Cymru award for *Trailblazers*.

Now retired from the media world, Don has been busy recording what he has learned about past times in his locality. He produces *The Garth Domain*, for which he has written millions of words in 60 editions of the 44 page magazine.

Don's first novel, *The Kissing Gate*, published in 2009, received much praise and is still obtainable from Gwasg Dinefwr Press. *Flight of the Cuckoo* is another product of his deep interest in local history.

FLIGHT OF THE CUCKOO

Don Llewellyn

Despair guided the lives of many; but there was hope – inspired by an awakening social conscience and the honourable efforts of the thinking classes – for this was the Age of Enlightenment.

CYHOEDDWYR
DINEFWR
PUBLISHERS

Copyright © 2013 Don Llewellyn

Published in 2013 by
Dinefwr Publishers
Rawlings Road, Llandybie
Carmarthenshire, SA18 3YD

The right of Don Llewellyn to be identified as the Author
of the Work has been asserted by him in accordance with the
Copyright, Designs and Patents Act 1988.

ISBN 978-1-904323-28-0

A CIP catalogue record for this book
is available from the British Library.

Printed and bound in Wales by
Dinefwr Press Ltd.
Rawlings Road, Llandybie
Carmarthenshire, SA18 3YD

For Ceri

Chapter One

Catharine Griffith tightened her grip on her mother's hand as they neared the edge of the stream. About them was a sea of wood anemones and the air was filled with the combined fragrances of wild garlic and honeysuckle. It was easy even for a little girl to know that this was late springtime for that is how it was described the last time she had a birthday. She would always thereafter associate the anniversary of her entry into the world with primroses, bluebells and the call of the cuckoo.

Today, in the month of April 1766, she had become six years old and felt she knew nearly everything there was to know about life. There was the house she lived in; there was the farm where her beautiful mother toiled from dawn to sundown; then there was the church to which they walked weekly to hear sermons that told of Heaven and Hell, Glory and Damnation.

It was to the church that they were now heading for the early morning service. The reason for caution was the fact that on a previous occasion she had lost hold of her mother's hand and had fallen into the swirling waters swollen by a rainstorm.

One by one their feet found the stepping-stones and on reaching the far bank Catharine's mother gave her a triumphant hug.

They paused amidst the faithful outside the little church at Llanilltern before they entered to take their places on pews at the rear of the nave where the common folk sat. The curate, the Reverend Garmon Rees, conducted a service which left those present in no doubt as to the fate that awaits the ungodly at the end of their lives. Wrongdoers would be punished with unspeakable tortures – but the righteous would be rewarded with everlasting bliss.

Catharine did not understand all of the clergyman's grave words but she listened intently.

'It behoves each of us,' said the curate, in sombre, almost sepulchral tones, 'to heed the word of the Omnipotent One . . . for come the day of reckoning we shall all have to face His supreme judgement.'

As he spoke, the cleric was leaning forward in the pulpit and Catharine for a fleeting moment seemed to catch his direct gaze.

The little girl's young mind accepted what the clergyman was saying as the ultimate truth; it would be some time before she developed her own views about good and evil, right and wrong.

At the end of every service the curate thanked local families for attending, including the Thomases of Penyboidy, the Jenkinses of Trenewydd, the Williamses of Llanfair, and the Prices of Parc, whose home a mile away was known to everyone for its connection with 'crime and punishment'. The curate couldn't have known that the Prices and a few others would soon be transferring their allegiance to the Independent chapel called Taihirion, recently built a few hundred yards away. The tiny church of St Elldeyrn, however, would go on serving the spiritual needs of the mainly farming folk who had observed their devotions there for countless generations.

As they came out of the church, together with other poor parishioners, Mary and her daughter moved instinctively away from the well-heeled. After saying their farewells they quickened their pace for there was much work to be done at Pantycelyn Farm where Mary toiled hard to earn enough money to keep them both alive.

In the distance they could see a group making their way across the fields from that other house of worship.

'Why don't those people come to *our* church?' asked Catharine, as they walked. 'Are they bad people?'

'No, no,' her mother responded quickly. 'They just worship in a different way.'

'I wonder where *bad* people go' thought Catharine for a moment. She wondered why anybody would want to leave St Elldeyrn's, for it was a beautiful place; everybody loved the curate and the worshippers were mostly gentle, warm-hearted folk.

On hearing the arrival of Mary and her little girl the hogs in the pens of Pantycelyn were squealing with hunger and knocking each other over as they fought to be first in line to be fed. Some order was restored when the troughs were filled with slops and waste from the farmhouse kitchen and Mary moved on to the next task. Twelve milking cows were already waiting in the corner of the meadow known as Cae Crwn, their udders looking as if they were about to explode. Catharine opened the gate and let them into the yard. The animals proceeded to the milking shed where, without fail each beast went to its personal bay and immediately began to consume the bundle of hay that had been placed there by the mother and her child before they left for the church.

As Mary, sitting on a tiny stool, relieved each cow of its morning quota of milk, she taught Catharine how to grip the teat and exert gentle pressure by squeezing it firstly between index finger and thumb and then with the others in turn. The little girl would take over and in no time, even with her small hands, she mastered this most ancient of rustic crafts. With Mary carrying full pails on a yoke about her shoulders and Catharine struggling with a pewter jug, they made several journeys to the dairy house where Mrs Pritchard, the farmer's wife stood at the door with arms folded wearing on her face an expression that spelt impatience and no little disdain. As the two weary workers went past her on their first visit to the dairy, she said sourly, in an attempt at English:

'Slower than snails it is you are. It's the whip that wretches like you do need annassafact.'

Each time they returned with more milk there was another cruel comment. However, Mary refused to be riled and simply winced. Although she understood not a word, Catharine, on the other hand, felt a surge of hatred rising inside her and was already planning retribution when she would be old enough and big enough to right what she saw as wrongs against her wonderful mother. As they poured milk from the pails into large wooden churns, the woman she had heard described as *'gwrach y fro'* (hag of the vale) continued her diatribe:

'Get on with it, thou misbarel westrals of low order!'

Addressing Mary directly, she added, 'thou art worse than the whore who bringed you into the world and deservin' of nought.'

Then, turning to the little girl, now clutching her mother's hand tightly, the hag continued, 'and were't thou a boy yud soon be down the bell-pits naked and diggin for yur life and die-in before thou reachest ten year!'

Holding a milk paddle in the air as if it were a battleaxe, she drove the pair out of the dairy, telling them to hasten to their next tasks for there was much to do before they would be allowed to go home.

In minutes mother and daughter were putting the milkers back into the meadow. Then they loaded a push cart with hay from the barn and made their way to the field where half a dozen oxen were lumbering by the gate obviously concerned that their daily ration had not yet arrived. With pitchforks (one long and one short) the pair went among the oxen scattering hay which the big clumsy creatures began to devour like huge eating machines. Both mother and child were pleased to see that task completed. It wasn't the oxen's heavy bodies which sometimes brushed against her as they moved around that scared Catharine; it was the immense horns curving out of their enormous heads, swishing like cutlasses through the air as they turned from one side to the other.

From the fields they returned to the yard where they sat at a bench and consumed a bowl each of oatmeal, begrudgingly provided by the farmer's wife. Mary's wages were three shillings weekly with minimal meals each day. Although her facial expressions spoke otherwise, the hag was happy with this arrangement for it exempted her and her husband from paying a portion of the parish rate.

Despite her exhaustion, Mary engaged her daughter in bright conversation whilst they sat for a few minutes' respite before returning to their tasks.

Catharine, looking tenderly at her mother, asked her what games she played when she was a little girl.

'Lovely games like hide and seek – and we had things like Jacob's ladder and cup and ball . . . and hoop and stick just like you have at home,' said Mary, putting her hand gently on Catharine's shoulder.

'Oh and I had two rag dolls . . . I called them my twins!'

'Did you work as well?' asked her wide-eyed daughter.

'Well that's how I learned to churn butter and to kill and feather geese and chickens.'

Her last remark reminded her that they had more work to do. After washing down the rest of the porridge with the tankard of milk they shared, mother and daughter went on to their next labours.

Several hours later they were still working strenuously. Mary had scythed the grass verges of the lane to the rickyard and trimmed the hedge alongside. She and Catharine had scattered chicken corn in the yard by the hen house and collected eggs from all around. Catharine found the warm eggs comforting as she clasped them one at a time in her tiny hands and took them to her mother whose wicker basket quickly filled.

When the afternoon's milking had been completed a mass of cow-dung was cleared from the byre and heaped in a corner of the yard. Mary was flagging even before she started the sawing and chopping of firewood. This, the hardest work of the day, still awaited them, yet the little girl noticed that sweat was already running down her mother's face as she frequently pulled back a wisp of her black hair from her forehead. Mary spent two hours sawing logs and now proceeded to split them. Catharine watched as her mother skillfully swung the axe and the pile of blocks behind her grew into a mountain of firewood.

The sun was setting over the oak ridge above Cae Crwn when the farmhouse door opened and instead of the wicked witch, her husband Amos Pritchard emerged. He crossed the cobbled yard and in the kindest of tones addressed Mary in their native language.

'My dear girl,' he said, 'you look so spent, you must cease work now. Take your little one home, sleep well and return refreshed tomorrow.'

Amos Pritchard was one of the congregation at the new chapel, Taihirion. He had been away all day at Cowbridge market.

Mother and daughter trudged homewards wearily and on arrival at their tiny single-story thatched cottage, Mary flopped onto her bed which took up most of the space along the far wall and stretched out full length. Catharine knelt at the side of her own wooden cot and with hands clasped, prayed to the Good Lord above. As she asked the Almighty to make life easier and better for the mother she adored, tears began to trickle down her cheeks. After she had said the customary 'amen' she turned to her mother and asked, *'Mam, beth yw hŵr?'* (what is a whore?) . . . but her mother was already asleep.

Catharine could not remember her father. Hywel Griffith was born in the cottage she knew so well; so had his own father and his grandfather. It stood on land which had originally been part of the Mathew estate from the days of the old Manor of Radyr and Pentyrch. There was enough ground to raise a few livestock and also to produce enough vegetables to sustain a small family. Mary and Hywel worked with great zeal to develop the holding and their future prospects looked promising when the family suffered a major blow.

Before his daughter was a year old, Hywel had been pressed into service with the King's Navy and was whisked off somewhere far across the seas. Catharine's mother told her many times how it had happened.

It was now five years past but Mary could recall every detail of the event. With a number of folk from the Llanilltern area she, her husband and their three daughters, went along the turnpike towards Ely to see a procession organised to celebrate the accession to the throne of the new monarch, George the Third.

They stood outside the Dusty Forge Inn and were enthralled to see long low carts carrying caged exotic animals. Alongside each vehicle harlequins and clowns danced their way forward to the music of various bands as constables and other law officers scoured the crowd for potential troublemakers. Huge playing cards depicting Kings, Queens, Knaves and Jokers were attached to men walking on stilts. Jugglers, tumblers and fire-eaters went by to cheers of approval, but it was the next group that moved the onlookers to applaud most enthusiastically. A detachment of the Glamorgan Militia was marching in formation to the sound of penny whistle and drum. Their uniforms were crisp and clean, each man holding his musket at an exactly similar angle over his shoulder and not daring to make eye contact with relatives in the throng who were waving wildly and proudly. As they went by, the soldiers' arms were swinging with metronomic precision.

Such was the impact of the marching militiamen on their visual senses, the crowd, now ecstatic with this rare experience of colour and pomp, hardly noticed the last group go by. They were not part of the organised procession but the twenty pigtailed men wearing woollen shirts with black and white hoops and cocked hats seemed to have a sense of purpose as they passed. They occasionally glanced at the crowd that lined the roadside. Hywel could swear that they were all looking him directly in the eye and he told Mary so.

Fearing the worst they left the proceedings early and used a short cut across Plymouth Woods before emerging at the lane that would take them to Llanilltern and their home. The narrow footpath was near the site of the Battle of St Fagans which had happened more than a century previously and had taken hundreds of young lives. No time now to ponder the stories of ghosts of the fighting men that were said to haunt the wood. Hywel felt in his bones that the navy gang was after him. Confirmation of this came when he stepped down from the stile less than fifty yards from his cottage. A group of burly sailors leaped out of the nearby bushes and as he was forcibly led away he was shouting to Mary telling her to look after their children and that he would be back one day and all would be well. Well, it was not. Mary would never see her husband again.

Before Catharine was born, her brother, twelve years older, had gone away to work in Brecon and the family lost touch with

14

him. She was still only a baby when her sisters aged twelve and eleven went to become live-in servants at big houses in the Vale of Glamorgan; she would never have older siblings at home again. Mary tried not to show it but she cried nightly over the loss of the young ones and their father from the home and the hearth.

The daily events in the life of the young Catharine followed a regular pattern. During hours of hard work at the farm the caustic commands from Mrs Pritchard and gestures of kindness from her saintly husband gave Catharine a good grounding in the vagaries of human nature and she quickly came to understand that life was brimful of challenges. There were families that had suffered even more than hers. She had known three or four children of her own age who would never again play with her. They used to roll their hoops down the slope in the lane to Lanfair House and they would all shriek with laughter when old Daio came out to pretend to chase them away with his stick. The fever came and took them away. She missed their laughter.

*   *   *

The daily drudgery continued and Catharine wondered now that she was ten herself would she soon be sent away to work like her sisters. There had also been nightmares about being sent up the dirty chimneys the hag had talked about but so far she seemed to be safe from all that.

Mother and daughter returned home after a typical day at Pantycelyn and, as usual, they both fell exhausted upon their respective beds. Catharine awoke amid the darkness of the early morning hours. She walked to the glassless window and looked at the night sky. The only illumination was offered by the full moon peering intermittently from behind fast moving clouds.

Turning to look at her mother's bed she realised that she had been awakened by her groaning and her calling out of her husband's name.

'O Hywel, Hywel, ble wyt ti 'nghariad i?' (O Howell, Howell, where are you my blessed love?) Her chest was heaving.

Catharine could see that her mother was gripping the woollen blanket so tightly her knuckles appeared to be bursting out of the skin on her hands.

Eventually, Mary opened her eyes wide and looking straight at her daughter, said, *'O Catrin, fy merch annwyl'* (my dear daughter Catharine) *'dishgwl ar ôl dy hunan'* (look after yourself).

Then she stopped moving and Catharine ran and ran and didn't stop until she reached Pantycelyn farmhouse and hammered on the door. The door squeaked open and Mrs Pritchard stood there. Holding a lantern above her head she shouted over her shoulder to her husband: *'Wyras y drwmpan sy 'ma. Beth alla'i wneud?'* (The whore's granddaughter is here, what shall I do?)

As Mr Pritchard appeared in the shadows Catharine blurted: *'Mae fy mam yn ffaelu symud'* ('my mother has stopped moving').

Amos Pritchard arrived at the cottage quickly and when Catharine who followed him got there, he was already coming out of the house and closing the door behind him. 'It's the fever,' he said. 'Your poor mother is the seventh in the parish to leave us since last Tuesday.'

Following the loss of her mother, Catharine had been taken, unhappily, into the bosom of a family at a large house, Plas Tyllgoed on the Fairwater Road. Purpose-built workhouses were being introduced elsewhere following acts of parliament in a genuine attempt to help the needy and to prevent irresponsible claims on a parish's poor rate. There were plans for such a scheme to relieve the poverty-stricken of the Llantrisant area but so far, on the eastern boundary of Cardiff there would be no such relief for some time. A few entrepreneurial families began to see a way of diverting some of the parish poor fund under the guise of charitable endeavour on behalf of the hopelessly destitute.

The Rev. Garmon Rees, curate of Llanilltern, out of genuine concern had requested that Catharine be taken in by the apparently benevolent Mathews family of Plas Tyllgoed. She would now begin a new life among half a dozen or so strangers ranging in age from six to sixty. With an outward show of compassion Martha Mathews promised to care for 'this tragic waif' with all the loving attention she would need. Mostly such places were havens of kindness but this one proved to be an exception. The wily woman waved goodbye to the curate who had brought Catharine to the door and then, gripping her arm tightly, led the girl inside the house.

Catharine took an instant dislike to the place and its proprietor. She was sure that this snarling witch-like woman would make her labour hard for her food and bed. She came to wonder if this was one of those places she had heard about called Houses of Correction – establishments for punishment and reform of the wicked poor. She ran away twice from Plas Tyllgoed and was beaten both times even more severely than the weekly thrashing she was having. She had no one to turn to for help and she wept until there were no tears left.

Catharine's daily tasks were in the preparation of food for her fellows who went out to work on farms and came back late each day. Year after year she toiled in a state of despair and blocked out of her mind any hopes she might have had of a permanent escape from the establishment.

The benefits of that nightmarish domicile were few, but one priceless privilege given to Catharine, albeit unwittingly, was the means of learning some of the English spoken under that roof. Catharine quickly absorbed what was known as *'yr iaith fain'* (the thin tongue) and although much of her vocabulary had, at first, a surfeit of ugly curses and threatening expressions, she slowly came to be reasonably fluent and to like the language very much. Even though she would always regard Welsh as her first and favourite means of communication, she felt sure she would never regret learning some of the Saxon's tongue. The daily grind in that house would have been unbearable whatever the language spoken.

* * *

Four years to the day her mother died Catharine had a message from a surly Martha Mathews to put aside the soup stirrer that had made her arms ache from turning heavy gruel simmering in a cauldron for the past hour on one of the open fires of the house. She was summoned to the front door where a handsome bright-eyed smiling man with skin tanned brown was waiting. He removed his tricorn hat and bowed as he beckoned her to go to him. A combination of intelligent deduction and her faith in dreams told her this was her father. He picked her up in his strong arms and when she kissed him on his cheek she tasted the salty tears that were now running down his face.

'We are going home' he said as they walked away. 'The cottage is still ours . . . I have checked with Mr Price and although it has been neglected for years it won't take me long to get it into shape. I have enough money now to buy a cow and perhaps a pig . . . even half a dozen sheep; chickens too.'

Catharine wondered if this was another dream among the many she had experienced lately, but the row of houses near Fairwater Green looked real enough, with wisps of wood smoke, as ever, curling from their chimneys into the blue sky.

She saw, too, St Fagans church, where a crowd was gathering for a wedding. Most convincing of all was seeing the gambo that went by with Amos Pritchard at the reins and his miserable hag of a wife sitting on the hayload behind him.

'*Helo Catrin*,' shouted Amos, '*Croeso'n ôl*' (Welcome back). Catharine gave a little wave; the sourpuss on the hay simply spat out something onto the road.

Hywel went on speaking to his daughter who was now looking up to him with nothing less than adoration. 'I heard about your mam from Dan Abraham when we met in Calais. He'd been pressed into service too but wasn't much vexed because his wife and his two sons had already died of the fever.' At this point he gave Catharine another hug.

When they arrived at the cottage Catharine could see that her father had already put the place in order. She had not seen it for over half her lifetime but it was not easy to get out of her mind the image of her mother lying lifeless on the bed.

Life took a happy turn when her father came home. It was a pleasure again to get up in the morning and breathe the fresh air. Hywel quickly built up his small holding into a place that would easily sustain them both. Catharine herself was going daily to Parc where their landlord, Samuel Price, lived, and his fellow local Justices of the Peace met and made their life-changing decisions. There she did various jobs as a general servant with both indoor and outdoor duties. Thus she quickly became familiar with the old mansion; every room in fact. Mr Price and his wife, Catherine (known to all as 'Madam Price'), were very kind, thoughtful people.

Time started to pass more quickly than ever and before she knew it, Catharine Griffith was fifteen years old. She knew it was birthday time again for violets were getting ready to peep out from behind stalks of grass on hedgerow banks; the bluebell carpet was appearing in the wood whilst sorrel and celandine competed for the shafts of sunlight coming through the trees. The final proof was the lone cuckoo calling from somewhere down in the valley.

Catharine was now the happiest she had ever been; hence she was singing a bright song whilst she washed linen from Parc in the brook one day. She sat on the bank of the stream dipping cotton clothes into the water and removing stubborn dirt marks from the fabric with her favourite rubbing pebble.

At such moments her thoughts often took her back over the events of her life and always there was a recurring theme in her musings. It was an ever present feeling about what she regarded as injustice. She wasn't at all sure of the cause of all the unfairness that seemed to follow her and her family but she constantly wondered if anything could be done about it. She didn't know it yet but she lived in a revolutionary age when injustice was being confronted by greatly differing forces in many parts of the world.

As she pushed the hand cart laden with basketfuls of washed linen up the drive towards Parc, she noticed that a coach had arrived and was standing on the forecourt of the house. A steaming cob was being unhitched from the shafts and led away to the stables. Clearly someone of importance had arrived, for both Samuel Price and his wife had come out to greet them. There were smiles and handshakes, hugs and kisses before the visitor, a tall man dressed predominantly in black but with white breeches and a green cravat, accepted their invitation to enter the house.

Dr Richard Price, one of the greatest philosophers of his day had come to see his brother Samuel for the first time in more than ten years. They had corresponded but Richard's work kept him in London, a prisoner of his own talents. There were people in England's capital who would have wished him away from there because he was not in tune with their political views – especially with regard to the treatment of the colonies.

The trouble brewing in America was Britain's greatest concern, and those who shared Dr Price's views were thought to be vile traitors. The Welsh philosopher was in fact years ahead of most political analysts; his beliefs were similar to those of Thomas Paine and a few others. The opinions he expressed in letters to his friend Benjamin Franklin in America impressed thinkers across the Atlantic to such an extent he would eventually be invited to become a citizen of the new republic. There is no doubt that Thomas Jefferson drew hugely from *his* correspondence with Richard Price when composing the wordage for the Declaration of Independence.

The Welsh sage was earning a reputation on other fronts too. A brilliant mathematician, he created the most advanced and reliable actuarial tables for use in calculating risk factors of concern to Life Assurance Companies and other financial bodies.

Today, though, at Parc, only brief reference was made to these subjects for the brothers were anxious to talk about the rest of their family back at Tynton, in the parish of Llangeinor near Bridgend, where their father had been a well-known Dissenting Minister. Richard had moved to London when his parents died and in his thirties received much praise for his work, *Review of the Principal Questions and Difficulties in Morals.* He continued writing and in 1765 was elected a Fellow of the Royal Society.

His *Observations on Reversionary Payments* astonished great mathematicians of the day. However it was for his *Observations on the Nature of Civil Liberty* that he would be remembered in America.

Catharine caught the name 'America' as she approached the library. She knew it was a distant land and wondered how far it was beyond Bristol; she had heard soldiers saying they were going to Bristol on their way to America.

When Catharine entered the library where the two men sat talking, she had no idea of the intellectual stature of the man in black, although she remembered that the other servants had talked of their employer having a brother who knew the Prime Minister and other important figures. The young maidservant had been sent in by Madam Price with a silver tray carrying a large coffee pot and china cups. She was told simply to place it on a low table and come out.

By now the men's conversation had moved to local affairs and on her way out of the room the little girl's acute hearing picked out the name 'Pantycelyn' and 'that devilish woman, Hannah Pritchard'.

Catharine realised they were talking about the 'Hag of the Vale', so she promptly stopped in her tracks and stood close to the almost shut door to hear more. She didn't know whether to laugh or cry when it emerged that the vicious woman had been sent to somewhere called 'Bedlam' after a series of incidents that 'defied decent description'. The Welsh spoken by the two men was far removed from the dialect with which Catharine was most familiar, but despite the 'big words' she understood fully the implications of what she had just heard.

The only reason for the subject of Hannah Pritchard being raised at all was because Sam Price had been explaining the dilemmas he faced as Justice of the Peace when some of the offenders brought before him were obviously not in control of their actions because of mental disorders. He had wondered if in these cases it was morally right to treat them as criminals and had sought the opinion of the intellectual giant who was his brother.

Richard's reply to Sam's question was not clearly heard by Catharine apart from a reference to the mental state of England's troubled monarch himself, King George, who was showing signs of incipient madness. It would be a number of years before the King would have to be relieved of his duties but the signs were there and Dr Price was one of the privileged few to have witnessed the problem that no-one dared speak of.

'When should loyalty give way to pragmatism?' said the great philosopher. Catherine would not have understood that even if she had properly heard it.

Each evening Catharine walked home from Parc. Tonight she went past the church at Llanilltern and down the lane towards St y Nill lake and crossed the stream where it entered the woods. As always, she smiled to herself as she saw the spot where she had plunged into the waters all those years ago.

On reaching the stile near her home she saw the light from a single candle in the cottage and moments later she entered through the only door. Grotesque shadows were dancing around the ceiling as the flame flickered in a breeze coming through the window. Her arrival was greeted by a deep 'moo' from the resident cow that lived in the end-part of the house. Her father was sitting on the edge of his bed with his head buried in his hands. Normally he would ask Catharine at this moment about what sort of day it had been for her. He remained silent, and as he slowly raised his head from his hands, Catharine could see, even in the gloom of the badly lit room, that he had been crying.

'*Beth sy'n bod, 'nhad annwyl?*' (Dear father, what is the matter?)

Hywel just sat there, shaking his head.

After a minute he got up from the bed and taking Catharine's hands in his, started to talk.

He explained the difficulties relating to buying and selling the produce of their smallholding. It was all a matter of timing. If a debtor was slow in settling an account, the problem would be passed on to a creditor who if he was the impatient type could make big trouble. The interchange of cattle, milk, eggs, salted pig meat and other farm produce was so fraught with unknown or unpredictable factors that creditors could be turned instantly into debtors themselves and vice versa. Then there was another exercise, probably devised by the Devil himself, that enabled the unscrupulous to take the law into their own hands. It was a ploy that had become the bane of honest folk as far as protection of ownership was concerned and amounted to no less than legalised robbery. This was called distraint, which was the permitted seizure of someone's chattels to enforce settlement of a debt. In practice it was not always the most deserving who benefited.

That very day, Hywel had come in from the fields only to find that the pigs' cots were silent and empty; so was the yard where the hens usually pecked their comical way around, and the gate to the main meadow was open with not a single cow in sight.

'I'm sure I know what's happened,' said Hywel, in a fiercely angry tone, now pacing around the flagstoned floor. 'Watkin Pugh has bought up my three main debts and he'll soon be on his way with our animals to Cowbridge market.'

He guessed this for he had heard of Pugh's reputation and had been warned it might happen.

'What can we do?' asked Catharine, now with her arms around her father's waist.

'I'll think about it,' answered her father quickly, 'down at the Dusty Forge.'

Before Catharine could protest, her father had gone. She was now more forlorn than ever, for although he had not touched any liquor since coming home, he had told her many stories of his life before the mast and his huge capacity for drink in those days. She heard about his escapades aboard ship, also ashore in France, Spain and Portugal. There was the fearful fighting to take the French island of Grenada and a tale too of Morocco where he had been thrown into gaol and rescued by his ship's company . . . not through his captain's kindness but because his presence was needed on a ship because half the crew had either deserted or had been killed in action. Since his homecoming he hadn't needed or wanted strong drink.

Hywel could hear the noise from the tavern long before he arrived there. Noah Penycae was struggling to make his harp audible above the sound of the singing voices, the ribald shouts of drunks and the grotesque laughing of women who were sprawling over everything – including the men.

Hywel was immediately recognised by a couple of his contemporaries, Shinco and Edmwnt, who beckoned to a barmaid to bring him a drink. Hywel declined her offer and pushed away her outstretched arm that held a jug of ale. He indicated that he wanted to talk to his two friends and they joined him outside the tavern door. He quickly told them of his plight and in minutes the three were on their way to Watkin Pugh's large farmstead, Penprysg, on the edge of St Fagan's parish.

Within half an hour they were at the boundary wall. They quickly decided that not only would the cows be the easiest to drive away from the grip of this rustler but they would also be the most valuable. The other creatures could be dealt with the next day when Hywel would come face to face with his tormentor.

There was not much sound coming from the cows in the enclosure apart from occasional lowing and a grunt or two. As they released the catch and opened the gate as quietly as they could, the cows moved out in an orderly group. The animals might have thought they were heading for cowsheds but the three men, each with a stick, guided the beasts out onto the roadway, pointing them in a westerly direction. With luck they would be in Llanilltern in under an hour.

Hywel felt a surge of satisfaction as the cows started moving steadily onwards. His pleasure was short-lived however, for upon hearing his name called from the rear, he turned to see a figure pointing a musket in his direction.

'I've been expecting you,' said the man with the gun. Then a shot rang out and Hywel fell dead.

Chapter Two

Catharine was not allowed to enter Parc on the day Shinco Jenkins and Edmwnt Rees were brought there to go before the Justices. She had no more tears left for she had wept for a whole week after she was told of her father's fate. In the short time she had known him she had loved him intensely and she knew that he was a good man. She had the utmost sympathy for the two friends who had helped her father on that night but neither was married, so there would not be any family complications were they to be pressed into the navy to serve in the Americas. She was not at all sure what their crime was said to have been. After all, if her father's action had been a legitimate attempt to recover what was his own property, then surely his two friends were equally innocent. Catharine Griffith's mind was swimming with unanswered questions about the nature of wrongdoing and the apportionment of blame.

Now she had another serious question to face: the urgent matter of how and where she was going to live. Catharine was still embittered by the blows that life was dealing out to her and she was now more determined than ever to react to the continuing challenges she seemed doomed to face. She owed the memory of her sweet mother a few strokes of reprisal but was always held back by her conscience which was as pure as spring water. However, it was what had happened to her father that was freshest in her mind.

Hywel Griffith was laid to rest at St Fagans in the presence of a score of mourners whose sorrowful voices filled the air around an unmarked grave in the north west corner of the churchyard. Heads were bowed in response to the priest's words which applied equally to the suffering of Jesus and the sacrifice of a young man who would be greatly missed.

Watkin Pugh had been arrested and charged with murder. For once in his life his wealth and influence would be of little help. There may have been inconsistencies in the dispensing of justice from time to time but, by and large, murderers were condemned from the moment they dealt the fatal blow.

Pugh was sentenced to death at the Great Sessions in Brecon and three weeks later, despite his protestations and appeals to his Maker, was taken on a wagon to the gallows at Stalling Down. His hanging was advertised in a news-sheet hurriedly produced in Cowbridge, and on the day of his demise five hundred turned up to bid him goodbye. Few would have known him but witnessing the last throes of the doomed was amongst the most popular of entertainments.

The kind Prices arranged for the Griffith cottage to be let to a young couple and Catharine was taken on as a live-in maid-servant at Parc. She shared a long draughty room in the roof above the stables with the other female servants. Access was by means of a wooden ladder which shook noisily when it was being climbed. Her bed was no more than a woollen blanket thrown over a straw-filled mattress which was losing some of its contents where it was torn.

Catharine Griffith was happy again and had resumed her Sunday visits to church, sometimes to St Fagans but mostly to Llanilltern where the services were in Welsh. Whilst Samuel and Madam Price rode in their trap down to Taihirion, the Independent chapel newly built on land which they had provided, the maids walked together with some of the farm labourers to the church. Strolling along, the lads would always tease the girls – often in a thoroughly bawdy way, making some of the young ones blush and others to squeal with delight. The young men's crudeness would end only after a stern rebuke from a senior maid accompanying them. Catharine and the other girls learned a lot from these sessions for they would hear tales from their male companions about the incidents which had occurred in the local taverns and other places, some of the stories being hardly credible. Catharine found it hard to believe that one young man paid nightly visits to Lady so-and-so and scaled the mansion wall to get to her room; neither could she credit the claim that a local Baptist minister was the father of at least three waifs who were regularly seen begging at the wall of St Fagans Castle.

Catharine also heard gossip on her visits to St Fagans village where she bought sugar, soap, salt, and other household requisites for her employer. Whilst she dutifully completed her shopping, on her way home, she often made a detour to see at close quarters certain houses to which she might return some day with vengeance in mind. In time this train of thought became obsessive, and because she knew it was intrinsically wrong, she hated herself for it, and every night she prayed that the Good Lord would teach her how to forgive fully. Hitherto, however, she was unable to prevent herself from mentally storing a number of wrongs she felt it her duty to put right one day.

At least, in Gwladys Harris, the cook at Parc whom she helped from time to time Catharine had someone to whom she could talk openly about her own confused thoughts. One morning she just blurted it out:

'What's a whore, Gwladys?'

'Ferch annwyl! Dear girl, why should you ask?'

'Well, Hannah Pritchard called my mother the daughter of a whore.'

'Believe me, my little one, your grandmother was not a whore.' The very expressive local Welsh word for whore was *trwmpan* and Gwladys, on using the term might well have spat if they had not been in the scrupulously clean kitchen of the mansion.

'Your mother's mam was a saint, and didn't deserve to be waylaid by that gang of scoundrels on their way home from the cockfighting at Bonvilston. The good woman fought like a wildcat but they overpowered her. Terrible it was.'

Parc had become a House of Justice during the occupancy of the redoubtable former owners, the last one being Morgan Williams, Madam Price's brother. Now in the possession of the Prices it continued in the same role. 'Justice', though, was in one sense a misnomer, for most of the wretches taken there would not have understood the language in which they were being tried. By this time the local gentry had become anglicised even though many could still speak their mother tongue.

The lane to Parc became every second week the route for a procession of alleged criminals. Some looked the part long before they were judged guilty, which was the fate of most. Some had already served custodial sentences and knew what lay ahead of them. These usually had a resigned look about them whereas others were loudly protesting their innocence to the world as soon as they had the big house in their sights.

On these days Catharine would manage to conceal herself near an attic skylight to watch the melancholy march. She would try to guess the nature of their crimes knowing she would learn later from her older colleagues about the sentences meted out. From her window seat she would attempt to identify the few that might be sent on to the higher court that she had heard was called The Assizes. Occasionally she would mentally transpose herself into the position of a criminal charged with some serious crime and wonder how she would react to the severity of her own punishment. These thoughts were sometimes accompanied by a strangely enjoyable guilty thrill as she imagined herself becoming a thief and even worse.

Gwladys the cook was the main informant and her reports never needed embellishment to make them colourful. Later that day when Catharine entered the kitchen Gwladys was half way through her account. She paused from her pastry making and, holding her rolling pin as one would a firearm, she told her colleagues that three men were to be shot:

'Yes indeed, it's musket balls for them. Dead they'll be before they reach the turf.'

On hearing the term 'musket' Catharine's heart missed a beat or two but she was still fascinated by Gwladys's gruesome narrative:

'Two of them were deserters from the militia and the other one had loosed French prisoners who were in his care.'

The others sighed sadly on hearing that for they knew that the last mentioned was a local husband with four youngsters at home.

Gwladys then went into full flow with her next report: 'Terrible whippins it'll be for them three from Fairwater. Them that took the bag of sovrins off Jabez the moneylender in the Dusty. Sixty lashes each they say . . . and the Constable wants to do it himself.'

Catharine tried to imagine Watkin Pugh, if he had been spared his life, receiving a hundred lashes with her having the privilege of wielding the whip!

Gwladys went on: 'Deborah Bevan and her husband Crad are going on a long journey. Yes, a long voyage. God knows where they'll take them. The Americas I expect. Aye, they said what they did was the worst crime of the week. They stole two loaves of bread from the pantry at St Fagans Castle. Caught they were and locked up in Cowbridge. Who is going to look after their little ones . . . only babies they are.'

By the time Gwladys completed the catalogue of crimes it was time for an event to which all the serving staff looked forward. It was the end of the month and Mr Price was due for his bath. Even among the local minor gentry there were several who washed their bodies all over only once a year, if at all, but Samuel Price was the fastidious type who believed in regular bathing. On the last day of every month with an 'r' in its name his tub was filled with steaming water by the maids. They would then retire giggling to the back room to await his call for a chunk of soap or more hot water. After he had scrubbed himself clean, to preserve his modesty he would stand facing the big open fire to await the warm dry cloths brought to him and placed on the floor to his rear. Throughout this exercise his rich baritone voice rang through the whole house as he offered every verse of an old Welsh ballad that recounted the wooing of the prettiest wench in Glamorgan Vale by a soldier returning from war.

All this took place under the fixed gaze of his wife, Catherine, the good Madam Price, who stood in the corner directing the operation. Her spectacles, perched perilously on the end of her nose, and the long, gold-headed cane she always carried gave Madam Price an air of authority that no-one dared deny. In fact, she was a kindly woman who took a great interest in her servants' welfare. Catharine Griffith liked Catherine Price very much.

The cook was the only servant who had a wash all over. This regular quarterly exercise took place in the big barn with Gwladys shouting commands to her helpers as if it was a ceremonial ablution to herald in the four seasons. Although they willingly helped the popular cook, carrying water and rubbing her down with her own dry cloths, Crisly the seamstress, Margaret the laundry-maid, and Lisabeth the scullery-maid all thought washing the body all over was unhealthy. Catharine thought she might try it one day.

The servants at Parc were treated very well by the Prices. Catharine became a 'maid-of-all-work' and soon learned the skills needed for pastry making, floor scrubbing, window cleaning, mending torn clothes and many other duties. She now saw the group of domestics as her 'family' – including the pathetic drudges that were sent from the workhouse to help at busy times. She even had some regard for the male servants who were lodged in the tumbledown sheds behind the pigs' cots – despite their coarseness. She continued to like some of their stories and she often laughed aloud at what they said to the maids.

'What do you think they call 'em fancy-dressed footmen in 'em big 'ouses?' said Jac Evan.

'Tell us Jac.'

'Fart-catchers! . . . that's because they always walk just behind the master or mistress, see.'

Several of the houses of minor gentry in the district employed butlers, valets and footmen. Parc had none of these, although Old Lewis often donned a red coat with twenty brass buttons and walked around as if he owned the whole place. He had no specific duties but as the faithful family retainer, he enjoyed more privileges than anyone. His oversized wig was always slipping out of control and so was his mind.

One moment he might be giving orders to the stable lads to saddle up a horse for an intended journey to Cowbridge Fair and then he would immediately ask to be excused for it was past his bed-time. Everybody loved him.

Cuckoos came and cuckoos went and as Catharine counted her age on her fingers, she felt she was finally saying farewell to childhood. For the first time she began to wonder about her future – about where she would live and with whom. Would she marry? . . . indeed, would there be romance at all?

Once more Catharine heard the cuckoo call and felt the joys of the spring air. The year was 1777 and she was about to begin the busiest year of her life so far. Now seventeen, her body was telling her she was becoming a woman. She often thought about the far off days of her infancy and in her prayers she thanked the Lord for the blessing of growing up in rosy health. Catharine Griffith would not have recognised it but she had also become a strikingly beautiful young woman, her twinkling dark eyes and cheery, pretty smile reflecting a thoroughly likeable inner self. She moved gracefully, and when she turned her head her ample hair fell in black ringlets about her neck and shoulders like the rippling waters of the St y Nill brook she knew so well.

On walks through the wood below Parc, singing softly, Catharine felt at one with the birds above. Hearing the twittering of darting finches and the sweet music of noble warblers somewhere in the thicket, she was sure they were conversing with her. She felt she had an affinity with animals too. Of the mammals that inhabited the copse she loved the red squirrel most. She would wait patiently at the foot of a tree just to obtain a fleeting glimpse of the creature which would hold her gaze with its huge eyes for a full second before scooting off along a branch with the speed of lightning. Among the domesticated stock, she had the softest spot for the donkeys that always came to her and nuzzled her in a display of affection. To her, asses did not deserve their reputation for foolishness; that was an attribute that better fitted a number of humans whom she knew.

Although she was maturing and life was getting easier, the idea of vengeance still occasionally entered her thoughts. She knew it was wrong, for in truth she wasn't naturally vindictive. Despite lasting memories of the hurt she had been caused, Catharine Griffith was developing into a kind and compassionate person. The teachings she had received at the parish church held firm in her head and she was always placing the needs of others before her own. Yet, from time to time she was forced to experience a fleeting pang of guilt as a strange feeling encompassed her whole being after wondering, if only momentarily, what it would be like to be a thief.

She was quite a pet with Madam Price who had made her a 'special' servant with more responsible duties. Their relationship was now akin to that of a young lady and a favourite aunt. Hardly a day went by without Catharine learning something of value from the inspirational mistress of Parc. They would sit for hours in Madam Price's favourite room beyond the library: a haven to which the good lady regularly retired to rest, to read – and to escape the inevitably male-dominated atmosphere of a home forced to double as a courthouse.

It soon became clear that Catharine had an innate talent for needlework and she quickly learned from Madam Price the latest techniques in embroidery. Together they made several samplers with scenes they had created themselves – in Catharine's case usually a young girl and a dashing young man would be depicted – whilst Madam Price's work mostly portrayed roses. Incongruously, wording – normally a required feature of samplers – was conspicuously missing from Catharine's work. There was no doubting however the high artistic standard of her products. Madam Price had carefully taught her the intricacies of both *gros point* and *petit point* stitching with the finest wool and silk as well as gold and silver threads. At other times, lace work occupied their busy hands as plain sheets, pillows, cushions and curtains were transformed into comely though functional items.

In the corner of the room stood a thing of rare beauty. Sturdy but elegant with polished wood giving way here and there to inlaid motifs of polished brass, it was a structure encasing an instrument that made glorious, sensual sounds. In response to the touch of capable hands it could produce heavenly trebles and imposing basses that combined in uplifting harmony. Madam Price was astounded by how quickly Catharine mastered the harpsichord keyboard and created impressively tuneful passages. The young girl was allowed to make music as often as she wished and more than once she was joined in song by Samuel Price himself who would generously compliment her on the sweetness of her voice. Catharine Griffith was rapidly proving she was a young lady of many qualities.

As a child Catharine had been proud to be entrusted to go shopping at St Fagans for groceries. Now she travelled much further afield on Parc business. Would the time be coming soon when she would take flight and see the wider world? She had already been to Cowbridge Fair and Cardiff town. Catharine no longer slept on the flea-ridden bunk in the stable loft. Her bed was now a soft feather-filled mattress in a little room on the same landing as that of her master and mistress.

She often thought about her sisters and wondered what they looked like now, if, indeed, they were still alive. How did *they* feel about growing into womanhood? She thought too about her brother whom she had never seen. Catharine had been given a selection of new clothes by Madam Price and she began to feel that she was being noticed wherever she went.

Life was becoming more interesting for Catharine Griffith. With the freedom of the house she often wandered from room to room taking in the different atmospheres. Madam Price's retreat was best known to her but there was much else to see. The main hall where rogues and rascals were dealt with was somewhat forbidding; the Royal Coat of Arms prominently placed above the wide fireplace imbued the room with grave authority even when unoccupied. She was familiar with the kitchen and its almost perpetual aroma of meat cooking on a spit over the open fire. This would give way on certain days to the heavenly smell of newly baked bread as the *ffwrn* in the sidewall of the fireplace was opened. In the large lounge there was always a slightly dusty, acrid tang hanging on the air and Catharine wondered if it was the result of Madam Price's addiction to snuff and her sneezing spells which lasted for about half an hour each night before it was time to retire.

On entering the library she would sense the masculinity which defined that room without fully understanding it. The few spaces on the book-lined walls were taken up by the portraits of ancestral personages with stern faces and eyes that followed Catharine as she slowly made her way about the room. Hanging in a line from the mantelshelf was a row of clay pipes of differing lengths and on the shelf itself a copper jar which carried a supply of the tobacco which Samuel shared with his friends who came over to talk most evenings. The furniture was sturdy with stout chairs and a heavy desk on which stood a globe of the world, that would, to the illiterate, seem no more than a pretty painted ball.

Also on the desk was an ink pot and a quill pen. Catharine loved quill pens and always marvelled at the skill of those who could produce those lovely shapes on paper by dipping the pointed end of the feather stalk into a pot of black ink and then scrawling what they called words across the page. It amazed Catharine that whereas for her it was just a scrawl, however beautiful, for others it meant sounds and meanings. When she was younger Catharine thought the words actually came out of the goose feather. She had been shown her name entered in English in the parish register at the church and she had many times since attempted to reproduce it on scraps of paper. She had tried to scratch it in the mud in the farmyard, and in the sand on the bank of the brook, failing every time. Her illiteracy was such that she wouldn't have noticed the difference in the spelling of her own Christian name and that of Madam Catherine Price. It was never going to be important though for most used the Welsh form Catrin in speech.

Chapter Three

Several residents of the district met regularly at local inns to partake of the good fare available to those who could afford to part with a penny or two. Most of the farming folk and successful artisans were good Christian men, but a few of those who gathered in the smoking rooms were often reactionary in thought. These would sit at the table or lounge comfortably in reclining chairs whilst ale was poured from a jug into their pewter tankards. They considered themselves a cut above those who populated the public bars and who, in their view, lowered the social tone of the neighbourhood. Yet, the conversation of these self-styled models of excellence, after a dignified start, would often degenerate to a level that would make even the basest ruffian blush. Everything from the behaviour of the monarchy to the state of the colonies would be debated along with the latest news from parliament. From the maudlin to the morbid, every aspect of local life would also come under their scrutiny. Talk of uplifting events would firstly raise their spirits but quickly the gossip would move to utterly depressing reports of fever, suicide, madness and murder. Such talk had been going on at the Plymouth Arms in St Fagans for five hundred years and it wasn't going to cease now.

'A nasty blast blowing up from the west they say. It's sure to flatten my barley.'

'Aye, and rain too. Well, the turnips need it.'

'Cowbridge market has upped the stall licence again. Brought my stock back . . . that's what I did.'

'Take 'em to Llantrisant. They're rough over there but they're fair.'

When the farming talk was exhausted, they moved to other matters.

'I hear that another deserter from our glorious militia has earned the right to have two hundred lashes' said Ioan John of Hendre Mwyndy.

'Deserves a thousand swipes and more,' said Aaron Owen, filling his church warden pipe, 'filthy traitor, that's what that young man is; a rotten egg!'

'He'd come back from America you know, and somebody heard him say he was glad them Yankees won the war.' As he spoke, Gomer Thomas positioned his arms as if he was holding a musket. 'I'd have him shot, myself.'

Heads turned towards the door as Yorath ap Rhys, the doctor from St Georges, came into the lounge in a bustling manner that suggested he couldn't really afford the time to stop for a drink. In fairness, he *was* a busy man, for sickness raged in the area and there were daily deaths . . . sometimes of the middle-aged and older, but mostly of the very young. The discerning might have wondered what percentage of those who died perished as a result of the treatment rather than the malady.

All in one movement Dr Rhys put his bag down, mopped his sweaty brow with the back of his sleeve, and flopped into a chair that had been vacated the moment he was seen to enter the room. He reached out an arm and instantly his personal tankard, frothing with ale, was put into his hand.

Always at this moment, the farmers would allow him to take a gulp of the beer before relating his day's work so far. They loved hearing details of the ravages of disease upon the bodies of his patients; of fits and fevers; of the withering of limbs, festering sores and the goriest of physical injuries. He hadn't had time to wipe the white foam from around his mouth before he was urged to start his recitation of events.

'Well,' he said, using his sleeve again, 'it's been a bad day. Old Shadrach the pigman at Culverhouse left us this morning. He'd have made a hundred next Hallowtide. In his bed for four years he was and the long lingering got him in the end. You should have seen his arms . . . as thin as cords they were and the rest of him was all sores. I don't know what the lice will do now he's gone.'

He stretched his arm again, the common procedure for requesting a refill of a tankard, and a serving wench duly obliged. Another swig, more foam about the mouth and off he went again.

'There was a case of severe ague in Peterstone and next door to that someone who went down with a seizure. Both died before noon and I left both families arguing like mad dogs about the wills before either corpse was cold. Then they found a little boy who was drowned by the waters of the Ely at St Fagans. The villagers had been out all night searching for him. He was trapped in a culvert just this side of the Drope where a stream joins the river. Then it was over to St Andrews to pronounce a little girl of seven dead. Malnutrition that was, sure. As I was leaving that house I could hear the child's mother weeping loudly. She had told me the girl was the last of her three children to die. Her husband was away on sea . . . he had been pressed into the King's Navy.'

There was more to come.

'I was sorely exhausted by now and was slowly riding down Crofft y Genau lane when I was intercepted by a messenger coming down from the direction of Rhydlafar. He was shouting, long before he came alongside me, "Doctor, Doctor – quick as you can to Pentyrch! There's bad fever on a woman there . . . she needs cooling physic now!"'

'I'm the doctor' I said, 'and begging your pardon sir I'll decide what remedy is required. Now where can I get a change of horse?'

'Just here sir, I shouldn't wonder sir, at Rhydlafar Farm. Luther Thomas . . . he's a good man.'

'And so he was, for within a quarter of an hour I was on my way up the long hill to Pentyrch.'

The doctor took out a large handkerchief and wiped his eyes several times before he went on. He was basically a principled and compassionate man even though his experiences had hardened him to withstand the shock of seeing so much suffering.

'I arrived at the cottage on the slopes of the Garth in good time but the woman had already died. I was told she had had a feverish fit about an hour before. She had hugged each of her five young ones and then she screamed out just once before falling flat on her back on her straw bed. Dead.' Dr Rhys got up slowly from his chair, gathered his bag and made for the door, pausing to say:

'It was the sight of those five little ones' faces as they sat around the bed just staring at their mother. Their father is dead too. He fell down a bell-pit last year and broke his skull.'

Yorath Rhys lowered his head and continued quietly: *Fel y dywedodd Iesu,* (as the Good Lord said), *"Gadewch i'r plant bychain ddyfod ataf fi ac na waherddwch hwynt"* ('Suffer little children to come unto me . . . and forbid them not.')

There were a few 'amens' and the customary pause when the good doctor left but before long the men returned to their usual crudeness.

'Did you hear tell of Wilson's bull runnin' amok in Peterstone on the way to Llantrisant Fair Wednesday last?'

As Richard Garnant asked his question he caressed the behind parts of a wench who was pouring his ale. She pulled away sharply only to receive the same treatment from Tomos Dafydd before leaving the room to go for a refill of the ewer.

'Oh aye,' said Twm Twyn yr Odyn, 'I heard about Willie's bull. Damned thing had a fit or somethin'. First it scattered everything that could move in the village, with sheep jumpin' into the Ely and chickens who didn't know they could fly, wingin' it into the trees.'

'Aye, sure,' said Dic Garnant, 'they had to rope it round its privates in the end with four of Wilson's men hangin' on as the animal raced away. Last anybody saw of 'em they was on their way down the lanes to Pendoylan.'

'Iesu Grist,' (Jesus) said Ben Treharne, 'I expect the men ended up in the Red Lion and the bull went among Shanco Tan'rallt's cows in the meadow by the chapel. They must have thought it was their birthday, them cows!'

Will Penyglog who always tried to show his superior knowledge of important matters could be relied upon to change the subject: 'I hear the king has been visited by two doctors who decline to express the truth for fear of ridicule. No doubt they'll send for some Prussian medicine men to tell his courtiers that he's as mad as a Madagascan monkey,' said Will, stretching his legs below the table.

'Aye, they know their own kind . . . and they're not fearful of telling truths, them Germans,' said Dic Bassett.

'God save the King' said Evan Hopkyn, raising his tankard, spilling most of its contents.

The talk then moved to foxhunting – a subject that often entailed bare-faced exaggeration.

'I know there's some big liars around these parts,' said Jac Rhiwperra, 'but did you hear about that pack from the hills coming down last week. They say the chase went twelve miles from the Garth to Wenvoe before Reynard went to ground!'

'Aye indeed,' agreed Isaac Tŷ Du. 'The bounder was torn to pieces down at St Andrews.'

Not all of those involved in tavern talk had a taste for brutal stories involving humans or dumb animals but there were those who seemed to revel in tales of the hideous.

Catharine was fully aware that life had dealt her many privileges as well as tragic set-backs. She often had sessions of self-analysis which in no time at all became self-abhorrence when she looked back at some of the things she had thought of doing in the name of sweet reprisal. In her nightly dreams she continued to act out the role of a petty pilferer and as time passed she felt less guilty. She began to feel that there was a thin line between justifiable vengeance and unacceptable vindictiveness. However, tales she had heard about the abominable cruelties some people suffered, especially children working down bell-pits made her feel that God was smiling on her.

Every day Catharine marvelled at the way that the Prices were going out of their way to be kind to her. She was more like a member of the family now than a servant. She was as eager as ever to please her employers and she didn't hesitate when she was asked to go on an errand to a place she had dreamed of visiting one day.

Bristol had always seemed to her to be at the far end of the world. From the high ground above Parc she had seen large ships in full sail slowly moving up and down the Severn Channel twelve miles or so away. Old Lewis told her they would be either going to or coming from 'Brista', as he called it. Some would be going to 'Americee' and others coming from the southern oceans where the cannibals who liked eating sailors lived. Catharine recalled once going with Old Lewis to a house in Pentyrch called *Brista Fach* (Little Bristol). It was a sort of distribution centre for goods, especially leather, for the east Glamorgan trade. They brought back to Parc a variety of items at the behest of Madam Price who knew everything about what had come over the water.

Catharine had no idea then that she would one day visit the real Bristol. She had heard so much about it that her impending trip filled her with a mixture of curiosity and no little trepidation. Catharine was pleased that she wouldn't be going alone; she would be accompanied by a servant who had come to Parc about a month earlier.

Sarah Phillips who was also seventeen had been in various institutions since she was abandoned by her mother when three months old. She had been left in a wicker basket at the entrance to Raglan Castle and found by a passing tramp who sold her to a man and woman in Abergavenny who wanted to take on a child. Her adoptive parents died in an outbreak of smallpox before she was four years old and she was soon given to a group of women who were long-term inmates of a House of Correction in Newport. The intention was to give the lives of the retired prostitutes some purpose for living. They taught her well. When she left them as a fifteen year old to work in London she took with her all the subtle skills of her guardians' ancient profession. Although she was now back in south Wales, in respectable service for the time being, it was her intention to 'work' Cardiff or some other coastal town in the future.

'I'm known as "Raglan Sal", what's your name?' she asked, as they walked in the direction of Cardiff town.

Each was carrying a sack slung over the shoulder but there the similarity ended. Catharine was wearing clothes which were of much higher quality than Sal's. She wore buckled shoes whereas Sal walked barefoot. They both proceeded with an agile gait and both had pretty faces – although Raglan Sal's showed signs of premature ageing. Before long Catharine would learn the reason for this.

The pair stopped for refreshments at the Dusty Forge on the Cowbridge turnpike two miles from Cardiff town using some of the money that Madam Price had given them for the journey. Catharine's choice was a mug of dandelion and burdock, whilst Raglan Sal had a tankard of strong ale; then another! Sal showed no ill-effects as they continued their journey.

Within twenty minutes they arrived at Cardiff Bridge, a notorious gathering place for what Gwladys the cook had called the 'Ladies of Darkness'. Sal was quick to say that this was where, a while before, someone she had known had been murdered. She was pointing to the spot further down the river where the body of the unfortunate young woman was found on the mudbank when Catharine leaned over the bridge parapet wall and was violently sick.

This was the moment that Catharine Griffith felt she had entered the adult world at last. She feared that there might be a large number of lessons to be learned in the future about human nature. She couldn't possibly have guessed how many lessons there *would* be.

They moved on with Sal supporting the flagging and still nauseated Catharine. As they walked past the ruins of Cardiff Castle some ravens rose from the ivy-covered walls and Catharine, still in a stuporous state, saw them as harbingers of great gloom; their raucous throaty cries seeming to represent a malignant and merciless world without hope. Raglan Sal thought the birds were quite beautiful.

As they neared the wharf on the river bank where the Taff flowed into the *Môr Hafren* (The Severn Sea), they immediately spotted *The Siren*. It was a two–masted schooner which was much bigger than Catharine had expected. It was moored by hawser to the pier that had stood the test of some of the highest tides in the world for half a century. It was motionless but already the deck-hands had started unfurling the sails.

Whilst shadowy figures darted about the deck and others began their perilous climbs up the masts and rigging, there was much whistling from men holding two fingers in their mouths. Others were shouting their commands loudly but few words were understood by the two Welsh wenches. The sailors' language was that of the Saxon, but, no doubt, the terminology was from the nautical vocabulary.

A breeze arose and within an hour the big boat was being slowly eased away from the pier and turned carefully to avoid collision with the dock wall. A small ketch and a sloop went ahead and the schooner duly followed. As soon as they were safely out of the Penarth Road and beyond the Sully Island swells and currents, they headed for the Steep Holm Rock before turning to port and heading upstream for the mouth of the River Avon.

The two young women sat on wooden crates which they noticed contained empty glass bottles. Catharine became fascinated by the on-board activities of both passengers and crew. Raglan Sal took it all in without a blink as if she had seen it all before. Catharine was now beginning to realise that her new friend had gained much experience of the world.

Among the multifarious travellers were people of different colours of skin. Catharine had not seen a single non-white person during her early years at St Fagans and Llanilltern. It was only on arriving at the Cardiff Quay that she had seen a truly black man for the first time. He was carrying a large barrel of something that must have been heavy for he was struggling with it. She remembered thinking that he would have coped more easily without the young white man who was following him closely and raining kicks on his buttocks as he struggled with his gargantuan burden. She was surprised that there was no reaction from the worker to this unreasonable treatment.

Now, on *The Siren*, a bronzed barefoot boy of about ten years old sat in the rigging singing an obscene shanty about sailors and south-sea island women. Catharine wasn't sure she understood the song. Raglan Sal clearly did for she swayed with laughter at every line. Even if she couldn't properly interpret each word, she obviously liked the song's general message.

The captain stood on the deck with his eyes fixed firmly on the expanse of water ahead. He was mouthing inaudible instructions which were passed on to the crew by the loud voice of the first mate who stood alongside his skipper with a telescope seemingly stuck to his eye.

There was a bigger swell out in mid-channel and as Catharine watched the bows of the boat rise and fall she was once again nauseated but this time she had nothing to discharge from her digestive system, so she just hung on and hoped it would soon all be over. Throughout the journey, Sal was quite relaxed; she laughed and joked with the deck hands who were giving her much attention as they went about their duties.

After about ninety minutes on the open sea, their destination became visible: the Avon.

Against the sound of much piping and bosuns' whistles the mouth of the river was cautiously approached. A flotilla of small boats awaited the arrival of the schooner at the jaws of the Avon where furious cross currents could send the ship, as big as it was, crashing onto one of the broad banks of mud.

The timing of the ship's movements had to be perfect with regard to the turning of the tide. The races and rips at the meeting of these two waters could be ferocious. However, busy hands had already been manning the halyards and lowering the sails. Now there was much hurling of coiled ropes and lashing to bollards and before long the ship was being gently towed by dinghies and skiffs up the narrowing river on the incoming tide.

The busy port of Bristol was now to be seen ahead. The masts of a large number of de-rigged ships of all sizes in a network of docks filled the skyline. Because the Avon was an intensely busy river a priority system prevailed. It was necessary for every incoming and outgoing vessel to work to a precise timetable. Hence the smile on the face of The Siren's master as his ship was freed from its attendant towboats and pulled quietly by hawsers ever nearer the jetty which had been allotted to it. The big boat edged to the wharf wall with hardly a crunch as timber met stone and finally became still. The crew tossed their hats triumphantly into the air and cheered.

Catharine looked at Sal. 'All this only to get a couple of bags of sugar,' she said, quietly.

'Sugar? Bloody sugar? Is that all we came for? Bloody sugar? You never told me!'

'You didn't ask,' said Catharine, adopting the manner of the one in charge. She thought that she had been letting her seniority slip a little.

They each paid their shilling to a gruff sailor who was collecting fares in a wooden pail and stepped off the ship onto the gang plank that had been raised.

Then Sal made a puzzling remark.

'Well,' she said, 'that's the last cash I'm parting with today.'

Although Catharine was somewhat bewildered she didn't ask Sal to explain her remark.

On dry ground once more they wobbled a few times before getting their balance and after climbing a high flight of stone steps they were suddenly overcome by surroundings the like of which they had never before encountered. Well, certainly Catharine had not.

All around there were tall buildings with people quickly entering and leaving with bundles of papers or else carrying all manner of bags. Carts, some piled high with wooden boxes or jute sacks rattled over the cobblestones. Flat handcarts with fish of many varieties went by leaving a stench upon the air for a few moments. The aromas changed as the two young women proceeded up a narrow street. Firstly there was a warehouse which, in its doorway, had open barrels full of spices of many kinds. They could identify another building long before they saw it for down the street the heavenly smell of coffee was wafting in almost unbearably delicious waves. Then, an alehouse from which the combined whiff of hops and yeast floated. For a while there were no nice smells to conceal the putrid pong from the roadside gutter down which mounds of human excrement were moving slowly. The offensive stink didn't subside until they passed a workshop where men were varnishing coffins.

'I'm not sure which of the last two smells I liked better,' said Sal, as they went by.

Catharine just shook her head.

'Can I ask you something?' said Sal, stopping Catharine by putting her hand on her shoulder and making her friend face her.

'Go on, ask!'

'Well,' said Raglan Sal, with a sort of mock severity in her voice. 'I don't want to be awkward but where the hell are we going?'

'I thought you'd never ask,' answered Catharine.

'Well, tell me then.'

'I can't.'

'For the sake of Jesus . . . why not?

'Because I don't know!' she tilted her head downwards and went on: 'You see, I've been looking for a sugar factory or something . . . they said it would be along here somewhere. It's got a big clock on the building and there's writing on it.'

'It wouldn't be the Bristol Havana Sugar Refinery would it?

'It would, yes it would.'

'Well, look behind you!'

Catharine did as requested. 'Oh, the clock,' she said, . . . 'it was above our heads all the time.'

'Yes, but look at the writing for Christ's sake!'

'I'm not bad with numbers but I can't really read,' said Catharine, trying hard not to whimper, 'especially English words.'

Sal now knew that her friend was illiterate. She put her arms around Catharine's shoulders and squeezed her tightly. 'I'm sorry, I didn't know,' she said. 'What with you living-in with the nobs I took it for granted, see.'

'How is it that *you* can read then?' asked Catharine, looking at Raglan Sal with renewed interest.

'Well, I've been around a bit.'

'Yes, I can tell that, Sal,' admitted Catharine, and from that moment she knew she was going to learn a lot more from the girl called Raglan Sal.

The pair walked into the refinery and were almost overcome by the heaviness of the air inside the building. There was a strange, sickly and distinctly unpleasant atmosphere – although it didn't affect the workers who were buzzing about the place like hornets. Along the far wall there was a line of pedestals on which cauldrons sat above burning coals, their contents bubbling. The young women were told that cane juice was being boiled to produce sugar in the form that they would be familiar with. At the front of the open building was a gigantic pile of refined sugar packed into cones that reached almost to the ceiling. Catharine remembered that her mother had told her that common folk did not have sugar when she was young but that had all changed now.

A big young man, stripped to the waist, was putting the cones twenty at a time, into the kind of hessian sacks that the two young women had brought with them. They moved nervously towards him (Sal rather less nervously) and asked for their two bags to be filled. Each cone weighed about two lbs so they would be carrying home forty pounds each. They had both been given cash to enable them to pay separately for security reasons. The bags were duly filled and Catharine handed over her two shillings to the man. She was astonished, and very perturbed, to see Sal take him by the arm and walk with him to a partition some distance away. A while later the man returned to attend to the next customer and Raglan Sal, with a look of triumph on her face, indicated to Catharine that they could now leave.

If the worldly Sal of Raglan thought her friend would be indifferent to her behaviour, she was mistaken.

Out on the street, Catharine lost no time in making her feelings felt.

'You are a whore!' she screeched, happy that no-one near them would understand her for they were, as ever, conversing in their own language. And once again the word *'trwmpan'* carried much more venom than 'whore'.

'I am what I am!' shouted Sal, in English, for once, as if she wanted the whole of Bristol to know.

'Now I know why you said that about not needing to spend any more money. You filthy whore!'

'I'm sure you'll change your mind about me one day,' said Sal, quietly, picking up her sack and slinging it onto her slim shoulders.

Catharine shouldered her bag too but she continued to utter oaths regarding her companion as they walked off with their loads down the cobbled roadway.

Just before the street started its final descent to the dockside there was an empty bench where they dropped their bags together and sat down.

After a pause, Raglan Sal, looking at the ground and not once raising her head to catch Catharine's reaction, launched into her life's story. As Catharine heard the details, sometimes pathetic, sometimes gruesome, of Sal's colourful past, she began to feel shame for having attacked her.

When Sal had finished her sorry saga she turned to face her companion.

'Are we still friends?' she asked.

'Yes, and I'll tell you why,' answered Catharine between sniffs. 'I have no right to condemn you for your way of life. It's not for me . . . but I know it goes on everywhere. I used to have nightmares about my grandmother being wrongly called a whore. I never thought I would ever get to sympathise with those of the "night" but you have opened my eyes.'

At this point she took Sal's hand and said with closed eyes: 'There's something I must tell you. I've been planning to be a thief. I dream about it.'

'Uffarn dân!' (Hell-fire), swore Sal, rising to her feet, 'what do you pinch?'

'Well, nothing yet.' Catharine also stood. 'I'll probably take wigs, powder, combs, buttons, kerchiefs, soaps, and lots of other small things . . . always things I can carry. Once I'll have started I don't think I'll be able to stop myself.'

'What about money?' Said Sal. 'Will you purloin money?'

'Oh no, never money, that would be real stealing.'

'Who would you take from?'

'In my dreams it's only those who have offended my family. In real life it would be a satisfying way of getting back at them.'

'I think we are very much alike after all,' said Sal, once more shouldering her bag. Catharine did the same and soon they were off again. Friends.

It was dusk by the time the pair proceeded towards the dock once more. They had each eagerly devoured a large hunk of cheese and bread from the alehouse and drank a tankard of beer. By that time the public house was stinking with the sweat of men from whose mouths came the pungent fumes of rough cider and other pollutant liquids. Lying on the floor of the big bar in pools of urine and vomit were several twitching bodies mostly of women whose clothes were shredded.

Other females, with grotesquely painted faces and low bodices from which bulbous breasts were trying to escape, were snaking their way through a throng of seafarers in the bar openly seeking business.

Catharine and Sal had gone out to eat their food in the guttered street which was only marginally less obnoxious than the bar.

Pointing to the ale-house, Catharine said, 'You have never been as low as those women in there, have you, Sal?'

'Oh, lower, much lower,' said Sal, turning her head away.

There seemed to be nothing more that could be said on that matter so they began to ponder the problem of where they could spend the night. The schooner wouldn't set sail until the morning ebb-tide so they had plenty of time.

'I suppose if I was not here you would walk the street tonight would you Sal?'

'Yes, it's addictive you know. Just like stealing!' Catharine saw the funny side of that and laughed along with Sal.

They arrived at the sea wall and put down their bags. It was as good as anywhere to get an hour or two's sleep, so they gathered some rags that had been discarded nearby and used them as makeshift pillows. To the peaceful sounds of lapping water, and occasional scrapes and squeaks from the woodwork of ships moored the other side of the wall, the tired pair fell into what would be a short-lived snooze.

They were awakened by a mysterious cause. It was something that challenged their auditory senses before touching chords of sympathy within their gradually waking minds. Although they could not immediately identify the actual sound they were sure it was caused by the human voice, or, in this case, voices. The pair looked at each other questioningly and the truth of it faded in. Some distance away, a hundred or more African natives, huddled in the hold of a ship, were humming a sorrowful song. The ship had come from the Cameroons with a variety of commercial goods for Bristol business companies and would now soon be leaving the port with its immensely valuable human cargo. In many cases ships of the trade, having left Bristol in the first place, called back there *en route* to the Americas. The two young women would have no knowledge of the wider implications of the enterprise that had made it possible for them to obtain those cones of sugar for their employer.

Other sounds began to gain supremacy as Catharine and Sal rose to see much activity all around them. Men were carrying kegs of brandy, boxes of cured tobacco, rolls of fabric, nets of potatoes, sheets of leather and crates of all sizes onto *The Siren*. A big man with tattooed arms was waving and pointing vigorously as the items were positioned around the ample deck. The goods were bound for Cardiff where traders would be waiting with greedy anticipation.

They boarded and Sal, despite what she had vowed earlier, paid for both in advance for their return journey. The only occurrence worth noting during the crossing as far as Catharine was concerned was that one of the sailors looked straight at her friend and smiling broadly said, 'You are a Cardiff Bridge girl aren't you?' Raglan Sal placed her finger on her lips to persuade him to be quiet.

The Cardiff Town Quay down river from Cardiff's Westgate was a welcome sight for the intrepid travellers as the boat moved slowly up the Taff. It had been a long day, made even longer by the schooner having been obliged to wait out in the channel for the tide to turn. Now they stepped onto the wharf wall amid a clamour of Welsh voices and felt glad to be home.

There was still some distance to go and off went the pair down the Cowbridge road with their shoulders bent under their loads. As they passed over Cardiff Bridge, Sal ducked her head lower than usual to avoid being recognised by any of the figures who were standing at strategic places, some leaning against the parapet, others standing on the river bank in the shadows of the bridge pillars.

'You needn't have hidden yourself,' said Catharine when they were well beyond the bridge and heading for Canton. 'I now know who and what they are, thanks to you.'

'Well, I didn't want to embarrass you,' said Sal, putting down her bag for a breather.

At that moment it was their very good fortune that Twmos *'troed clwb'* (Tom club foot) came by with a cartload of turnips and was heading for Parc. He stopped and helped them onto the vehicle and they made the rest of the journey sitting on a mound of hard and moving vegetables that bruised their legs. They didn't mind for it saved them carrying the sugar for the last five miles.

At Parc they took their sacks to the foodstore, then Sal went to the servants quarters while Catharine retired to the house where Madam Price wanted to hear every detail of their day in Bristol. Unsurprisingly, Catharine declined to give her *every* detail!

The paths of Catharine Griffith and Raglan Sal didn't often cross in the course of their daily work at Parc but one day the latter was at the well pumping by hand, filling leather water jacks and earthenware pitchers when Catharine walked by on her way to saddle a horse for a shopping trip to St Fagans for small items.

'Hello, my fellow traveller,' said Catharine, pausing with the saddle, girth and bridle draped over her arm. 'How have you been, Sal?' she said.

'Doing my share of work of course,' said Sal, mopping sweat from her brow with the back of her hand. 'What about you, do they ever give *you* real work to do?'

'Look, Sal, I've been thinking, maybe I could get Madam to give you some jobs with more responsibility so you can move up the ladder a few rungs to start with. You are far too bright to be pumping water from a well.'

'Listen, Catharine, save your breath. I like you very much and I think we'll be friends for life, but I've made up my mind. I'm leaving ere long.'

Sal pumped the lever a few times and water gushed from the spout.

'Leaving? Where are you going and why?' Catharine had a look of genuine concern on her face.

'The answer to the where bit, is Gloucester. I've heard tell there's good money in that town, and I know some of the girls who are already working the streets there.'

'My God, so you're going back to the profession,' said Catharine with a shocked tone, 'I should have known you would.'

'Come with me Cath and be part of the real world . . . not the one the vicars and ministers think is out there. I'll look after you. What's more,' she went on, 'you could do some thieving on the side if need be!'

Catharine wasn't sure if she should have been offended by Sal's last remark but she simply shrugged her shoulders and said, 'Well, do whatever you think best, but be sure to get the papers sorted out before you go.' She was referring to the serious matter of documentation that tied a servant to a household exempting the employer from paying a portion of the parish rate in the way that the Pritchards claimed on behalf of Catharine's mother so many years ago.

Raglan Sal's reply was unequivocal:

'They can wipe their backsides with those papers. I'm off!'

Chapter Four

It was a lovely summer morning when Catharine walked out to the forecourt of Parc to find the pony and trap harnessed and ready to go.

'*Siwrna dda!*' (Have a good journey) a voice called out and she saw Old Lewis the retainer a few yards away, doffing his tricorn and bowing. His wig fell off as it always did, revealing the shiniest pate in Glamorgan if not Christendom. He picked up his headgear, turned his bent frame round and made towards the house, still muttering, '*Siwrna dda!* . . . *Siwrna dda!* . . . *Siwrna dda!*'

Catharine called back, 'Thank you, Lewis,' and soon the pony was trotting.

She had lately made several unaccompanied journeys and felt proud that her employers had sufficient confidence to send her alone to distant places in the county. This time her destination was the busy Vale port of Aberthaw; the purpose of her visit was not entirely clear but she was told she simply had to collect a package.

Catharine Griffith looked a picture as she sped along, her black suit matching the colour of her own hair and Robin's smooth shiny coat. She wasn't entirely sure of the way but knew she had to go southwards. She wound her way through bendy lanes with high hedges. She had seen few people on the roadside who might have helped by pointing her towards Aberthaw. True, there were some workers bent over their tasks in fields but they were out of shouting distance. The gateway to a 'big house' appeared on her right and another a little further down the road on her left near a sign for 'Bryn Cadwaladr'; then another some miles later had a sign that read 'Trewallter'. As none of these names had been mentioned in the instructions she had been given regarding the best route, she realised she must be on the wrong road.

She twisted westwards and entering Llancarfan the pony started to sweat. She knew there would be more hills to climb before they could drop down towards the coast and she began to feel concerned for Robin's welfare.

At last she saw two figures ahead on the wayside so she slowed the pony to a walk and stopping alongside the woman and little girl she realised they were gypsies. She politely asked them the way to Aberthaw. The woman's completely blank expression told Catharine that she couldn't answer the question.

The little one suddenly piped up: 'My mother can't speak Welsh, but I can,' said the girl, adopting a proud look.

It was then that Catharine realised that she had been using *Aberddawan,* the Welsh name for her destination. The girl said the place she wanted was about an hour away walking and could be seen from the ridge which would be half way there. Catharine knew then she should cover the distance in a quarter of that time, so she thanked them, and with a flick of the reins, the pony took off again. Sure enough from the ridge she could see the busy port ahead with a number of vessels of various sizes and shapes bobbing off-shore.

Catharine guided the pony down a long lane which eventually split into ramps leading to jetties at which loading and unloading of cargoes was taking place. A strong aroma of pitch mixed with the salty air gave the place an aura suggestive of adventures on the high seas. Squawking seabirds, some circling, others diving, added to the busyness of the place. The boats here mostly plied trade across the Bristol Channel to Minehead, Bridgwater and a few other Somerset ports. Also there were of course regular sailings to Bristol, the city with which South Wales did its biggest commercial business.

It was the Bristol trade that Catharine believed was the reason for her being at Aberthaw, looking around desperately trying to find a man who was supposed to meet her with an important package for her employer. She became conscious of staring eyes wherever she turned and she began to feel uneasy about being the only female in sight. All around her, uncouth men stinking of chewing tobacco which was frequently being spat from cruel-looking mouths were rolling barrels of liquor or else carrying sacks of flour and shouting oaths, which, although unintelligible to Catharine, were surely venomous.

Catharine heard the native form of her name being called out. *'Catrin! Catrin!'*

A strong arm encircled her shoulders and gently pulled her around to face a tall handsome man. He went on: *"Sdim amser i'w wastraffu.'* (We have no time to waste).

Taking a small blue paper package from his coat he gave it to Catharine, saying: *'Ewch 'nôl 'nawr heb oedi! . . . a diolch!'* (Go back without delay . . . and thanks!)

The striking looking man raised his hat to wave goodbye, and as he turned on his heel one of his coat-tails moved to reveal a sword swinging at his side. Catharine sighed and was reminded of her first meeting with her father who had also raised his hat in a gentlemanly manner.

At the jetty the sword-bearing stranger boarded the biggest vessel which, no doubt, would soon be returning to Bristol.

Catharine drove as far as the ridge at which she had paused on the way down. She decided to rest Robin for half an hour before continuing. She was tired herself and soon dozed off where she sat with her head bowed. It must have been an hour or more before she awoke – and that was because the trap was shaking violently. Worse, there was a hand across her mouth preventing her from shouting for help.

She realised immediately that her assailant was one of the burly workers she had recently been watching at the jetty. He was mouthing menacing noises and trying to remove her outer clothing. With a surge of energy born more of anger than fear, she reached around the back of his neck for his pigtail and gripping it with both hands she yanked his head backwards. At the same time she brought up her knee with such force into his nether regions that he yelped in agony and fell backwards off the trap.

The pony needed no instruction from Catharine; it headed northward at full speed leaving the marauding old salt writhing on the roadside. Catharine couldn't be sure that the attacker had been after her body or the package. She blushed thinking that she might at least have felt flattered had it been the former! She soon collected the reins and went over in her mind the events of the day which had started with a fond farewell to Old Lewis in the courtyard. Catharine looked forward to arriving home, knowing that the old man would be there as ever to greet her with his cheery smile and kind words of welcome.

She guided the trap through the gate and upon arriving at the frontage of the house she knew instinctively that something was wrong. Old Lewis wasn't there, but Samuel Price was, with his hat in his hands, together with Madam Price and their son, John, a well-built man in his early thirties.

'My goodness,' mused Catharine, 'the package I have for them is more important than I thought.'

Mrs Price moved forward and took the pony's reins whilst her son and heir helped Catharine down from her 'carriage' with conspicuous courtesy.

Samuel Price was weeping and looking down at his feet as he addressed Catharine.

'Dear girl, you have come back to a saddened house this evening.'

'Tell me why. Tell me why, please!' pleaded Catharine, almost sure there would be bad news about Old Lewis.

John took the pony to the stable and his mother moved over to take Catharine by the arm.

'Mae'n flin 'da fi ond mae Gwladys wedi marw,' said Madam Price, quietly.

'Our wonderful Gwladys dead? Oh no!' Catharine was falling to the ground in shock but Mr and Mrs Price took hold of her, walked her to the house and sat her down in the big drawing room. Mrs Price sent Lisabeth to bring a tumbler of water for Catharine but before she returned, Samuel Price had already opened his cabinet and taken out a bottle of his best French brandy.

Catharine sipped the cognac from a priceless cut-glass goblet and wondered how it was that she, a wench from the poorest background, could ever have expected to be sitting in such luxurious surroundings and being fussed over by persons of a higher caste. Then her mind reverted to the situation that obtained twenty minutes earlier and she suddenly got to her feet.

'Gwladys!' she shouted. 'For God's sake, what happened to Gwladys?'

Mrs Price indicated to her to sit down and she complied while Samuel Price began his explanation.

'Mrs Harris, that is, Gwladys,' said Samuel Price, 'was set upon by two youths in the Star Lane when she was walking home from her sister's home in St Bride's. We had let her go because her sister is not long for this world. And now . . .' He failed to continue so his wife picked it up:

'Yes,' she said, 'now Gwladys has gone to heaven first. Both of them good and godly women.'

Samuel regained his composure and said, 'Gwladys came here bloodied and sore, but we didn't expect her to die. She told us what had happened and who had done it. Then she fell down and never took another breath. Old Lewis was inconsolable when he heard and he went straight to his bed sobbing.'

'So you know who did it!' said Catharine, quickly rising to her feet. 'I shall want to know!'

Samuel Price swiftly went into his Justice of the Peace mode: 'Catrin, Catrin. This will be a matter for the law officers to deal with. I've already sent a man to inform the Sheriff.'

'The law! The law! I don't want to hear about the law! The law has never done anything for the common folk. My father was shot dead when he was doing the lawmen's work for them. To hell with the law!'

Catharine burst into a flood of tears, and it was only after shaking for fully a minute she realised she had gone too far. She then begged the Prices for their forgiveness. She said she should not have spoken thus, adding that she loved them dearly and they weren't like any other landowners and employers she had ever heard about . . . they were good people . . . Godly people, and she would go to her grave grateful for their kindness to her . . .!

'Amen,' said Samuel Price.

Catharine left the room with a sheepish look but before she reached the door she took from her waistcoat the small blue paper package she had collected and handed it to Samuel Price. His hand shook as he gently took it from her. *'Diolch,'* (thank you) he said, before beginning to whimper again.

'Amen,' said Catharine Griffith.

'Amen,' said Madam Price.

'Amen,' said Lisabeth who had been listening behind the door.

It was not long before the servants at Parc found the identity of the two youths who had attacked their beloved friend Gwladys. One night before sleep called, all the servant girls lay in their beds offering ideas as to what punishment they would like to inflict on the perpetrators of the crime which had sickened them. Only one declined to disclose her intentions: Catharine.

On the long walk at midnight to Fairwater Green where the youths lived in adjoining cottages, Catharine wrestled with her conscience. The two young men had been soaked in gin and laudanum when they made their brutal attack and as Catharine left Parc her intention was to cause them anguish and pain. If nothing else was possible at least she might enter their abodes and remove some possessions.

As she proceeded, her feelings certainly didn't mellow as far as the culpability of the two youths was concerned. Yet she was less sure that she had a right to pass judgement in the first place let alone administer the punishment. Words from all those sermons at the church resounded in her mind with a clarity they had not possessed when first heard. By the time she reached the far end of St Fagans she had recalled three times the curate's voice declaiming the Ten Commandments. Then she heard again Christ's Sermon on the Mount and immediately turned back. That night, as she lay in her bed, it was in the twilight zone immediately before sleep that she wrestled once more with her sense of reasoning and she began to wonder if she was in fact going mad. Common sense eventually prevailed and she felt relieved that she had aborted her plan for reprisal. Sleep came only after she had convinced herself that crime and punishment were matters far beyond her understanding. However, in her slumbers she once more adopted her *alter ego* and quickly lost herself in a fantasy world among the criminally acquisitive.

The next time Richard Price visited Parc, Catharine was introduced to him as the brave young lady who had collected 'that document' from Aberthaw.

'It was nothing,' insisted Catharine. 'I didn't even look at it to see what it contained.' She might have added that it wouldn't have helped – because of her illiteracy. It occurred to her that Raglan Sal, despite her earthy career, would have been better equipped than her to meet such clever people.

'Well, let's just say it is a changing world' said Samuel Price, 'and that note was a letter of thanks from some very courageous people who will bring about those changes.'

During Richard's last visit another man of letters came to Parc. It was the formidable littérateur Edward Williams of the southern Vale. The pair had met in London and it was clear from the tone of their conversations at the big house that they were like-minded with regard to social justice and the 'Rights of Man'. Unitarians, they advocated freedom from formal dogma or doctrine. There was no doubt that they had supported totally the colonists in their war against the British and that they felt the Americans deserved their freedom from the shackles which had been imposed on them by parliament and a sickly monarchy. Also there was no question that they would back the revolutionaries in France; they were assiduous members of the vanguard in the war against class tyranny wherever it ruled. Catharine would have loved to possess the intellectual capacity to question them about such things, but she was now more conscious than ever about the gulf between the educated and the ignorant masses to which she knew she belonged.

The snippets of conversation she had overheard when the pair of philosophers were talking in the library were far beyond her comprehension, yet despite that, in general, she felt she was getting a better understanding of what was right and what was wrong – or at least of what other people considered to be right and wrong.

Catharine had ample opportunity to see the two intellectual giants at close quarters and was able to make comparisons. Price, the older of the two, and the taller by far, was attired as usual in black which, together with his shock of white hair gave him a ministerial air. She would learn later that this personage was known in the literary, scientific and philosophical communities of London, Oxford and Cambridge as 'The Friend of the Universe, the Great Apostle of Liberty'.

The physical appearance of Edward Williams – who is remembered by his bardic name of Iolo Morganwg – was far less striking than that of Dr Price. He was a small man with no interest in sartorial niceties. His hair was usually bedraggled and he always seemed to have pieces of paper protruding from various pockets in his waistcoat, tunic and overcoat. He also had made his mark in London where he counted among his friends leading poets of the day and was known to them as 'The Bard of Liberty'. The fact that he was later proven to be a forger hardly blemished his well-deserved good name as an antiquary.

Whereas Price's voice was commanding, even thunderous at times, Iolo offered no more than a squeak. In their writings however, they were both ground-breaking geniuses. This was unknown to Catharine, yet she had no doubt that the two men were deeply involved in matters beyond her comprehension. She now realised she might never know the true significance of the package she had brought safely to Parc. She would always wonder what Madam Price had meant when she was told by her in barely audible whispers that the item she had collected was from a 'new world'.

If anyone was going to reveal the truth about that package, it would not be Samuel Price, for he left this world for the next in July 1777. This was an important date for the Prices because the American Republic with which the family was inextricably linked was now exactly one year old.

Samuel had risen on the morning of the 10th of July with few cares that might spoil his day. Many of his social class had successfully negotiated the purchase of shares in tobacco plantations in Virginia and cotton estates in North Carolina long before the American Revolution and it is more than likely that he had done similarly.

Perhaps too, like his friends, he had invested in shipping groups sailing out of Bristol, Newport, Cardiff and Aberthaw. Their commitments to the Bristol enterprises would have felt very safe indeed as the shipment of slaves had doubled in the previous five years and the figures were still increasing. Also the vessels sailing out from the Vale of Glamorgan were mobile treasure chests for they brought in the most profit-making commodities of all: coffee and tobacco.

Aberthaw was also the channel through which suspect produce, even illicit and seditious literature, could be handled. With corrupt customs officials all in the pay of avaricious merchants, a degree of law and order had vanished from Aber-thaw. However, Samuel Price and his agents were incorruptible and he went about *his* business there well inside the restrictive limits of the laws of the land. This was just as well, as he was a Justice of the Peace himself.

Samuel still had his nightgown on when he entered the library for his morning weakness. He always started his day with a generous glass of whisky that gave him the happy air which would inform his behaviour throughout the morning. A similar dose of the 'medication' would then set him up for the afternoon.

On that morning, one year and six days after the Declaration of Independence in America, he downed his morning elixir with his usual measure of joy and promptly fell prostrate.

After losing consciousness for a few minutes he recovered and, realising he was on his own in the room, he got up and tried to walk across to the fireplace to reach the pull-cord in order to raise an alarm. He found he couldn't keep his balance and crashed into every piece of furniture. Just one tug of the corner of the thick cloth table cover and he sent a dozen china ornaments flying across the room. By the time he himself fell into the spacious fireplace, a large bookshelf had come crashing down sending tomes flying in all directions. The noise was eventually noticed by none less than Old Lewis who was passing the open French window on his way from some garden duty. Normally it would have offended the rules of etiquette for him to look into the room but a simple glance told him all was not well with his master. He leaped across the slabbed patio and into the library where by now Samuel Price was lying dead. Once again the old retainer was inconsolable.

Dr Yorath ap Rhys was sent for and he was immediately concerned about Madam Price who was weeping loudly and having an attack of the vapours. There was nothing he could do for poor Samuel. *His* earthly sojourn was over. However, his widow needed to be calmed quickly and without hesitation the doctor brought out a small phial of laudanum, itself a potent mixture of alcohol and opium, to which he added a tincture of absinthe and administered the cocktail to Madam Price by forcibly opening her mouth.

Far from becalming the woman the liquid caused a sudden personality change and those who had come to the library were entertained for a good ten minutes by her cavortings. She appeared to be enacting a dance worthy of Salome. The silk handkerchief in her hand was waved daintily as she pirouetted and tripped around the room. Throughout this performance she wore a smile borrowed from some different life. When she returned to this world she flopped into a chair and sighed. The effects of the drug had worn off and she was now ready for the doctor's reflections on her husband's passing. He didn't disappoint her.

'It was an apoplectic fit that saw Sam off. Only wish I'd been here to see it. They can be very entertaining, those fits. Looking at the way he rearranged the furniture it must have been a mobile one. Oh yes, that's what it was, an apoplectic fit. Mind you, a blissful way to be disconnected from the mortal coil . . . no pain to speak of and it was all over before you could say King George the Third. Could have been worse. Take old Barnaby Hughes for instance up there in Pentyrch. He was a puddler at the Ironworks. He was stirring molten iron all day and working in heat worse than the fires of hell. Yet he took ill after he cut his leg and it went to gangrene. I helped the sawbones take his leg off three Michaelmasses ago but he slowly withered and in the end he died of the long ling'ring, shouting for St Peter to let him in.'

'Thank you,' said Madam Price, as she rose from her chair and retired to her bedroom to pray.

Five days later Mrs Price wore black all over including a lace bonnet which had frills that framed her face and a gown that went to the floor waving in folds at every turn of her hip as she walked.

Now the elegant lady sat in the library to receive one by one those who wished to pay their respects and to commiserate with her over the loss of her husband. She sat in her slowly rocking chair, holding in one hand the fan that her son had brought back from a foray into Calais with his militia unit a while back. She offered her other hand to be kissed as each person was directed into the library, the same time giving her face a dainty flick from the fan before thanking them for coming.

She would describe time after time the way her husband had been found by old Lewis . . . how Samuel had had a fit and how the place would never be the same again. Neighbouring farmers called as did some of Samuel's business associates. His fellow justices of the peace and magistrates arrived and before long the broad yard before the house was full of broughams, traps and whinnying horses. Relatives, some of whom hadn't been seen for years, turned up and each of them embraced Catherine Price.

Not one person had entered the library without a nod of the head from old Lewis who had found an old black coat for the occasion and was enjoying a rare 'butleresque' opportunity. He stood stiffly by the door, turning only to introduce each visitor. Invariably he had the names wrong but no-one complained.

Throughout the proceedings Samuel lay in his open coffin on a table near the French doors. Everyone had to pass him on their way out and all reacted differently. Some just gave him a glance, some knelt and prayed; others touched his hand before going out. Only a small number spoke to him. Usually this was a brief comment about Sam's passing into the arms of the Almighty and the ecstatic life he could look forward to in heaven. However, William Hughes, his lifelong friend, approached the coffin and promptly launched into a tearful recount of countless happy mutual experiences.

At first this was acceptable for it was clear he would greatly miss Samuel . . . but after five minutes he had not yet reached their tenth birthdays so he just had to be moved on. He was still describing long gone happy days when Old Lewis took him by the arm and helped him out through the French window.

One relative was noticeably absent. A dozen of Samuel's family had come up from Bridgend and several from further afield but his brother Richard was not among them. The philosopher now resided in London where he was regarded with considerable awe even among the intelligentsia. He could, of course, have easily made the journey had he been in the country. In fact though, he was half way across the Atlantic by then, on his way to Pennsylvania in response to an invitation from his confidant Benjamin Franklin. Sewn into his clothing was a package containing the letter from his American friend. It was wrapped in blue paper.

Despite Samuel Price's Nonconformist affiliations his funeral took place at Llanilltern Church. It was the biggest event held there since the burial of the previous occupant of Parc, his brother-in-law, Morgan Williams, who, like his predecessors, made sure the name of his residence was a byword for penal justice in the locality.

Most comfortably-off landowners were good men who truly cared about the fate of delinquents. They believed that the processes of law should include means for the rehabilitation of repentant criminals. Unfortunately, a minority of law-enforcers appeared to value property higher than human life and occasionally their negligence led to tragic miscarriages of justice. Samuel Price, however, had been one of the good men, renowned for his fairness and his charity.

His sending off was a grand affair. As the widow Catherine remarked, 'Such a pity he couldn't be here . . . he would have loved every moment.' If the urchins lined up outside the church wall had heard that they would have laughed their clogs off . . . if they'd possessed clogs.

Each of the four black horses that drew the hearse wore a plume of red upon its poll and from the forehead to the nose a neat white blaze. The enterprising master carpenter, Jacob Stradling, supplied the fine animals as well as the coffin. He was a miserable man and therefore perfect for his role as driver of the hearse. He sat high up front looking like a black beetle.

The expression on his face was designed to sadden the most optimistic of souls. His horses, trained to perfection, walked with a respectful gait.

When the hearse came slowly to a halt near the church gate, the curate emerged from the shadows and spoke to Jacob so quietly that even the nosy couldn't hear – despite stretching their necks. Then ensued what appeared to be a competition between the funeral director and the priest to find who could produce the saddest frown. Even though the Rev. Garmon Rees was a naturally sorrowful soul, Jacob won by a mile for it was his job to be gloomy; he probably practiced before the mirror each morning.

Whilst the parish church of St Mary in St Fagans had for some time favoured monoglot English incumbents, the tiny church of Llanilltern, historically a chapel of ease in that parish, was given Welsh-speaking curates – for the regular congregation was largely monoglot Welsh.

It was a fine morning as dignitary after dignitary arrived and made their way into the little church which was soon full. There was no room for the poor on this occasion. There were no servants allowed in except one. Catharine, for the first time in her life, sat in the middle of the church and, not for the first time, wondered why she was being afforded such privileges.

The coffin was eventually led into the church by the curate and close relatives of Samuel Price J.P. The cleric turned to the congregation and began his eulogy. His precisely spoken quotations from William Morgan's translation of the Bible helped convey the basic message of his sermon which was the need for rectitude in life.

'In a world increasingly controlled by the forces of evil, the greater the need for good men.' With a sideways glance at the coffin, he said: 'Samuel Price was a good man; I have known no better.'

Yet, although going on to say that he would personally miss his presence in church on Sundays, he couldn't resist referring to the fact that Samuel had lately supported in more ways than one the establishment of the Nonconformist meeting house at Taihirion. At this point the curate cleared his throat and looked for a moment as if he was in need of a convenient spittoon. Perhaps the reason he desisted was the presence of those numerous relatives of Samuel who had come up from Bridgend, all of them leading lights in the Congregationalist movement!

The Rev. Rees went on to say that he would miss the rabbits and pheasants that Samuel regularly sent down to him, also the fine whisky and brandy which would be brought out when he, as curate, called at Parc during his parish visits. In an attempt at making a jocular remark, he added: 'I preferred the whisky to the cognac but I am just a poor priest, therefore, a beggar . . . and beggars can't be choosers.' No one laughed.

Finally Garmon Rees called the congregation to stand to sing a dirge whilst Sam's oak box was carried out to the graveyard. By the time the other mourners and the curate, whose facial expression was now at its gloomiest, stood at the grave's edge uttering his incantations, the yard was full. He then reminded those assembled that a spread awaited them at Parc with plenty to eat and drink. The invitation of course did not apply to the ragged horde outside the graveyard wall.

The spirits soared in more ways than one up at Parc that afternoon. Apart from the fact that everyone seemed to be in a jolly mood, the contents of several glasses flew towards the ceiling as Theophilus Pwll Du, standing in front of the hearth, got into full flow, emphasising every pompous remark with extravagant gesticulations.

The boastful squire of Pwll Du estate rarely behaved in a way becoming of a gentleman of his social and political status. He appeared now as a comic figure, attempting to steady himself by clutching the hilt of his sword ever more tightly as he swayed. Each time he flung his drink away he immediately called gruffly upon the servant to bring more. The little black boy in a red coat with big buttons bowed each time he returned with the tray, his huge smile showing gleaming white teeth. It was fashionable to have black servants in 1777 and Jones of Fonmon had loaned this one to Madam Price for the day.

As it happened, Theo was ranting about a recent increase in charges made by the Bristol and Gold Coast Company for the transportation of slaves. His plantation in Antigua would feel the effect of such an imposition.

'It's a blasted affront to our dignity,' he said, turning and spitting into the fireplace which was empty on account of it being summertime.

'Do you know,' he went on, 'that each of those black bounders costs half a guinea to be taken to Virginia? Cows go for two shillings! . . . Where's the sense in that?' he said, spitting once more for emphasis.

'Well,' said Shôn Pen y Goetre, 'you make a good point but you have to consider that most of the cows make it to the other side which is something that can't be said about them blackies.'

With that remark he patted the head of the ebony-coloured boy who was passing with another trayful of drinks.

'Now that them Americanees are on their own over there maybe they'll find it too costly to ship 'em over from Africa, and they'll start using them Hispanics on their plantations.'

'Aye, or them redskins. They've got plenty of them over there!'

'Your conversation is degenerate, sirs. This house is deserving of better talk.' John Price, Samuel and Catherine's impeccably attired son, had moved into the company of those close to the fireplace.

'Furthermore, gentlemen,' he said, 'should we not be lamenting today the passing of an honourable man, to whit, my glorious father?'

John, an elegant looking man in his thirties, was standing arm in arm with his wife, the daughter of Peter Birt of Wenvoe Castle. By this time their home was the sumptuous Llandough Castle and visits to Parc were these days rather infrequent. When John *did* call it was usually to remonstrate with his mother with regard to her legendary extravagance. A good man, he was secretly proud of his mother and her philanthropy; however he was wont to remind her that the supply of money was not limitless. Furthermore, he was becoming extremely uneasy with the slavery trade, which was the basis of nearly all local wealth. He had started attending the Unitarian church at Dinas Powis and had heard a sermon that had rocked his mind with regard to the whole business of capturing Africans and ferrying them to the other side of the ocean to work for the rest of their lives in the custody of often sadistic masters. He could no longer look at a cotton dress, or see a man smoking a pipe without wondering about the human distress that made these things possible. He continued:

'There are many things that are about to change with regard to society. I am afraid the common people are going to rise up wherever they are the victims of injustice.'

'You are an insult to your class, sir,' said Theo Pwll Du. 'I would have you whipped, sir, for such remarks. Retract them now or I shall offer you a duel, sir . . . and that will bring an end to you and your ungodly, dastardly ideas.'

'If you were not as drunk as a bee in a foxglove, sir, I would take you up. Please calm down and go home.'

Theo might have taken the matter further if he had not, within a couple of seconds, collapsed to the floor in an unshapely heap. Some of his closest friends lifted him and conveyed him to his carriage which was waiting outside. As he was unceremoniously dumped into the vehicle, his driver, a young man in royal blue livery, had the semblance of a smile on his jet black face as he flicked the reins and turned the carriage towards Pwll Du.

John Price sensed that Theo Pwll Du was not the only one to have objected to his statement. Amid menacing murmurs backs were turned to him and few men shook his hand as they left. He knew that he had not heard the end of the matter. He did not fear a gun-duel for he was an excellent shot with the pistols he had brought home from his time in the seizure of Grenada and other conflicts; nor did he know of an equal as a swordsman for he had perfected his fencing skills when at the military academy in Gloucester. There were other ways though in which his new enemies would seek to destroy him . . . but he had no idea as to what they might be.

It was now mid-January and cold winds were blowing from the east to give problems to the ewes which had been introduced to rams at the end of October. Not all farms of the upper Vale of Glamorgan had cover for livestock when the snows came down. At least at Parc there was some natural shelter with the rising ground of the Graig holding off northerlies and the grove of beech and ash on the eastern edge of the estate defying the worst of the wind known as *'Gwynt traed y meirw'* (The wind of dead men's feet). Even so, the winter of 1778 was bitter.

It was fully dark when Catharine crossed the yard to the stables. She pulled her thick woollen shawl tightly around her shoulders as the first flakes of snow of the winter were starting to fall. She knew she couldn't stay long at the other servants' sleeping quarters for she might not get out before being trapped by the weather.

She climbed the rickety ladder which gave a squeak each time she placed a foot on a rung. Even before she stepped up to the loft floor there were other squeaks; also some happy laughter. She knew immediately that the girls had visitors from the male servants' draughty dormitory and they would be persuading the wenches to keep them warm for an hour or two. It had happened before . . . in summertime! She had no wish to stay except to pass on a message to Sal.

'Sal?' said Lisabeth. 'You sure you want Sal?'

'There's something I want to tell her,' said Catharine.

'Rhy hwyr, cariad. Mae hi wedi cwnnu ei chwt.' (Too late . . . she's hopped it!')

'Well, she did warn me' thought Catharine as she stepped out into a blizzard. Her disappointment was as bitter as the cold wind that was now cutting through her as she struggled across the yard to the house. She had been told by Madam Price that she was considering giving Sal a better position as Catharine had hoped. Her adventurous friend could be half way across the country by now. She liked Sal and she said a prayer for her before she tucked herself into her bed warmed by a copper bottle containing hot water and placed there by Old Lewis.

Before going to sleep every night she went through the same ritual of recalling incidents in her life and asking herself the same unanswered questions such as why she was being treated with such kindness here at Parc. She was sure she hadn't done anything to deserve special favours.

Her last thoughts were usually about her mother and her father, leading to dreams in which she experienced the fulfillment of her vengeful intentions. Those ideas just would not go away.

The huge log fire blazed at the Plymouth Arms and as usual the talk to start with was distinctly agricultural.

'Well, if this snow keeps up I shan't be making it back to The Drope tonight,' said Jac James. 'Old Charles will have to get off his rear end again and milk those cattle. It won't hurt him, his cottage is only a mile away up by the Persondy.'

He emptied his tankard and made the usual sign that he wanted a refill. Once again the serving wench dodged the out-stretched arms of 'gentlemen' to get past them with the ewer.

'What do you mean "those cattle?"' said Isaac Lewis . . . 'you talk as if you had a great herd down there. God knows you've got two cows and no more.'

'Aye, well, I did have more but I was distrained again by that dung-heap from St Donats, Miles Morgan. He said I'd done 'im on the exchange with that hay I sent down. He said it was all ragwort, milkwort, foxtail and bloody buttercup . . . hardly any grass. "You killed my cows" he said . . . "so I'll take yours." And he bloody did! Came in the night with his big sons. Old Charles and me would have been no match for 'em.'

'In the byres they should all be on a night like this,' said Humphrey Phillips the constable who was stretched out nearer the fire than anybody.

'I'd stick to arresting people if I were you, Umff,' said Ben Treharne, 'you know as much about farming as a judge's arse.'

The constable was ready to rise to that remark but Wil Pen-glog was quicker to get his words out.

'I hear they are going to send a thousand French prisoners back next month. They'll be sailing out of Bristol so I wonder if there's a penny or two in that for us. It's all paid for by parlia-ment after all.' As he spoke he was patting his coin pocket to indicate he could sense a chance of making money.'

'Well I hope they don't send 'em back before they finish that stone walling over in Peterstone. They're doing a good job 'tis said.' Dic Penywaun seemed genuinely concerned . . . about the wall, not the Frenchmen.

'Aye,' he went on, 'they also did a good job on those two wenches from the Dusty Forge who were sent out with cheese and bread to them when they were working.'

'Ah, and there was I thinking that pair were simply putting on weight!' Theo Pwll Du laughed at his own jocular remark but no-one joined him so he quickly changed the subject. His hatred of Sam Price's son had festered for six months since he was put down by him back at the funeral and he so much wanted to get his own back.

'What do you think should be done about that scum John Price, then?' he said with a scowl before taking a long swig of ale. 'He's been spreading it about that we good folk are sinful for investing in the trade of blacks doing honest work in Americee. I'd have the rat shot if it was up to me, but I'm sure you can come up with subtler ways of removing this sharp thorn from our flesh.'

'Whipping?'

'Ducking?'

'The stocks?'

'Hanging?'

'No, no, no!' said Theo, getting up and moving around the group, engaging each of them with a look that spelt painful retribution. 'Don't worry,' he said. 'Just leave it to me. It might take a while but I've got an idea.'

Chapter Five

Catharine's duties were mostly confined to the comfort of the house interior but occasionally she helped with outdoor chores – like carrying water from the well and mucking out stables and cowsheds. She no longer took washing to the brook but did occasionally get an opportunity to take her favourite strolls through the fields and along the woodland paths. On these occasions she would think about her life to date and shed a tear here or break into a giggle there.

As it was springtime again she knew she must now be eighteen years old. She'd heard the cuckoo that morning and memories flooded back. She could remember all but three of her anniversaries thanks to the bewitching call of that bird and now with most of the trees in full leaf and spring flowers blooming everywhere, she was as happy as she had ever been. It was dusk and she should have been making for Parc but it was such a balmy evening she decided she would make it as far as the bank of the stream before returning.

She arrived at the footbridge over the runnel and once again recalled the time she fell into the water just there when she was a child. She sat on the bank and wondered about life. It was at that moment she heard a man's voice singing a beautiful, melodious English song that touched and soothed her senses.

She looked towards a break in the trees whence the sweet sound had come and saw an outline of the figure of a man dismounting from his stationary horse. The figure moved towards her and as it entered a ray of light from the now setting sun she immediately identified John Price. The slight swing of his sword as he stepped forward gave her that tingle she had experienced before.

He doffed his hat with a dignified sweep of the arm and said: 'I am John Price . . . I am on my way to visit my mother. I'm told she wants to see me. You are her helper are you not?'

She liked the fact that he hadn't used the term 'servant' and simply nodded.

He went on: 'You should not be on your own away from the safety of the house, especially at this time of day. May I suggest you return forthwith?'

She ignored his question and felt she wanted this moment to last forever. She had seen John Price only from a distance previously and hadn't realised how handsome and manly he was until this moment. Her mind searched for something that would prolong their meeting. 'What was that song?' she said, with her head bowed.

'Oh, just a ballad about finding love. It's all there in the words: both the heartache and the joy.'

'Could you sing some more?' said Catharine, immediately feeling she was being a little too cheeky.'

'Sorry, but I must go' said John Price. 'Forgive me.' Replacing his tricorn hat as he stood up, he gathered the reins once more and put one foot in a stirrup, the brass buckle on his shoe faintly glistening as it caught a beam of the dying light.

Just before he mounted he once again advised Catharine to go home. 'They will surely be missing you up there,' he said.

Receiving a gentle touch of a spur and a slight tug on the rein, John's horse obediently turned towards Parc, which was several fields away up on the hillside.

Catharine, still emotionally charged by the song, couldn't stop herself calling out: 'Who were the words for?'

'My dear wife, of course. Who else?' shouted John. He heeled his mount and sped away to the mansion.

A full half hour later Catharine was still out walking the woodland path and with the night sky now lit by the moon and the stars she went over and over in her mind the event that had just taken place. Reliving the moment when the handsome man had sung his love-song she pretended that the words were intended for her and not his 'dear wife'. Most of the males she had lately come into contact with were uncouth examples of humanity. Oh would that she could meet someone of John Price's calibre; she would allow herself to be swept off her feet and taken away to another life where joy was permanent . . . and just as importantly, she would no longer be driven to seek vengeance.

Suddenly, she saw a horse cantering towards her from the direction of Parc, silhouetted against the sky. As it went past her the rider leaped from the saddle, his tricorn hat leaving his head and rolling along the ground nearby. As he bundled Catharine to the ground, she felt strong hands ripping her clothes from her. She struggled bravely but her assailant was far too strong. She screamed and he quickly wrapped a piece of her displaced clothing around her face, stuffing most of it into her mouth. She kicked wildly and he forcibly wound his much heavier legs around hers. Going through her mind in rapid succession were several moments from the past of which this episode reminded her only too clearly. The attack she had survived on her return journey from Aberthaw was one . . . and the other she could only imagine – that of her grandmother being brutally attacked as described to her that time by dear Gwladys the cook.

Suddenly her right arm was free and her hand touched a stone that was lying on the ground inches away from the writhing pair. She grabbed the lump of rock tightly and swung her arm in the direction of her attacker's head. The man went limp and as he fell away she noticed that he was wearing military style riding boots . . . she had half convinced herself they would be brass buckled shoes. She was well away from him when she heard him groan and despite the darkness saw him disappear into the depths of the wood.

It was a very dishevelled, muddy and utterly forlorn Catharine Griffith who struggled to make her way back to Parc up the sloping grassy fields. She was exhausted and had to pause frequently to recover her breath and to regain her composure. After a hundred yards or so she felt she could go no further. She might have fallen asleep had she not heard the rumbling of approaching horses and the unmistakable sound of cartwheels.

Before she could really assess what was happening, two dragoon guards had dismounted, and picked her up. As they took her gently to place her in the cart, the other riders made themselves known to her.

One said he was a bailiff to the Sheriff of the county and was delighted to have been able to come to her aid. She recognised another as being a regular visitor to Parc, the loutish rustic squire, Theo Pwll Du. Catharine had no reason to doubt that they were there in her interests and gladly allowed them to take her to the big house. It was only when one of the dragoons grabbed Old Lewis roughly by the collar and pointed him towards the library demanding that he bring out the vermin that she became uncertain of what was going on. She couldn't be sure now that these men were her rescuers. John appeared at the door with his mother behind him.

'Tie him up,' said Theo, 'and put him in the cart.'

Madam Price now moved forward and tried to stand in front of her son. 'Be away with you all!' she screamed. 'What is your business here?'

'We have come to arrest your wayward son. He has ravished a poor defenceless servant girl and we came along just in time,' said Theo Pwll Du with an undisguised look of triumph on his face.

'You are making a grave mistake,' said John, standing boldly upright. One of the dragoons attempted to grab John's wrists in order to lash them together but was flung to the ground unceremoniously by his intended captive.

Old Lewis started shouting curses at the visitors but was soon silenced by a blow across his face from the back of one of the other dragoon's fists. He fell to the ground and as John immediately bent to offer him aid, he too was struck – this time with the butt of a musket and he collapsed with blood running profusely from the side of the head. Catharine, up to this point, had been speechless with fear and anger. Now she was raining blows on the chest of the grotesquely smiling Theo.

'No, no, no!' she wailed, 'that man is not my attacker! He was bigger and he was wearing boots. Let him go you brutes!'

It was of no use. The armed soldiers, the bailiff and Theo took John away despite continuing loud protests from a weeping Catharine and a bewildered old Lewis who was sitting on the mounting stone aside the front door shouting oaths that would have shocked even Raglan Sal.

Madam Price's temper began to cool. Helping Catharine and Lewis into the house, she said calmly, 'Don't worry about my John; he can look after himself. What we must do now is try to find out what mischievous plot has been hatched. For a start, I wasn't expecting him. I wonder who told him that I wanted to see him.'

After Old Lewis had washed himself at the tub in the cold-room next to the dairy he was given as a treat a large measure of the cognac which had been Samuel's favourite. Catharine, meanwhile, sat with the lady of the house and related the whole of the evening's events to her.

'Oh, yes,' said Madam Price, 'my son is a pure romantic – but he is also a good man. I know his views on certain matters are not popular and I'm sure that is the reason for what went on tonight.'

'What will happen now ma'am?' asked Catharine, now red-eyed and wretched.

'Well,' said the cooler than ever Madam Price, 'we shall have to gather the evidence and see if we can identify your assailant. Your memory of boots rather than the buckled shoes that John wears is a good start.'

Then, lowering her head slightly, she went on: 'It's a pity Sam's not here to sort it all out . . . but don't worry, we'll get to the bottom of this. You should go to bed now my dear. You'll feel better in the morning.'

Catharine complied with Madam Price's request and was soon beneath the woollen blanket on her bed. She had hardly fallen asleep however, when she heard knocking. She awoke sharply and after gathering a cloak about her shoulders she opened the door.

'Sorry, Miss Griffith,' said a breathless Old Lewis. 'You'd better come back to the front of the house. Something's happened.'

Catharine was surprised to see that the two dragoons had returned. So had the Sheriff's bailiff. On seeing the fourth figure, she stepped back startled, for she immediately recognised the military boots of the beast who had assaulted her.

Madam Price was quick to assure Catharine that all was well and that she need not be alarmed. In any case, the man was tied up with his arm in the firm grip of one of the dragoons who spoke a moment after Catharine had joined them:

'We found this devil wandering about the woods after we left you. Look at the lump on his head! Full of confessing he was and demanding his payment from that squire Theophilus fellow who hopped it when he saw that his plan had gone all wrong, see.'

The dragoon now speaking with his head bowed, went on: 'Fact is it was *us* who got it all wrong and arrested an innocent man. And that Theo's run away. Don't worry though, he won't get far. We'll catch him in no time and put his legs in spikes. Looks like we should apologise to one and all here. We didn't know any better. We'd been told a terrible lie by that squire when he called out us dragoons. He said that Mr John Price was planning to waylay the servant lass, see. But nobody had reckoned with the girl clouting this 'un like that and freeing herself from him. Oh I'm fair sorry you've had this trouble, my girl.'

At this point Catharine glanced briefly at the new prisoner's face and was sickened. He simply turned away to avoid her gaze.

'Where's my son?' said Madam Price, in a firm tone.

'Well, ma'am, he's safe enough I'm sure. He was being taken on to the lock-up in St Fagans when we caught this 'un. Escaped by now I shouldn't wonder . . . he's a wily old soldier, your son ma'am. I'll wager he's gone home to his wife in Llandough Castle.'

With that comment the wily soldier himself joined them. He hugged his mother who was clearly relieved to see him despite her earlier expression of confidence. Then he saluted both of the dragoon guards who stood immediately to attention returning the gesture. He took old Lewis's hand, shook it firmly and added a hug for good measure. John finally turned to Catharine and took her hands in his.

Looking into her eyes, he said: 'I hope one day you will find a good man who will look after you. You have had more than your share of bad ones. Sleep well.'

He went to the door and Catharine received a familiar *frisson* as he removed his hat with a characteristic sweep of his arm. 'I bid you all farewell,' he said. 'My dear wife awaits me.'

There was an air of disbelief when the drinkers at the Plymouth Arms discussed what had happened up at Parc. And they were all down to their usual level of respect for their fellow man.

'That John Price surely got away with it then!' said one.

'Aye,' said another, 'but more like that Theo bungled it didn't he!'

'Talking of the Squire,' said Dic Garnant. 'What have they done with him?'

'He's in Cardiff Gaol. He'll be there for five years they say. Serve him right for not planning it properly. Can't help feeling sorry for that lad he asked to do the job, mind. That wench hit him good and proper with a rock they say.'

'Aye, he's got a lump on his head as big as a croquet ball,' said Twm Twyn yr Odyn. 'What are they going to do to *him*, does anybody know?'

'I heard he's going to get sixty lashes and the Cardiff Constable is going to do it,' said Gomer Thomas. 'It'll be the whip I expect. Or could be the cat. Anyway for sure, they won't hang him . . . for it wasn't as if he *stole* anything, was it!' They all laughed at that.

Chapter Six

Catharine was lying awake in her bed again and going through recent events in her mind. She could see the starry sky through the window and apart from the bleating of lambs that had lost their mothers and the occasional calls of tawny owls, it was a quiet night. Sleep just would not come. She had relived her chores, and painfully recalled her physical struggle with Theo Pwll Du's stooge.

One image however came back repeatedly to haunt her. It was of a tall handsome man with a sword at his side, singing words of love which, although not intended for her, nevertheless aroused her emotions in a way she had not experienced before. She felt she was inevitably moving towards a time when fate would bring to her some kind of romantic liaison. John Price's words were there all the time at the front of her mind: 'I hope you will find a good man who will look after you.'

For a while, every time Catharine visited her fellow servants in their quarters in the stable loft they insisted on her relating her recent escapade in every detail.

'What is John Price really like?'

'What does he feel like? . . . has he got soft hands?'

'What does he smell like? . . . I heard he washes in lavender water.'

'Did he kiss you?'

'Are you sure it wasn't him that came back to pull you to the ground?'

However firmly Catharine kept to the absolute truth she found that there was a natural tendency for people to believe only what they wanted to believe.

When Catharine's thoughts wandered to the incident involving the squire and his puppet she had no confidence that their punishments would be as thorough as some were suggesting. She had long suspected that there might be a variation in the levels of severity of punishments meted out to different echelons of social class. Also, in her more charitable moments she felt she could not fully approve of brutal whippings, whether the victim be poor or prosperous. She had heard it said that an inordinate number of lashes whether it be with whip, birch or cat-o'-nine-tails, often proved to be fatal. Doctor Rhys was called more than once to administer pain-killers to victims of this punishment and to attempt to heal their wounds.

Even the regulars at the Plymouth sat open-mouthed as the doctor described the fate of Edward James, one of the militia-men who had accidentally released a number of French prisoners that were in his personal custody. Perhaps if he had appeared before Justices of the Peace or even a judge at the County Assizes, he would have been treated fairly, if strictly. But this young soldier was tried by a military court set up by the Glamorgan Militia who needed to recover a good reputation that had been lost in recent months due to the loutish behaviour of its serving men.

'Don't you know?' said the officer in charge of the trial, 'that if those Froggies had remained free they would have raped countless local females and roasted their children on spits . . . after drinking their blood.'

With such arguments against him, Edward James didn't have a chance.

The doctor described the state of the young man's back when he was called to the barracks where the soldier lay unconscious on the floor of a punishment cell.

'He had been lashed until his bones were bare. It was like being at the butcher's. This was somebody's son. I wanted to be sick. Hard to believe that anyone could inflict so much pain in such a gratuitous way on a fellow human being, and I said so to the officer in charge. His answer was that the militiaman had ceased to be a human being when he committed the crime of freeing prisoners who were enemies of the realm.'

Catharine's world was still mostly confined to the enclosed acres of Parc. No doubt she would have been given the opportunity to have more excursions to the outer world if only she had asked, for she had a degree of freedom her fellows lacked. If her dreams were to be believed there would be new horizons for her but she would have to be patient. The cuckoo once more told the world of Catharine Griffith's advancing years. As a twenty-year-old she had more questions than ever to be answered.

She became more and more curious as to the reason for the comparatively mild conditions of her service. She still worked hard, often physically, but this was of her own volition. She never felt constrained to pick up a shovel, brush, or pitchfork, or indeed to carry heavy pitchers of drinking water from the well but she did all these things as if they were obligatory. There were times when she fell asleep in seconds at night after a gruelling day shifting dung or chopping wood just like her mother used to do all those years ago. But she knew that she could equally have stayed around the house, talking to the other servants whilst they worked or, indeed, her employer who was an inveterate chatterer. Samuel always used to say about his wife: *'o's dim trai ar ei gweud!'* (her talk never subsides).

Madam Price was a frequent visitor herself to the kitchen, the dairy, the stables, the barns, the fields; in fact, anywhere at Parc to talk to anyone who would listen. She had kind words for everybody and when inevitably the subject of recent crimes was discussed she was not averse to finding an excuse for some of the wretched individuals who came up before the Justices. She knew that in some cases the law-breakers were given penalties that far outweighed the seriousness of their misdeeds. She believed in retribution for evil done, but strongly opposed punishment born of spite. She often said that of all the virtues the most ennobling was mercy.

When Madam Price was not to be seen around Parc she was, as like as not, on some errand of compassion for she frequently took succour to the poor and comfort to the ailing. She was careful not to be seen to be interfering in the business of the justices' court at Parc but she often influenced the decision-making of the magistrates if she felt strongly about a case. When Samuel was alive she saved more than one poor soul from undue punishment, but also if she heard that tyrants, bullies and unscrupulous manipulators were attempting to buy their way out of trouble, she would quickly make her views known so that true justice prevailed. Her direct contact with the Justices of the Peace was less since Samuel had gone, but she was still a matriarchal figure given that she considered the whole judicial dominion at Parc to have been her family's responsibility since her own brother had held sway there.

It was against Catharine's nature to think of herself before others but there was one privilege she enjoyed even though it was denied to everyone else. She loved horses passionately, and when she was asked if she could regularly exercise Dandi the gelding that had belonged to John when he lived at home, she was ecstatic.

The pony was now in its twenty-second year but he was as fit as ever. Being a cross between Welsh Mountain and Exmoor, he was of the hardiest stock so he was never stabled. It thrived on the fields where the winds came whistling from the east in wintertime. But Dandi loved the month of May as well for his winter covering had then gone, replaced with a smooth and shiny coat that made him look half his age. Catharine loved Dandi and the feeling was mutual for one call from her would bring him galloping from distant fields as if his life depended on it. He would then stand stock still while she bridled and saddled him.

There was one little trick he would sometimes play on her and that was to inflate his ribcage when she fitted the girth. On riding away he would deflate his chest and the saddle would slip to one side or the other, causing his rider to fall off. But Catharine was a natural when it came to horses and she quickly made a deal with Dandi. Prior to bridling him she would give him a carrot or a lump of sugar and he, in turn, would acquiesce in the process of fitting the leatherwork.

She would often get away for an hour and one of her favourite routes was up over the Graig to Pentyrch and then to the Garth Hill where she would gallop Dandi across the ridge feeling she was on top of the world. When they were at the highest point where the ancient mounds stood she could look southwards across the Severn Sea to the distant Somerset hills; to the west, she could see the Carmarthenshire Vans and to the north, the Brecon Beacons. She knew the names of these places because Old Lewis had pointed them out on their several visits to the high ground of Pentyrch.

Catharine was aware that lying beyond the Monmouthshire hills to the east was a different land – called England. She had made that one visit to Bristol with Raglan Sal but that was by sea. She wondered how far it was to England by land and then to London and if she would ever go that far in her life.

The longest journey Catharine had ever made alone was that trip by horse and trap to Aberthaw with Robin but the furthest she and Dandi went together was to Penhow, the other side of Newport. They were accompanied by Ianto the groom, a gruff middle-aged man who rode a cob called Caesar. The purpose of their visit was to collect some bottles of physic prepared by a ninety years old woman who lived in a cottage in the wood beyond Penhow Castle.

A feature of the trip was the way that Caesar at every opportunity tried to barge into Dandi, causing Catharine to use all her skills in order to prevent a collision. Annoyingly, Ianto never once took action to prevent such an occurrence and Catharine put that down to his need to emphasise who was in charge of this mission. She smiled to herself when she decided that this was another example of the childishness that some people retained in their advancing years. She often these days mused about this aspect of human nature although she would not have been able to put a name to it. She was still learning about the differing attitudes, behaviour, and aims of other people. Above all, no doubt from living at an establishment responsible for 'Justice' she continued to ponder the questions arising from 'crime and punishment'.

Nothing could have prepared Catharine for what happened next for it was most apt considering the thoughts that had been flooding her mind as they approached the northern edge of Cardiff.

There, on some rising ground near the crossroads at Mynydd Bychan, which some called 'The Little Heath', was a scaffold and from the gibbet a body hung in chains. The corpse was turning slowly in the breeze, with the head bent to one side and Catharine saw a face still bearing an expression of agonised despair. The eyes had gone and crows were still circling above hoping to continue their plunder. A host of flies were one step ahead of the birds. Both riders urged their mounts forward and slowed down only when they came upon a man walking at the roadside.

'Who is that back there?' asked Ianto, leaning out of his saddle and pointing his crop in the direction of the sad sight.

'Don't speak no Welsh,' said the walker. 'Talk to me proper and I'll tell you. What is it you wants to know?'

'Who's the unfortunate one?' said Ianto, in English, 'what did he do?'

'Don't know about unfortunate,' said the man, ''e deserved what 'e got.' He moved closer to the two horses and lowering his voice he went on: 'Thomas Arthur, that's who it is. A bad 'un 'e was. Put an end to the widow Watkin up in Cyncoed. That's what 'e did. Murder 'er 'e did, see. In early June it was. They tried 'im at the Sessions and croaked 'im all within a month. They 'ung 'im up down there on Stalling Down in the Vale. But the locals 'ere wanted 'im to 'ang around 'ere for a bit so they could throw things at 'im, see. So they brought the body back 'ere. Startin' to rot 'e is. Best thing for 'im I says.'

Ianto thanked him and nudged the cob onwards. Catharine, feeling somewhat nauseated, had already moved on.

They arrived at the cottage in the Gwent woods and after getting no answer to a gentle knock, Ianto hammered on the door and shouted, 'Come out, you witch!'

It was then clear to Catharine that Ianto and the woman knew each other for surely he would not otherwise have been so abusive.

A truly witch-like woman came to the door and Catharine was immediately reminded of the 'hag of the Vale' from her childhood: the one who had been so unkind to her mother at Pantycelyn farm.

This one might have been witch-like in appearance but she was kindness itself to her visitors. They were asked inside and given mugs of some soft drink which Catharine could not identify. Then the woman and Ianto chatted in Welsh about old times. It appeared that they knew each other at a place Catharine felt might have been Cowbridge House of Correction. It was explained that they were both employed there: Ianto as a warder and guard, the hag as a cook.

'Still taking this poison then are you?' said the hag, addressing Ianto and cackling as she spoke.

She then turned to Catharine and said, 'if I were you I'd take it too, it's saved many a life.'

'When we were at Cowbridge we met Will Edwards,' said Ianto. 'He was being corrected as far as they could but he ended up in Cardiff Gaol. Anyway he was descended from the physicians of Myddfai in Carmarthenshire and he had some special remedies. Shênad here got the recipe for one from him. Mind you, she won't tell us how she got it from him, but she did!'

'Aye, that I did,' said Shênad, giving that cackle again, and starting to hand the pair bottles filled with a greenish coloured liquid.

'What's it for?' asked Catharine innocently.

'What's it for? What's it for? . . . didn't this good man tell you?'

'It's for everything,' said Ianto, for Catharine's benefit. 'It'll cure headaches.'

'And piles,' added Shênad.

'Constipation too,' said Ianto.

'Rheumatism, without a doubt,' said Shênad.

'Don't forget scrofula,' offered Ianto.

'And worms,' said Shênad.

'Dropsy . . . don't leave out dropsy,' said Ianto quickly.'

'Alright, alright,' said Catharine, 'but we are collecting for our mistress, Madam Price. What does *she* want it for?'

'Not for us to know,' said Ianto, finishing his drink with a flourish.

They packed two canvas bags with the bottles and after thanking the hag, mounted their horses and left, taking an alternative route back for neither wanted to pass the scaffold again.

Their mistress was waiting for them in the yard when they arrived. The first thing she did when they dismounted was to remove one of the bottles from Ianto's satchel and drink the contents in one swig. 'It's what Samuel used to take,' said Madam Price. 'He swore by it.'

Catharine couldn't help wondering if that had caused him to have the fit before he took his last breath!

By the time the cuckoo called in 1784 to herald Catharine's 24th anniversary, not much had changed at Parc except for the sad demise of two of the serving staff. Both Lisabeth and Jac Evan had died from the smallpox. They were replaced by two youngsters from the workhouse, thus saving the parish finances a goodly sum. Phoebe, the cook who had replaced Gwladys, also passed away despite a stringent attempt by Dr Rhys to let blood from her by means of an incision in her scull. He had decided that her recent uncontrollable fits of temper were caused by 'bad' blood. She screamed so loudly that Madam Price felt obliged to go to the servants' quarters where the grisly operation was being carried out, to offer her assistance. The cook was dead by the time she got there. All three were buried on the same day at Llanilltern. And life went on.

Summer had well set in and it was time to bring in the hay. They had been at it for three weeks; now just one field remained: the nine acre called *'Cae'r Odyn'* (the Limekiln Field). Everyone

at Parc was involved in one way or another; also friends came from neighbouring farms to help.

A row of ten reapers moved slowly forward down the field, their scythes swinging with perfect rhythm as grass fell from the blades. Old Shinco Llewelyn, the lead scyther, set the timing of the mowing movement and kept everyone entertained with his rendering of traditional harvest songs as he went along. From time to time, but only when a ballad had come to a natural end, Shinco would take from his pocket a sharpening stone and apply it to his scythe. The others followed and this exercise also had a song to accompany it. The voices would alternate as they honed the blades with the whetsones, after dipping them into pots of water held by servant girls standing behind.

At the meal-break, Catharine brought from the house the pitchers of cider and nettle beer to which the workers had looked forward since the first blades of grass were mown.

The crowd of helpers would gather up on the headland and sit together to partake of the food and drink. It was mostly cheese and bread but occasionally there would be treats like '*teishan ar y maen*' . . . made with Welsh-cake mixture but with a dollop of thick cream on top.

The afternoon's mowing was always less well organised. The effects of the cider and nettle-beer not only reduced the scythers' productivity but it heightened the risk of mutual injury from implements over which they now had far less control.

All hands helped with the turning of the hay, which would be started two full days before the gathering. Thirty and more walked the field with their pitchforks twirling the cut grass over and over again. When the 'bringing in' eventually started each *gambo* went steadily across the field as huge forkfuls of hay were pitched onto it. An experienced loader ensured that the grass was loaded tidily to prevent it falling off. On the estate of Parc, the hay was then always stacked in front of the hedge below *Cae Wrth Tŷ* . . . the field near the house.

Another skill came into its own at this stage . . . the construction of the hayrick. The mown grass was compacted and after the stack grew to its maximum size, a perfectly symmetrical and rainproof straw roof was thatched to the top. For some years since John Price had come back from a military mission to France the stacks at Parc were round with conical roofs instead of the traditional pitched, ridged and gabled style of old. There were more than a dozen haystacks to see the farm's stock through the coming winter; also to supply less successful neighbours.

On the last evening of the hay gathering there would be a *Twmpath* at Parc. This was a concert of often impromptu acts: singing, clog dancing, fiddle playing and harping.

The entertainment would go on well into the night and Madam Price would watch and listen from the comfort of a chair placed especially for her on a slightly raised platform at the end of the barn. There was no stage as such for all the activity took place on the huge stone slabbed floor.

Madam Price always liked the dancing which was well-organised even though some of the movements were improvised. She would wave her gold-topped cane in time with the music, and generally give signs that she was enjoying herself – and that all was well with the world. She was not going to let the loss of the man to whom she had dedicated her life in any way reduce her enjoyment of traditional merriment.

Madam Catherine Price had, herself, been familiar with some of the set routines which involved six boys and six girls weaving a pattern as they moved to the music. Various gestures from the participants as the piece progressed had great meaning – for the dances often related incidents in Welsh history. That is how it went year after year.

And so it was, once more, on midsummer's night 1785. With all tasks completed, the workers at Parc gathered at the big barn

where makeshift seating was arranged, leaving enough space on the floor for the harpers, the fiddlers and the jiggers.

A group of dancers from Nantgarw were particularly entertaining this night. Even though they had earned their reputation in the halls of the 'mighty rich' of Glamorgan they were more than willing to take to the floor before the minor gentry. In fact they could be seen too at the fairs throughout the county where spectators were mostly from the peasantry, a class that was well represented at Parc.

Before the proceedings got fully under way, Daniel Siams, *Eos y Fro* (the Nightingale of the Vale) stood, near the triple harp being played by his wife, Hannah *'Telynores Elai'* (the Ely harper). This meant that a high standard would be set for the evening by this pair of leading local musicians.

The introduction on the harp was played and silence ruled as Daniel began to perform. He walked as he sang and the 'Nightingale of the Vale', brought forth sweet sounds worthy of that avian minstrel. Dan's words thrown to his audience as he sang his way around the barn told of ancient times when the Cymric folk ruled the whole of Britain; when the good Christian Welsh fought off the pagan invaders until they were swamped by numbers and power. When he recalled the tragedies of those long ago times, Hannah produced low-pitched stormy passages from her strings. When the sun came out in the saga, the harp tinkled with silvery sounds. Dan wound up his heroic tale in the centre of the floor with a resounding conclusion and a bow to the enraptured gathering most of which by now had partaken of liquid refreshment of the mind-loosening variety.

The Nantgarw dancers were enthralling as they demonstrated their latest routine, which involved an intricate pattern of movements and the not infrequent squeal of a girl as the dance told the story of the love of a poor peasant wench for a squire's son. The waving of fluttering handkerchiefs and the girls' coquettish expressions enhanced the telling of the tale through meaningful movements.

To begin with, Catharine Griffith sat with her fellow servants quietly in a corner of the barn, bemused as suitor after suitor came up and took away her friends to dance or sing or both. Not once was she envious of her friends being chosen before her.

Once more it was the turn of the Nantgarw dancers, some of whom had not taken to the floor in the earlier performances. This time among the men dancers was a figure from which Catharine simply could not avert her gaze. He wore a white shirt with a frill down its front and a narrow red cravat around his neck. His tight-fitting breeches helped to emphasise shapely calf muscles on legs which descended neatly into his highly polished clogs. His masculine charm was plainly evident as he moved with grace and exquisite timing.

As the dance was completed, he bowed elegantly to the young lady who was his opposite number in the formation and led her from the floor holding her hand high, by the fingertips, before disappearing into the crowd of onlookers who were now clapping and cheering. Catharine stood bewildered with the image of the young man refusing to stay out of her head.

Chapter Seven

Catharine once again sat in the attic window at Parc to watch the parade of the pitiable. Several of the men had their hands tied behind their backs. Strangely, the few women amongst them held their tied hands in front of them. All of the prisoners received kicks to the rear from laughing guards who walked alongside. Others limped, and were egged forward with the help of the stock of a musket pushed into the small of the back. Catharine was shocked to see one of the prisoners return a kick. The response from the guard who suffered that humiliation was to strike out with the stock of his musket once more. This time, however, the target was the prisoner's head. In moments the poor man was bleeding profusely and his white shirt quickly developed red streaks. Despite the vicious blow, the victim refused either to fall to the ground or even to subdue the smile that lit up his face.

Catharine immediately wanted to go down to remonstrate with the guard but recalled Samuel Price's words: 'Catrin, Catrin, this is a matter for officers of the law!' Even so, she went as far as the front door and had a closer look at the prisoners gathered in the yard. The man who was bleeding was standing proudly upright before he was kneed in the stomach by the same guard who had struck him with the musket butt. He was then grabbed and forced into an outbuilding to await the call to the courtroom to face the magistrates. As he was leaving the yard he turned to face Catharine full on and she felt a huge shiver through her backbone as she recognised him as the handsome dancer she had constantly thought about since the night of the *twmpath* a full month earlier.

She could not have foreseen what would happen next. A clearly irate Madam Price, waving her cane, emerged from the house and made her way to the courtroom. Within seconds two justices were out in the yard and receiving a most vehement verbal onslaught from the furious woman. Again, within seconds, the man who had been so aggressive a little earlier was brought before the mistress of Parc and the justices.

A sergeant stepped forward and removed the musket from the cowardly guard who, as he walked away, received some kicks to his rear parts, the first one coming from Madam Catherine Price! It transpired that she had also been watching the arrival of the trialists and had been appalled that the standard of behaviour set by her late husband had dropped to an unacceptable level.

This was not the end of the matter, for within a short time the white-shirted prisoner himself had been released on the instructions of Madam Price. Catharine Griffith didn't see him leave but she retained in her mind that last image of him, smiling despite the pain which he was clearly feeling at that moment. She went to bed that night with an ocean swell of her recent emotional spasms running from anger to peace, from bewilderment to understanding – and from despair to hope. It was on a note of optimism that she finally fell into a deep sleep in which she dreamed sometimes of dashing men with tricorn hats and swords at their sides and other times of handsome white-shirted dancers.

Dandi was already waiting at the fence when Catharine walked from the stable yard with saddle and bridle at 6.30 in the morning. He seemed to have an uncanny knowledge of the weather and must have known that today was going to be a lovely late Autumn day and if he didn't play any tricks on Catharine they would most likely go on a nice long run. Guided towards the

Graig above Parc, the pony knew that they were heading for Pentyrch once more and perhaps to the Garth ridge. In fact though, the furthest they were going that day was to a thatched cottage near Ffynnon Catwg ('Cadoc's Well') adjacent to Pentyrch parish church. She tethered Dandi to a hand-rail on the wall near the mounting stone outside the church wall before knocking on the door of the cottage. As she waited she could hear unfamiliar sounds from within: metallic clicking mixed with scraping noises and occasional musical tinkles.

The door opened and a tall man wearing a working apron greeted her in Welsh.

'Come in,' he said, shaking her hand, 'I'm John Philip, my brother will join us in a moment.'

Catharine entered a workshop such as she had never seen before. Vices of various types were attached to a bench upon which sundry tools were scattered. Around the room, some attached to the wall and others standing free, were clocks of all shapes and sizes. Pervasive ticking noises were interrupted by occasional chimes and one sound that startled Catharine at first but which she soon found very appealing indeed. It was caused by the cuckoo that thrust itself out of a clockface, called and went back inside as quickly as it had emerged.

'It's not my birthday surely,' mused Catharine, smiling to herself.

'I am here for Madam Price' she said, looking around the room, amazed. 'I believe you know what she wants.'

'Ah, yes' said John Philip. 'A long case clock with brass dials and a small plaque with a dedication to her dear departed husband.'

'That's right,' said Catharine. 'In dark oak wood.'

'Oh, yes, yes,' said John Philip quickly. 'Only the best for Madam Price.' He turned and called to his brother who must have been in the back room. *'Dafydd, der 'ma . . . mae merch yma ar ran y Frenhines . . . er, er,'* ('Come, David, there's a girl here on behalf of the Queen.') He quickly realised his little joke might have been rather insulting, so, facing Catharine again, he added: 'Well, when I say "queen" I mean your good lady is so, er, regal you see. Yes, that's it, regal. Yes indeed, regal.'

David Philip joined them and got down to business rather quicker than his older brother.

'Have you brought the necessary?' he said, noticing the leather bag at Catharine's side.

'Yes,' she said, 'but it's not in the bag. Too many thieves about you see.'

'Where is it then?' ventured John. 'Do you have it?'

'If you good men retire to the back room and come back in twenty seconds it will be here for you, plain.' The two brothers glanced at each other and went out. They thought they heard a shuffling of Catharine's clothing before they returned to find a small leather bag tied with a thong sitting on the table and Catharine standing with her arms folded.

'Go on, count it,' she said.

David reached for the money holder and counted out the coins passing each piece in turn to his brother. At the emergence of the last piece they visibly stiffened.

'There's only five sovereigns here,' squawked John Philip, 'where's the other five?'

'Payable on safe delivery and only if it arrives in working order,' said Catharine as she turned on her heel and walked out. 'That's the way it has to be.'

'Who says so?' shouted David Philip, who had quickly come to the door.

'The Queen says so,' she replied as she mounted her pony and turned for home.

A month later it was getting dusk when Old Lewis was heard rushing about the house shouting, 'They're coming! They're on their way! They are nearly here. Come out! Come out!' It sounded like a command from an officer in charge of some garrison that was under attack.

In minutes, several servants and labourers who had been in earshot of Old Lewis had downed their tools and gathered in the back yard. Eventually they were joined by Madam Price, who, apart from Old Lewis, was the only one who knew what was happening. Catharine should have known too but although she strained her eyes in the direction of the copse on the Graig to which Old Lewis was pointing, she had no idea.

Gradually emerging from the trees and joining the path that crossed the field down to the house were two men, carrying a heavy object – one at the front and one at the back. Every few yards the men put their burden down and took long breaths.

When they were about thirty yards away the kind Madam Price said to no-one in particular, 'Bring them drinks and other sustenance. They will be fatigued beyond reason.' Three servants rushed into the house competing for the right to fulfill their mistress's request.

Daio and Bryn had been hired by the Philip brothers to carry the clock all the way from their workshop in Pentyrch – a matter of about two miles over undulating fields and through the copse.

At last, the clock was placed on the spot reserved for it in the library and the two men were invited into the kitchen for food and more drinks.

Daio and Bryn were explaining to the cook and the other servants that normally they delivered clocks on carts even though the roads were mostly rutted and stony, thereby often causing damage to the delicate mechanisms. In this case the Philip brothers thought it wise to do as requested by Madam Price, because, they said, their fear of her was unbounded. Madam, passing the kitchen door, heard that remark, smiled and walked away waving her gold-headed cane in triumph.

It was a fruitful but turbulent time for many living at the eastern extremity of the Vale of Glamorgan. 'Long ling'ring', agues, smallpox, melancholia, fits, financial ruin, breaking of limbs, drownings, blood-lettings, floggings, public executions and infant mortality' were far from being unusual. There was still no limit to the variety of subjects that amused and entertained the worthy folk who continued to gather in the ale and smoking lounges of Cae Golman, the Dusty Forge and other taverns. At the Plymouth Arms the regulars were always agog for the latest gossip.

'I've heard tell that the Bailiff of Hensol, old Zacharias, has been dead a week now,' said Ioan John.

'Well I trust so,' said Twm the tiler, 'for was he not buried yesterday!'

Inevitably, this brought course laughter from the others. The most common way to change the subject of conversation was then used:

'Let's drink to the King's health!' said Ioan, sharply getting to his feet.

'Don't know about his health,' interjected Ithel Ynyswen. 'I think we are too late on that score. But let's drink to the King anyway.'

Half a dozen wenches dutifully filled the tankards held in outstretched arms.

'The King!'

Catharine was now twenty-six and inevitably she wondered why it was that a number of the much younger serving staff were going off to get married and having children – whilst she continued to wait and wonder if she would ever get swept off her feet in the way of her dreams. In fact she pondered over many things – for instance: how long cuckoos lived. Was the one that she could hear calling from the distant Plymouth woods the same bird as she had listened to in previous years?

There was, however, another question that made Catharine Griffith quite curious. She was aware of the various Nonconformist movements that were growing apace in the neighbourhood and wondered what was their policy regarding the teaching of right and wrong and the punishment of crime. She had heard talk of the Methodist meeting houses where Calvinism was the guiding moral force, despite occasional incursions from Wesleyans. She knew too of the strength of the Baptists, and the recent gathering of support for the Unitarians who sometimes held meetings on her beloved Garth Mountain. Always, in the background, were the Quakers whose attitude to Bible teachings Catharine had heard were very different from the rest. Of Roman Catholics, she knew very little indeed. She was though hearing much about a movement which had originated during the time of the Puritan reforms, the Congregationalists. (*Annibynnwyr* . . . Independents).

It was therefore with burgeoning interest that Catharine walked one Sunday morning from Parc and left her group that was mainly heading for the church at Llanilltern. She crossed the fields below Tydu and Rhydlafar before picking up the well-worn path to Taihirion. Madam Price would be there before her for she had gone ahead in the trap with Old Lewis. Catharine joined a big group walking along the path and wondered how they would all fit into the little chapel. They did so and a member of the congregation courteously gave up his seat for her. The Rev. Rhys Rowland, sermonised about the price of sin and so on, and Catharine listened in vain for any differences she might detect between his output and that of her church. She wondered if it was the Taihirion influence which had made

Madam Price and Samuel, merciful employers, but quickly dismissed that idea for she knew a number from the parish church congregation who were also very kind and compassionate. In addition she had always considered Garmon Rees the curate to be a very good man. Perhaps, she thought, we are simply what we are and that's the end of it. The only certainty was that Catharine Griffith was more confused than ever.

Madam Price asked Old Lewis to pull up the pony and trap alongside Catharine who had started walking home.

'If I had known you were coming to our chapel today I would have brought you along with me,' said Madam Price, pointing to the empty bench at her side as a way of inviting Catharine to join her.

As the servant took her seat, Old Lewis flicked the reins and the pony broke into a trot.

'Did you hear, Robin?' asked Madam Price. 'He whinnied when he saw you. You must be a good girl. Robin doesn't like everybody!'

After they came to a stop in the yard, Old Lewis helped Madam Price down from the trap and repeated the action with Catharine who thanked him courteously.

'You have gentle manners, Catharine,' said Madam Price as they turned for the house. 'Which reminds me that I wish to speak to you at length. Come and see me in the drawing room at 3 o'clock.'

'What could this be?' wondered Catharine as they went their separate ways. Perhaps I'll be told at last about that package? She had not the slightest inkling that she was about to experience one of the most dramatic life-changing events of her whole life to date.

As Catharine approached the drawing room, the long case clock was striking three and before it had stopped chiming, she was knocking on the door.

'Come in,' said Catherine Price, and Catharine Griffith complied with her request, taking the chair to which the lady of the house was pointing with her gold-headed cane.

Madam Price herself was sitting in her favourite rocking chair with a truly angelic expression on her face.

'Catharine,' she said, 'I have something very serious to tell you.'

'I felt it was going to be something important,' said Catharine, 'I could tell by the look on your face. Is it bad news?'

'That will be for you to judge' said the kind mistress of the house. 'But, I hope you will be pleased.' At that point she got up from the rocking chair, put down her cane and moving towards Catharine, who was also now standing, gently took her hands in hers.

'It's a long story, so forgive me if I hesitate in its telling.'

By now Catharine was a sackful of nerves.

Madam Price went on: 'You don't remember your grand-father of course – but he figures large in this story I can tell you.'

'Oh, please Madam Price,' thought Catharine, 'just get on with it.'

As if reading Catharine's thoughts she did move the story forward.

'You seem to know only about your grandmother and the vicious rumour about her inviting that assault when she was carrying your mother. Well, your grandad was dead by then but he will always have a place in our hearts.'

'Madam Price,' said Catharine, 'I'm sorry to be impatient but what are you trying to say?'

'Well, my dear girl, when I was very young, about four years old, *my* mother was attacked too, on the road from St Fagans. I saw it happen. One of the brutes was about to carry me off as well when a man riding from the direction of Pentrebane saw the scene and sensed the worst. He quickly dismounted and bravely set about the three assailants. Fortunately they hadn't had their way with my mother and the man who had grabbed me released me before running away with his equally cowardly cohorts.'

'What has all this got to do with me?' asked Catharine, perplexed.

'The brave man who saved us was your mother's father,' explained Madam Price. 'I didn't know myself until it was explained to me just before you came to work with us.' She sat back into her chair with a sigh as if she had just unburdened herself of the world's greatest secret.

She continued, 'I discussed it with Samuel and he agreed that we should help to ease your passage through life, as a gesture of gratitude.'

Catharine started to walk slowly around the room, slowly shaking her head and with a puzzled look on her face.

Somewhat alarmed, Madam Price asked: 'Do you see this as bad news? Have I offended you?'

Catharine stopped and, looking Madam Price straight in the eye said: 'I'm afraid nothing will ever be the same again, Ma'am. *Rydw i mewn trallod!*' (I am distraught).

'Why in God's name, are you so vexed?'

Catharine walked around the room again and then, flopping down into the chair, burst into a torrent of tears. Madam Price knelt beside her and said, 'What is it that troubles you about what I told you?'

Catharine rose again and moved towards the door. She stopped, turned, and said, 'Madam, for all these years I have worked for you, I thought I was being appreciated for myself and not for the repaying of a debt to someone else. Any notions I might have had that I was being rewarded simply for being good, have now drained from me – I bid you goodnight.'

In the early hours of the morning, Madam Price could hear the sounds of sobbing coming from Catharine's room but felt there was nothing she could do to help the girl. What was meant to be a welcome revelation had turned sour.

Catharine was in torment for days. She deliberately sought the hardest and dirtiest jobs which was her simple way of suppressing the feelings of guilt which had engulfed her very being since her meeting with Madam Price. The lady of the house decided it would be better if she kept her distance from the troubled girl for the time being.

Several questions were getting tangled in Catharine's mind. She wondered whether she would have so readily accepted the comforts that were afforded her if she had been aware of the reasons behind her employer's tenderness. Then she would lean to the view that the Prices were naturally kind and lenient and were to be admired. Even though she toiled hard, she was dazed by a confusion of thoughts that teased and taunted her as she went about her duties. Feeling weak from incessant self-reproach she knew it was time to seek help to find a way forward. There were few persons who could be relied upon for advice untainted by self-interest . . . and one of these was Old Lewis.

Catharine found the old man sitting in the tool-shed in the stable-yard, sharpening sickles and scythes. 'Miss Griffith,' he said, suddenly standing up, 'what brings you here?'

'I need your help, my old friend,' said Catharine, whose red eyes hadn't escaped the notice of the old man. 'I am desperate for help.'

'Well, well,' said Lewis, 'and there was me thinking you didn't want for anything in this world.'

Catharine told the old man everything about her meeting with Madam Price and the fact that she had been agonising ever since about whether she deserved the privileges she enjoyed.

Old Lewis sat down again and Catharine took the stool he pushed towards her. He said nothing for a while, simply sitting there with head bowed.

His silence led Catharine to think that perhaps it was a wasted journey. After all, most people thought that the old man had lost his mind anyway. Catharine though had always found the old retainer helpful; she felt too that he always spoke a lot of sense if you just gave him time to get his thoughts and words together. She would be patient with him.

The old man rose to his feet and stood, saying nothing; just staring out into the yard.

His visitor was about to bid him farewell when he started speaking.

'I've been on this earth a long long time,' he said slowly. Perhaps, too long. Who knows?' He cleared his throat a couple of times and went on: 'I was ten when Queen Anne of England died. I've outlived two Georges . . . and from what I hear of the present one I might make it three yet.'

Catharine began to wonder if indeed the old man's mind had gone, but he turned to face her and continued: 'I'm over three times your age and the surest thing I've learned in all my time on earth is that there are bad people and there are good people.'

Catharine, not being totally unaware of this fact, could do no more than just nod in agreement.

'Now then, what was it you came to see me about?' said Old Lewis, reaching for his sharpening stone and preparing to get working again. Disheartened, Catharine sighed and got up. She was about to thank the old man and say goodbye when he spoke crucial words to her.

'Good people, the Prices. All of them . . . and those that marry them as well. Nobody quite like them. God's people, see. Sam Price was the kindest man I ever knew . . . and Catherine Price is the best woman. Now go and be kind to *her* for a change!'

Catharine crossed the yard and ran straight into the house. She tapped gingerly on the door to the drawing room and was pleased to hear Madam Price's voice immediately saying 'enter'.

They met in the middle of the room and flung their arms around each other. They stood hugging for a full minute and when they parted, nothing was said by either of them. Nothing needed to be said.

Catharine and the good lady of Parc had become closer than ever after their fateful meeting. Catharine Griffith, serving wench, had finally become Catharine Griffith, lady's maid and companion.

Chapter Eight

Ianto the groom had scrubbed Robin until he shone and he even put a red ribbon on his bobbed tail before harnessing him to the trap which looked new now that it had been painted black and varnished by Old Lewis. Madam Price and Catharine, both carrying leather bags, climbed aboard with Catharine taking the reins this time.

This was the latest of several trips they had taken together lately; the first one, a few months previously, had been an eye-opener for Catharine. It wasn't until they arrived at a cottage in upper Pentyrch that she had understood the nature of their visit. Four dirty children, two boys and two girls in rags, came out to greet them. Catharine had never seen such thin bodies and she stared at them in a state of utter shock. Madam Price, on the other hand, picked up the children in turn and hugged them lovingly – and carefully, for they were hardly more than bags of bones. She then went into the house and beckoned to Catharine to follow her.

The scene within the cottage was awful. The children's consumptive mother was lying on the bed and having a coughing fit. Appearing at the side of the woman's mouth was a red trickle which became progressively worse with each rasping cough. Madam Price took a cloth from a nearby bucket which contained some potion or other – and after wringing it out, wiped the blood from the poor woman's face.

They then brought from the trap a basket that contained bread, cheese, a hunk of salted ham, six wine bottles containing fresh milk and apples and pears from the orchard at Parc. No words were exchanged, but the woman raised her hand as a gesture of thanks as they waved her goodbye.

Madam Price said, 'That poor mother will be in heaven by the morning. I've arranged for two homes on the estate to take in the children. The curate's sister will be happy to help; so will Jemima and Cledwyn at Tŷ Gwyn Farm.'

Catharine had lately come to understand that word 'good' more clearly than ever before.

The trap journeys were usually errands of mercy, and for amusement Madam Price would keep their destination secret from Catharine until they were nearly there each time. Today they were off again – and this time they took neither money nor food for they were certainly not visiting the needy.

They trotted on past the splendid Pencoed House, home to Welsh princes of Glamorgan in medieval times, and up the lanes to another mighty residence called Castell y Mynach. Despite its name the house had never been a castle or a monastery. It was, though, the home of minor gentry since it had been taken over by the Mathew family a century or so earlier.

'My kinsman lives here,' said Madam Price, with a hint of pride. 'Well, I think he's a relative. Anyway, it's a fine house!'

As they pulled into the courtyard, a manservant came out and took hold of the trap as the two women stepped down.

'Is William here? Or is he up at Penllwyn counting his sheep?'

'No, he's in the house,' said the servant, while placing a tub of oats under Robin's nose.

'Ah, well, he'll be counting his money then,' said Madam Price.

William John came out at that moment and invited the two women into the house.

'How are you Catherine?' said William, I haven't seen you since Sam's funeral. Oh, and who is this young lady?'

'She's my friend, Catharine Griffith, whose father was shot dead in cold blood by Watkin Pugh, Penprysg.'

'Oh yes, a bad business, that. At least he was fully brought to justice.' Changing the subject he said: 'I heard your remark about me counting my money. Come back in a year or two and that is exactly what I shall be doing. I've built a lime kiln and I'm going to spread the fields and grow corn. If the price of wheat holds I'll make my fortune.'

'Well, just think of old Fat Mathew who lived here a hundred and fifty years back,' said Madam Price. 'He was so wealthy they used to say that if his golden sovereigns were laid side by side, the line of coins would extend from here to the parish church in Pentyrch, two miles away!

'I wouldn't want to meet the same end as he did,' said William, with a pained expression on his face. 'Sat on a poisoned spike on a bench down at the forge, that's what he did!' As he spoke, he grimaced whilst holding his own posterior.

'Yes, that spike was placed in a cushion by a disgruntled employee,' said Madam Price. 'I hope your people like you!'

William laughed. 'Let's show you what you've come for,' he said, leading the way to the door. They crossed a large garden in the direction of the orchard and came upon a stone building outside which there were haphazard piles of barrels, assorted tundishes and tubes scooped out from wood.

They entered the building and immediately they were aware of a pungent but not unpleasant aroma. A huge stone circular apple press was being turned by a muscular, suntanned man who was stripped to the waist. A second man was placing apples in the path of the moving stone wheel and a third was gathering the resultant juice in earthenware pots which were then being carried away by a succession of young servant girls.

Catharine hardly noticed anyone else but the man at the wheel. His action was reminiscent of someone rowing a big boat; his rippling muscles bulged and relaxed alternately as he stretched his arms and wound the handle. William raised his hand as a request to cease working and the big wheel came to a stop. The winding man then turned to face the visitors and Catharine nearly fainted with shock for she realised who it was. He was even more handsome than he had seemed the first time she saw him – in the barn at Parc when the dancing troupe were leaving the floor. He smiled and she nearly fainted again – but managed somehow to regain her composure.

William, addressing Madam Price, said, 'This is Henry, Henry James. He will come to help you set up your press. When do you want him?'

'He can join us as soon as he likes,' said Madam Price. 'I have a shipment of apples coming into Aberthaw from Bridgwater in a few days. We have a stone; it's an old one – I think it was used for flour at Llanbedr Mill years ago.'

'I'll be pleased to come to you as soon as you wish, my lady,' said Henry James, and upon hearing his rich manly voice, Catharine's nerves tingled again.

Before they left Castell y Mynach, William insisted on showing them the old mural on one of the bedroom walls. It depicted the demise of a galleon at the Battle of the Armada and had been painted by a visiting Dutch artist soon after that time.

'I've seen it before,' said Madam Price, but I'm glad you had an opportunity to look at it as well.' She continued to talk the whole length of the return journey and had Catharine been listening she would have learned that it had been an ambition of Madam Price's late husband to have a cider press at Parc and that she had been making enquiries regarding that project. This had led her to Castell y Mynach and so on and so on . . . but Catharine was hardly listening. It was just as well that Robin knew the way back home for her mind was set on something quite different.

As he was classed as neither a servant nor a labourer in the accepted sense of the terms, appropriate accommodation had to be found for Henry James during his attachment to the estate of Parc. There was great excitement among the serving maids when they found his arrival was imminent. They too had noted his good looks and his impressive demeanour when he was at the *twmpath* and looked forward avidly to seeing him at close quarters again.

The newcomer was to lodge at Y Gockid, a substantial property half a mile away from Parc. He would be looked after royally there by the Hopkin family and already the talk had gone around the community that an Adonis was on his way. The trouble was that no one really knew what sort of a person he was. After all, he had been in the custody of law officers a short while ago.

Catharine herself was head-over-heels in love with someone to whom she had never spoken a word. She told herself repeatedly that it was irrational to be so besotted when she had seen him three times only: the first was a fleeting glimpse when he was accompanying a female dancer; on the second occasion he was a prisoner of the law and had his head cracked open; the third time, he was too busy fixing work to have really noticed her.

Despite her obsession, or, perhaps, because of it, Catharine these days was rather better adjusted mentally than she had been for a long time. In what had previously been that worrying hour before sleep took over, she thought much less about things that troubled her. She was able now to consider what she loved about life: flowers, trees, birds, especially the cuckoo that crossed the seas every April to celebrate her birthday – and the nightingale that brought music to the Plymouth Woods every summer. Half asleep she saw images from her ideal world:

beautiful ponies, young gambolling lambs, chicks and piglets, all outside in the open air where the sun was always shining. Moving indoors too in her half-dreams there would be things of delight: Quill pens producing magic, clocks with brass dials . . . clocks with nesting cuckoos. She saw kind faces with Madam Price always among them. Old Lewis as well – for he represented the wisdom that comes with age. Try as she would to prevent it, the last image she saw before slumber claimed her was always that of a thoroughly handsome man with rippling muscles and a smile that she felt could light up the darkest of rooms.

The new cider press was successfully installed under the supervision of Henry James. Catharine and Old Lewis took a big cart to Aberthaw to collect the first delivery of apples. Good cider apples were grown locally as well but these were of the highest quality and came from *Gwlad yr Haf* – Somerset. Each sackful of fruit weighed about seventy pounds and as the quayside workers carried them from the ship and loaded the vehicle, Old Lewis began to worry that the load would be too heavy for the ageing carthorse, Major, who had been chosen for the task. In the event although movement on the home journey was slow, they made steady progress.

Catharine could hardly wait to get back to see the man of her dreams. Their paths had not crossed since he started work at Parc but now, she fervently hoped, they surely would.

It was quite late in the evening when they got back. The sacks of cider apples were duly dumped near the new building which, to Catharine's bitter disappointment, was locked up. The brewers had obviously finished for the day and the man of her dreams had departed. She had little choice but to be patient so she decided to visit her friends in the servants' loft to catch up on the latest gossip.

Catharine Griffith was more than a little surprised as she climbed the rickety ladder to hear the voice of a man who was regaling the girls with tales, which, to judge by his audience's reaction, must have been extraordinarily interesting. The speaker had his back to Catharine as she arrived in the dormitory. There was no doubting his voice and when Catharine saw those black curls tightly rolled about the back of his neck above a crisp white shirt, she knew it was him. As he turned towards her his face erupted with a sunburst smile revealing the whitest teeth she had ever seen. Catharine's knees were threatening to knock as he stood up and took her hand.

'This is Catharine,' said Martha Jones, one of the younger servants. 'The one that really fancies you!'

'Ah,' said Henry James, 'I think we saw each other at Castell y Mynach last week.'

'Don't let me interrupt you,' said Catharine, trying not to show her embarrassment at Martha's remark, as she joined the other girls who were sitting cross-legged on the floor. 'Please carry on with your story-telling.'

'Surely I will,' said Henry – and he picked up where he left off in a tale about his escape from a pirate ship on which he had been held prisoner for two months. He claimed to have swum ashore when they called at some South Sea island to collect fresh water, stayed there for a year, married the native chieftain's daughter, became king of the tribe, had fifteen children all of whom had black curly hair, and eventually escaped by building a raft and paddling it back to Europe, arriving in a thunderstorm at Marseilles where he became a vagabond, travelling all over Europe as an advisor to princes and statesmen! He said he came back to Wales with only one thing in mind . . . and that was to find the woman of his dreams and settle down with her to a life on the open road!

He got up and said, 'It is late, so I shall now do the gentlemanly thing and leave you good people to have your sweet dreams.' As he began his descent of the ladder he blew a kiss to the assembled girls and then disappeared out into the night.

Catharine left a short while afterwards, the 'oohs' and 'aahs' of the girls continuing until she was out of earshot. Lying awake for an hour or more in her bed, she went over the day's events in her mind, inevitably recalling again and again that moment when he smiled upon her arrival at the girls' dormitory. 'Such curly black hair,' she thought. 'Such startlingly white teeth.' 'Such a radiant smile.' – 'Such a wonderful liar!' Once again, Catharine Griffith went to sleep with a smile on her face.

Events elsewhere were as interesting as ever. John Price, whose good name was under continual attack from reactionary groups, found that vicious lies about him were being circulated in fashionable society throughout Glamorgan. He was vilified even for having been seen in the company of Iolo Morganwg on a visit to London. The talk was that he should be put down before his advocation of rebellion gained too much support. In particular he was attacked in the press for what were described as attempts to undermine 'an industry that was fundamental to the financial well-being of the nation' – a convenient euphemism. John had often gone across the Bristol Channel to meetings in Bridgwater where anti-slavery feeling was growing by the day. In a few years there would be a huge uprising against slavery and it was thinkers like John Price that sparked the beginning of the revolt.

John Price was fully aware of the hate which he had generated and he remained fully alert to the dangers to himself that were caused thereby. There had been a few false alarms so he was ever watchful that one day there would be a serious physical strike against him. That was a misjudgment for he should have known that such was his prowess with pistol and sword, even wrestling, that few would dare stage a private attack on his person. He had, however, neglected to protect his family against possible attention that might be given to *them* as opposed to himself.

It was, therefore, with a deep feeling of self-reproach that he learned of the danger into which his wife and young child were suddenly plunged.

He found a note, scribbled on a crumpled piece of paper attached to the main gate of his home. It said simply: 'Prepare to be widowed and childless by midnight tonight – unless you post a notice on the cross at Llandaff renouncing your part in the Anti-Slavery Society.'

John's military training and his experiences in various hot spots taught him that he must keep cool. Panic at this stage would be disastrous. So it was, that after he had found the note, he went for a slow walk around the grounds of his big mansion at Llandough to collect his thoughts. His intelligence told him that it would not be in the interests of his adversaries to harm his loved ones at this early stage for they would then lose their biggest bargaining tool with nothing gained. Time was on his side, but he thought it would be wise to make it his priority to arrange for his family to be at a safe location. After walking for no more than five minutes he retraced his steps into the house and was horrified to find that his wife and little girl were no longer there. He took a deep breath and went around the house checking every room, niche and nook to be sure they were not being hidden in their own home.

Throughout history the turn of events has often been fortuitous rather than predetermined and what happened next was a good example. An old trusted servant of the family into which John had married – the Birts of Wenvoe Castle – happened to be in the herb garden, quietly hoeing between the parsley and the thyme without a harsh thought in his mind, when he saw his master's wife and child being manhandled into a trap and driven away at speed.

Putting 'two and two together' as he put it, Siôn Bowen recognised the trap as one belonging to Robart Gwilym, of Hendre'r Coed. He had seen it at the coachmakers in Ely when he was there collecting axle grease a few days before. Surely there was only one trap in the county painted yellow, green and red. Siôn lost no time in telling John Price.

John thanked him for the information and borrowing his buggy which was harnessed and waiting, rushed off towards Hendre'r Coed, but then slowed down to think the matter through. He quickly decided that Robart couldn't possibly be implicated in the abduction – for was he not a stout supporter of John in all his causes? The fact that Siôn had seen the distinctive trap raised all sorts of possibilities, but it took only a second to choose the next move. Making a slight detour, John Price drove to the coachmaker's yard and pulled up on seeing a man carrying a pot and paintbrush.

In answer to John's quickfire questions, the coachpainter said, 'No doubts about it, I did the job for a big man with red hair – wouldn't give his name. As long as they pays me I'll paint 'em any rainbow colours they wants.'

A minute later John was on his way once more. His return took him past his own house again where Siôn was still working in the walled garden and took the precaution of calling over to tell him where he was heading.

'Give me half an hour,' said John – and Siôn' replied with a nod.

It wasn't too far to Pwll Du mansion where Erasmus, the red-headed giant, was running the home farm of the estate in the absence of his father, squire Theo.

John trotted the buggy at a respectable pace towards the yard and then slowed. He thought it would be unlikely that the captives were held at the house itself. It would be too obvious. He turned his attentions to the outbuildings one by one, but met with no success as he walked around, pushing doors open. John was taking great care for he knew of Erasmus's reputation as a fighting man. He did though afford himself a wry smile when he saw, protruding through the open doors of a cart shed, the tail end of a highly coloured trap that shone with new varnish.

Firstly John was aware of a huge shadow darkening the corner of the yard where he now crouched, listening for any tell-tale sounds that might have come his way. Then the shadow took on a distinctly human shape, indicating that it was from the frame of a very big man standing behind him. If that wasn't enough to cause John alarm, the fact that the shadowy shape now included a raised arm holding what looked like a sword made him leap to his feet. He too drew his sword and turned to meet his opponent who was bringing his weapon down with great force through the air where John's head had been a split second earlier.

The swordplay that followed was of rare quality for both men had become proficient in the art whilst serving in the Glamorgan Militia. However, whereas John had left the service with his gentlemanly reputation intact, Erasmus had been dishonourably discharged after severely injuring two men in a tavern brawl, one of them a senior Dragoon officer.

John knew that if it came to an exchange of physical blows he would be no match for the brute; but as long as he was fencing he was fully confident he would eventually master Erasmus for the big man would surely tire. The sounds of clashing steel and regular grunts from the larger of the two men filled the air as they wove their way around the yard. Never doubting his supremacy, John played with his opponent who, after five minutes was breathing heavily. Lunges from Erasmus were becoming clumsier and every strike easier to parry; every doublé; every clashing of foibles; every bind; every feint, resulted in John's favour. At last, following a feeble envelopment from Erasmus which led to a total loss of his balance, the big man's weapon flew from his grasp. John Price stepped slightly to the side and with a dexterous sword-point flick removed a large patch from the giant's breeches. This was followed at lightning speed by a similar action and an even larger patch fell away. By now the snorting monster was trotting heavily around the yard with John in close pursuit. Soon he was without a scrap of cloth covering his manhood, dancing like a deranged creature and begging for mercy: 'Don't kill me, for God's sake don't kill me – I'll do anything you ask!'

'Where are your prisoners, you disgusting bladder of lard? – you toxic weed, you slithering serpent. Where are they?' said John, carefully sheathing his sword.

'In the cellar, they are down in the cellar!' said Ginger, now down on his knees with his hands clasped together in a pleading gesture.

'If I were to fall for that, I'd be as witless as you are!' said John, who now seemed to be towering above the crouching figure. 'Now tell me the truth, where are they?'

'In the stable loft, that's where they are! Aye, in the stable loft!'

'Not the tithe barn?'

'No!'

'Not the milking shed?'

'No!'

'Right, for the last time,' said John, moving as if to unsheath his sword again. 'Where are they?'

Erasmus would have answered with another lie had not the sound of cantering hooves caused them to turn their heads. Six burly men rode into the yard and dismounted. One of them was Siôn Bowen, another was Robart Gwilym of Hendre'r Coed. Each of them agreed with what John Price stood for and would give their lives for him.

'Put him up on the roof,' said John, 'I'm feeling merciful today!'

'No, for God's sake, I'll tell you where I've hidden your dear family – I will! – I will!'

'Not necessary, you noxious parasitic worm. I *know* where they are,' said John, causing the group to give him a curious look. 'Stick him on the thatch and tie him to the chimney. I'll make my way to the lime kiln . . . just look at his boots!'

The evidence had been there all the time. Wet lime stuck to his leather boots would certainly have been removed by Erasmus at the first opportunity. Clearly he had been to the kiln not very long before John's arrival.

John's wife and daughter both burst into tears as he opened the little iron-barred door to the kiln and entered by bending low. The prisoners were covered in lime and their skin had started to burn. John promptly untied them for they were lashed together at the wrists. They felt sure that the prayers they had been reciting since they were shut in the white cell had been answered by the Great One above.

They soon recovered their composure and as they approached the yard they could hear curses and pleadings from the direction of the roof. John removed his tricorn hat and covered his daughter's eyes as they walked to the waiting buggy, but it was too late.

'Why isn't that man wearing breeches?' asked the little girl. He'll catch his death of cold.'

'I hope so,' said her mother and father in unison.

Chapter Nine

Referring to John Price's recent escapade, his mother told everyone proudly that her son was unremitting in his personal war against injustice, and was about to leave for France although it was still a dangerous place to visit. Madam Price could not be sure of what business her son had in going there – especially at a time of serious social turmoil. Although she was a very well-informed person by the communication standards of the time, she probably wasn't aware of quite how serious that turmoil was.

There was sensitivity with regard to the aid the American colonists had received from France, also the Dutch. However, there was no state of war presently between France and Britain, even though a degree of diplomatic nervousness still prevailed. John Price's purpose in going to France was definitely not a military one. He had seen action in many places fighting for king and country but now held the view that wars were futile; his interest was in social change. Now, a 'man of the people', he was considered to be highly dangerous by those who were desperate to maintain the old social order. John was fascinated by the current rumblings of revolt in France. What he had learned from his uncle Richard assured him that he would find many in France who agreed with the remedies for social injustice that he himself favoured.

The 'experts' down at the Dusty Forge of course knew exactly why John Price was crossing the English Channel.

'That devil is up to no good again,' said Wilson Jarvis, a Somerset man who was over in Cardiff to raise money for a ship which was to sail out of Bristol in a month heading for the Gold Coast carrying corn seed and salt. It would then cross the Atlantic with a much more valuable cargo.

'No doubt if he was here 'e'd say we was all evil for tryin' to make an 'onest penny!' said Jarvis. 'The man's a pest. He should be hung up by the testicles.'

''E wouldn't 'ave any if I 'ad my way,' said Tommy Tucker, the butcher from Crockherbtown in central Cardiff, 'I'd take my cleaver to 'im.'

'Anyway 'e's going over there to find out 'ow to stir things up see,' said Jarvis. 'Mark my words, 'e'll be comin' back with ideas about killin' the king and God knows who else.'

Tom Tucker agreed. 'Aye,' he said, shaking his head, 'so somebody's got to do 'im in. It's going to be a tough job though. Even Big Ginger messed it up, the damned fool. Three days 'e was up on that roof before anybody went by. When he was brought down the straw thatch had scratched a map of the world on 'is arse! Cryin' like giant baby 'e was.'

On hearing that John Price had gone to France, Catharine eradicated him from her dreams. This was made all the easier by the fact that one Henry James had now moved to 'front of stage' in her mind.

It sometimes seemed to Catharine that events in her life were almost predictable. She by no means possessed clairvoyant powers but things she expected to occur often happened. Given the proximity of the cider press to the stables where Catharine spent a lot of her time, it was always likely that she would encounter the human being who had recently monopolised her thoughts.

Ianto was brushing down Major whilst the animal tucked into an enormous mound of hay in his stall at the end of the stable which was the domain of the bigger carthorses. Catharine, meanwhile, was shovelling dung, a task made somewhat harder by Major, who added to her burden from time to time. She had five stalls to clear before dark, so she increased her pace. Her work rate had slowed because of Ianto's insistence on her listening to the latest gossip that he felt the need to pass on. His stories were often about farmers' disputes or about vagrants being pushed from one parish to another, and sometimes about severe punishments meted out to law-breakers for comparatively minor offences. Catharine rarely, if ever, knew the persons whom the gossip described. However, this day almost as soon as he began to recite one story, she felt in her bones that she knew the person involved. It wasn't the string of crimes he was said to have committed – or indeed, the fact that he came from the parish of Eglwysilan. It was the fact that his black hair was said to curl about his neck and that he was the biggest liar in the world!

Ianto finished his work and walked home to his cottage in Groes Faen some three miles to the west. Catharine had completed her work too and was swilling the stable floor with water from pails she had earlier filled and carried from the well. She was about to leave for the house when she heard footsteps approaching the stable from across the yard.

She was not in the least surprised that the figure now filling the doorway, backlit by the setting sun, was that of the folk-dancing, pirate-fighting, native-ruling, raft-rowing, tale-telling vagabond who seemingly couldn't tell the truth if his life depended upon it.

Was this the moment, she wondered, when the first part of her dream would come true? Was this the moment when he would take her in his arms and sweep her away? He bowed and asked if he could walk with her. If his spellbinding voice hadn't drawn her to him, the way he held out his arm for her to take it certainly would have – and they walked across the yard together as if they had been a devoted couple for an age.

He took her to the door of the main house, delicately released his arm from hers, stepped back and bowed gracefully, whilst sweeping his arm in the manner of a gentleman of class. After he bid her goodnight with that captivating voice, she entered the house and quickly ran up to her room along the landing. She got herself to the window seat just in time to see the departing Henry James walking out of the yard. He turned and waved; she responded with a little flicker of her fingers.

Catharine could hardly feel the touch of the ground as she strolled about the estate. The couple had not met for a few days but Catharine's one encounter with Henry James, though brief, sustained her hopes and inspired even more dreams. There were many unanswered questions gently simmering in her brain . . . but they could wait. That they should meet again soon was inevitable.

She walked along her favourite path and smiled once more as she passed the spot where she fell into the stream as a little girl. She went along the edge of the wood and again sat on the bank of the brook where she had been given an unexpected rendering of an old song by the dashing John Price. This time there was no song; no image of a sword-carrying figure emerging in the sunbeams through the trees. What happened was totally different but a million times more exciting.

As Catharine sat taking in the glorious sights and sounds of nature, she felt two warm hands cover her eyes. The voice which came from immediately behind her was mesmeric as it delivered the words of a poem in English.

'I see your face where e're I glance –
In soft-edged clouds and waving corn.
In your sparkling eyes when butterflies dance
And the shine of your smile in a sunlit dawn.'

'That's beautiful,' said Catharine, not attempting to remove his hands.

'Sh! there's more,' said Henry, taking his hands away and turning her by the shoulders so that she faced him.

> 'I hear your voice in happy sounds –
> On laughing wind, in swaying trees,
> In every place where pleasure abounds
> Like birdsong on a summer breeze.'

After a pause, Catharine said, turning their talk back to their native language, *'Ai barddoniaeth yw e?'* ('Is that poetry?').

'I trust so,' said Henry, 'although I don't know if William Cowper or Thomas Gray would agree!'

The names might have been those of local ditch-diggers for all Catharine knew, but not wanting to show her ignorance, she said nothing for a moment or two. Then she asked him. 'Do you write Welsh poetry as well?'

He looked straight into her eyes and then released a waterfall of words in the ancient British tongue, so musical yet so intensely meaningful that she wanted the world to slow down so that she could enjoy this highly romantic episode all the more.

Henry took Catharine's hands and they got to their feet and faced each other. 'Do you know what day this is?' asked Henry quietly. Catharine couldn't find her voice so she simply gave a slight shake of her head in response.

'It's the first day of the rest of our lives!' said Henry, raising his rich voice a little. He looked up to the starry sky, paused for three seconds, then bent to kiss Catharine in an embrace that remained for a long long time.

They eventually drew themselves apart and walked hand in hand up to Parc. They kissed again at the door and Henry, with his characteristic bow, said farewell to a young lady who had been transported into a world that even her wildest dreams had not foreseen.

Catharine met Henry several times during the weeks of autumn. They walked the woodland paths until the weather cooled, whereupon they sat amid the hay in the big barn and at all times Henry James was a model of what Catharine understood to be 'gentlemanly' behaviour. He held her hands; he lightly stroked her hair, he hugged her gently; he kissed her sparingly before they parted. In addition, he filled her mind with tales about his life on the ocean waves; huge journeys he had undertaken overland; wild animals he had faced both in tropical jungles and in frozen wastes. He was a natural story-teller with a wicked ability to convince listeners that even his most outrageous claims were true. By now, Catharine Griffith was deeply in love with Henry James, and when she heard from the other servants that he had hinted he would soon be going away, she planned to challenge him privately about it. She held out little hope that she would get the truth from him.

As Christmas 1786 approached, with the apple pressing over, the remarkably versatile Henry James was retained at Parc by Madam Price for winter work. He was an able woodcutter and almost single-handedly repaired all the fences on the central estate; he also went out to help some of the tenant farmers in similar work. Unwilling oxen which had caused many a driver to pack his bags and leave, were taken in hand by Henry and quickly became totally co-operative. He ploughed several fields with these animals – one day turning over the Graig – the trouble-some three acre rock-strewn piece of hilly ground that stretched from the back of Parc to the edge of Coed y Carw (Stag's Wood). This impressed everyone for it had not been ploughed in living memory.

He repaired thatch; white-limed walls; repaired tools; greased cartwheels; groomed horses and supervised cheese and butter making. He brought logs for the yuletide fires, also ivy and mistletoe with which Madam Price decorated the hallway, passages and rooms of the house to brighten it up for the coming festive season. He grew in everyone's estimation.

Henry organised a concert in the barn where the mid-summer *twmpath* had been staged. He brought dancers from far afield and they all appeared to know him. He sang solos and took part in duets and before the evening's activities came to an end he gave a recital on the three-stringed harp. He ended the evening with a very agile clog dance with a besom. Henry James was the talk of the place.

Such was his popularity and such was Catharine's familiarity with him that as they walked together on Christmas morning to Taihirion chapel she thought she could now ask him the question that required an answer more than any others.

'Are you leaving us?'

Caught off guard, Henry could only mutter, 'Yes, of course, one day.'

'Why were you under arrest that day and brought before the justices?' Henry's answer staggered her.

'Because I am a thief,' he said.

'Please tell me the truth' said Catharine. 'Don't tease me!'

'That *is* the truth,' said Henry, who was getting down on one knee. Taking hold of one of her hands, he looked up into her eyes and said, 'Yes, it is the truth.'

Catharine looked away, bewildered and not a little forlorn. He was behind her now but she said, 'what do you steal? Is it money?'

'Only occasionally. Usually it's small items which I then *sell* for money. Are you shocked?' Henry asked as he raised himself up.

He could see clearly that she wasn't – for she linked her arm with his and led him into the chapel.

The sermon reminded the congregation of the birth of their Lord and the message of Peace that was fundamental to Christian teaching. It went on to condemn avarice by citing Jesus's example of frugality, a point that made a few of the more prosperous members shuffle nervously in their pews.

In full flight, the preacher found his *hwyl* at which point the delivery of his words was much more akin to singing than to speaking. This style of preaching had recently been adopted by several of the Nonconformist ministers and the Independents of Taihirion were at the forefront of the trend.

As the preacher's voice trembled with passion he inevitably touched upon the *Deg Gorchymyn* . . . the Ten Commandments. As he came to utter the phrase *'ac na ladrata,'* (Thou shalt not steal), Catharine gave Henry's hand a friendly squeeze.

Only five words were spoken by Catharine as they parted that night. Standing in the main doorway at Parc, she buried her head into Henry's chest and said simply and quietly: 'take me away with you.'

Chapter Ten

The little bar-room at Cae Golman Tavern in Pentyrch was always buzzing with gossip. Frequently the talk was about vessels coming to grief in the vicious currents of the Bristol Channel; a number of farms in the Vale of Glamorgan had fireplace beams made from timber salvaged from wrecks. This night the talk was about yet another marine disaster. Bound for Bristol from South Carolina a vessel had foundered in a high sea and was cast against the Bendricks near Sully. Few tragedies brought out the worst in men's minds more than a wreck with a high potential for the looting of its cargo. Even the most steadfastly moral citizens appeared to suspend their belief in the eighth commandment when the opportunity for plunder arose. Maritime misfortune for some – was bounty from heaven for others.

Several of the Cae Golman regulars had been to the coast the day before and had brought back souvenirs that should have shamed their souls. One was wearing a pair of buckled shoes that had been washed up on a pebble beach; another had a perfect pair of calf-skin breeches, yet another was showing off a variety of trinkets that had floated to the shore in a sealed wooden box – all of these previous personal possessions of humans who were now probably lying on the sea bed.

Nobody referred to the tragic circumstances which had effected their new possessions; only annoyance that their intentions had been thwarted by the brisk arrival of law officers at the scene.

'It was that Jones of Fonmon and Pryce of Dyffryn who raised the alarm,' said Twm Pen yr Heol, tapping his clay pipe out on a stone at the side of the fireplace, 'but by the time the dragoons got there from Cowbridge there were hundreds on the beach – farmers, most of 'em. They were boating it out to the wreck and bringing back sack after sack of flour.'

'Aye, God's work it is,' said Will Caerwen, 'the Vale farmers have had it hard for too long. I hear they were selling the wheat for less than sixpence a bushel on the side of the road by St Andrews before daybreak!'

'Can't blame 'em,' said Dic Harries, Maes Teg. 'A great providence for poor folk – only wish I could have gone down there myself.'

When talk of the recent wreck reached Parc, there was a mixture of views expressed by the serving hands as to the rights and wrongs of looting a broken ship. One person, however, averred adamantly that stealing from the dying was totally wrong. That man was Henry James, the self-confessed thief!

Catharine Griffith was unsure of the cause of it but without doubt she had started to see life differently. She was now overwhelmed with every emotion when she thought of the Adonis who had entered her life but strangely she still felt there was something missing. As she matured she had gradually reduced those vengeful feelings which had troubled her thoughts for so long. She was also more tolerant of traits she had previously seen as reprehensible in others; the concepts of right and wrong had become less difficult to ponder than they had previously been. She was, however, an intelligent young woman and occasionally doubts entered her mind regarding her own interpretation of the circumstances in which she found herself. She did wonder if her judgement of all matters was now essentially linked with her infatuation for another human being: in this case, a flawed human being. Was this why the idea of stealing gave her few qualms? Was it the fact that during her time of wishing retribution on those who had caused her family pain she had herself considered stealing their property?

To any impartial observer, the answer was simple: Catharine Griffiths was so besotted with Henry James that reason no longer applied. Curates and preachers could have sermonised until they were purple in the face; it wouldn't have mattered, for Catharine was being controlled by the most powerful biological force in nature. So what was missing?

Life at Parc could hardly be faulted. Catharine enjoyed benefits denied to the huge majority of the local populace. She worked hard, slept well and was robustly healthy. She was well clothed and well-fed. She had many friends in an establishment that was years ahead of its time with regard to the benevolence of the employer. She, alone among a number of attractive females, had secured the attentions of an irresistible heart-throbbing newcomer.

Henry was still reticent about his plans for going away and Catharine felt disinclined to repeat the daring question she asked him at Christmas. New Year came and went with little exciting happening apart from the visit of the Mari Lwyd. The group turned up as they had always done at about an hour before midnight. When Sam Price was alive they could be assured of a strong poetic challenge and were kept at bay until a truce was agreed on the stroke of twelve, whereupon the visitors would be led to a table laden with food – and liquid refreshments of all kinds as well were given to the thirsty singers and poetisers. Once again it went well. The servants, called in to help, were also allowed to partake of the fare.

Catharine and Henry continued their walks along the wood-land paths, also around the fields near the house. On the edge of the wood beyond the Graig were the remains of an old stone wall. Henry offered the view that this must be part of the ruins of an ancient fortified building pointing out the uninterrupted views to the south – the most probable direction from which alien forces would approach in times of conflict. He also showed Catharine two springs from which water amply flowed. In addition to the deep well in the yard at Parc these *ffynhonnau* would have been invaluable sources of water for such a fortress. His opinions, delivered without a trace of pompousness, confirmed Henry in Catharine's mind as an expert in many matters. He might exaggerate somewhat the tales of his experiences around the world but there was no doubting his versatility, for that was being proven daily before his doubters' very eyes. All his several skills must somehow have been acquired and retained; but where, when and how? These were further questions to which she would love to have answers. She suspected that his many abilities came from the fact that he was a much-travelled person.

Leaving Parc was now foremost among Catharine's ambitions. She had long wondered if she would ever go far away from the place which, despite its relative cosiness, or rather because of it, failed to satisfy the spirit of adventure which the young woman had noticed gaining strength within her. It was a sudden surge of demand for excitement rising from her inner soul which had prompted her words to Henry that day: 'Take me with you.'

Deep snows came in February, 1787, and brought everything to a stop. There were no markets so the farmers' priorities were keeping their animals alive and using their stock of feed sparingly. A gang of workers from Parc cleared the long lane as soon as they were able. Thereafter, the hayricks were diminishing daily as gambos, one after the other, came up the cleared track and went away fully laden.

One problem had been of concern to Madam Price and her workers. It was the fate of the sheep on the high ground of the

Graig. Well, it would have been a worry if Henry had not fore-seen the problem. He had gone up there with Old Lewis and a few others to cut a clearing in the wood a month earlier, the purpose being to create a protective fold for the ewes. There was snow aplenty but the trees made a solid defensive wall against that fearsome east wind. It must have been, crucially, three degrees warmer inside the wood than it was outside where the wind screeched in anger for a whole month.

The melting of the snow in February was heralded by the bleating of lambs from the Graig. The few who had lost their mothers to dogs, foxes, or the bitter cold, were brought to the comfort of the big kitchen at Parc and were treated royally until strong enough to face the outside world.

Catharine was still seeing Henry at the end of each work-ing day. It was now well into the month of April and some migratory birds had arrived. House-martins flew from their nests in the eves of Parc and returned with beakfuls of clay to make running repairs of damage which had occurred since they were last there. Swallows ducked and dived high above the yard, and flycatchers went shyly about their business just within the safety of the copse. If anyone approached the house, rabbits would be seen scurrying about, their white scuts bobbing as they ran to safety.

The pale green of new foliage started to appear on trees and hedges and the first primroses showed their beautiful faces to the world. It was altogether the season of renewal and this was reflected in a new determination displayed by Catharine Griffith to change finally the direction in which her life had been heading. Help came in that respect from the most likely person.

Henry met her at their usual rendezvous, under the oak at the edge of the stream. He stood with a hand on each of her shoulders and after a pause he held her eyes in his gaze which as ever, was captivating. Catharine felt that if he asked her at that moment to fly to the clouds – she would fly to the clouds. If he asked her to help him steal the Crown Jewels, she would have agreed without hesitation.

'Will you come away with me tomorrow?' said Henry, quietly, gently tightening his grip on her shoulders.

'I will, I will,' she said, taking his hands in hers, and adding: 'but does it have to be so soon?'

'Well the sooner the better,' he said, adding, in the Saxon's tongue: 'parting from so many friends will be such sweet sorrow.' She did not know he was paraphrasing the greatest English bard, or that the phrase was adapted from the ultimate example of a tragic love story.

'I should like, if I may,' said Catharine, reverting to their native language, 'speak to Madam Price – for she has been so kind to me.'

With the faintest of frowns, Henry nodded and said, 'I suggest you see her tonight.'

Catharine tapped lightly on the drawing room door and she trembled a little as she heard Madam Price's kindly voice inviting her to enter.

'I understand you wanted to speak to me, child,' said Madam Price. 'Please sit down, dear girl.'

Catherine felt that in view of the seriousness of what she was about to say, it would be inappropriate to sit. Instead, she stood before the lady who had been much more than her employer. She had been her guardian, her mentor and her surrogate mother, since she was a child and she did not want to hurt her.

'Madam,' she said, with a shake in her voice, 'the time has come for me to leave you and I am wretched with my thoughts, for you are the person who has been most gracious to me for most of my life.'

Few things vexed Madam Price, but when annoyed she had different ways of showing her displeasure. One was to remove her *pince nez*, make a sharp comment, followed by a haughty toss of the head immediately returning the glasses to her nose. Another was to rock in her chair with hands clasped together – staring fiercely but saying nothing. In this event she reacted in neither of these ways. She moved quickly and clasped her arms around Catharine, uttering words that would haunt the young woman for years to come.

'*O Catrin, cariad. Duw a'th fendithio*' ('God bless you dear Catharine'), Madam Price said, 'wherever you go, be sure to remember your time here. I wish you all the good fortune you deserve.'

There were no further words for a while. They stood entwined, weeping.

Eventually, they unlocked themselves from the embrace and sat down, both very much relieved.

'I have been expecting this for some time,' said Madam Price, 'ever since that handsome young man came here. I could see that you were smitten.'

Before leaving, Catharine thanked Madam Price for all of her kindnesses over the years and promised she would always try to live according to her guardian's high moral standards.

Lying in her bed at Parc for the last time, Catharine was kept awake by a tumble of thoughts about her past. For an hour she relived the highs and lows of a life which had provided much pain, but also joy. About to leave her own 'patch' – probably forever, she would have to brace herself for the wrench of leaving behind all those things with which she had been familiar: people, friends, gossip – even, perhaps, the very language she naturally spoke. She would be in the care of someone she thanked God for bringing him into her life. However, before she fell asleep, a thought or two surfaced about her partner-to-be who was a self-confessed robber and again she wondered if she had finally lost her understanding of what was right and what was wrong.

Chapter Eleven

The morning of the pair's departure was cool but bright. There were tears when Catharine said goodbye to her fellow workers at Parc and most were shed by Old Lewis who sat on a log shaking his head and murmuring sadly to himself.

Catharine and Henry stopped just once and turned to give a final wave to their friends as they left the yard. Catharine had no possessions apart from some spare clothes in a bag which her partner now carried for her over his shoulder, and some coins she had saved which she kept in a small leather purse tucked into a pocket she had made inside her dress.

As they walked on only one of the pair knew where they were going. Catharine had put her faith unconditionally in the man striding along with her. She didn't even know where they would be staying that night. She could have asked but was in fact enjoying the mystery of it all. So far, the terrain over which they tramped was familiar to her for she had walked and ridden these lanes before. After they passed the farm of Llwyn Dafydd Ddu, however, she could see that they were heading for the hill country.

Soon they were dropping down to the bottom of a valley from which the old Castell Coch (Red Castle) ruins were visible up on a wooded hill. As they paused to absorb mentally the sheer beauty of the landscape, Catharine was delighted when she heard a sound that she instantly recognised as having personal significance for her. Indeed, it was the call of the cuckoo. She could not have been happier at that moment for it was a serenely beautiful morning and she was in the company of the man she adored. And now the spring visitor called to tell her she was twenty-seven years old.

They came to the bank of a river of about forty yards width where they rested again for a while.

'This is the Taff,' said Henry. 'In all my travels I have never seen a faster flowing stream. The water rushes down from the mountains of Breconshire and it can't wait to get to the sea. Sometimes you'll see salmon speeding upstream. *They* can't wait to get back to the beautiful hills and their spawning grounds.'

Towering above them was the eastern end of the Garth along which Catharine had ridden many times. She had always approached the ridge from its western end but now seeing the hill from the deep valley of the Taff she was surprised that it was so high. As they proceeded northward along the river bank they soon came upon a hive of human activity. It was the Pentyrch Ironworks which was by far the biggest employer in the area.

Workmen as busy as ants darted about amidst a variety of sheds; horses were pulling wagons laden variously with iron-ore, limestone rocks and timber logs, whilst men pushed handcarts piled high with coal. Hissing noises came from inside one shed; the sound of hammering on metal from another. The pair could feel the heat from a row of furnaces as they went by and were caught in a crossfire of shouts from hard toiling men.

The sounds of industry were fading as they neared the spot where a crude river ferry operated linking the Garth side of the Taff Gorge to the quaintly-named hamlet of Portobello on the eastern bank. A simple oar-less rowing boat was pulled along a fixed rope, and the elderly lady who worked it took dozens safely across for one farthing per person every day. When she saw the pair approach, she rushed to Henry and held him in a fond embrace.

'I knew his mother, God rest her soul,' she said, looking at Catharine. 'Are you Henry's wife?'

The last remark threw Catharine off guard but her man stepped in to save any embarrassment: 'Not yet,' he said, smiling radiantly, 'but she might be, one day.'

As they stepped into the boat it gave a wobble but the woman steadied it and started pulling on the rope. The river was often unkind to travellers and there had been a number of fatalities in recent years. Today though, it was as calm as it could possibly be. As they alighted from the boat on the far bank, the lady said, 'no charge today for old friends.'

'How do you know that old woman?' asked Catharine.

'Well, I come from this side of the river and I know a lot of people.'

A few yards from the river's edge on its eastern side was a rickety old shed – no more than a bundle of wooden boards clumsily nailed together. Its door, hanging on one rusty hinge helped to make the building appear very uninviting indeed. After a brief hesitation, Catharine agreed to take Henry's hand and they went inside. A circular slabbed stone bench surrounded a bubbling spring the waters of which were being turned to a foam as they were thrown upwards.

'This spot has been visited since ancient times by people in search of cures,' said Henry, his voice echoing as he spoke.

'Cures for what?' asked Catharine, her own voice also sounding as if it belonged to someone else.

'Aches and pains, mostly,' said Henry, 'but also problems of the heart . . . such as lovesickness.'

'Ah, now I know you are not being serious!' said Catharine, 'there's no cure for that, it is said!'

As they came out again, Henry spoke: 'This place is known as the Taff's Well – and I was brought down here firstly by my mother. In later years I came with friends.'

'Girlfriends?'

'Oh, yes,' said Henry, deciding to tease her. 'We used to take all our clothes off and jump into the water together.'

'Were you cured?'

'Of what?'

'Lovesickness?'

'Well, as you said, there's no cure for it!'

Catharine slapped him on the shoulder as they came out of the shed and walked on.

They were now proceeding up the eastern flank of the river following a well-worn path which, in places, was hardly worthy of the term 'roadway'. As they left the Well of the Taff behind them, they picked up the track that was the main, almost the *only* route to Merthyr Tudful, the biggest township in Wales. Up this very thoroughfare, countless foreigners had gone to seek their fortune in the industrial hell-hole that the town of Tudful the Martyr had become. Down this track came donkey and mule trains carrying coal in panniers to the ports of Cardiff and Aberthaw. Big wagons pulled by up to four horses carried heavy loads of pig iron. There was too, a steady stream of pedestrians.

The pair met a variety of souls moving southwards, some striding out with the confidence of seasoned travellers, others who, by the expressions on their faces, clearly had no idea of what to expect around the next corner. As it happened, Catharine Griffith, going in the other direction, was also entering the unknown.

'What is this place called?' asked Catharine, as they came upon a group of houses at the foot of a sudden rise of ground to their right.

'Nantgarw,' said Henry, in a matter of fact way.

Catharine drew in a breath. 'This is where your dancers came from!'

Henry nodded.

'Is this where *you* come from?'

'No,' said Henry, 'but I first joined the cloggers here some years ago when I came back from London.'

'What were you doing in London?'

'I was in gaol,' said Henry, unabashed.

This was leading to subject matter that Catharine instinctively felt would be better left to another time. She was happy and feared risking the shattering of a dream that was so far turning out to be true.

'I was born up there in the hills near Eglwysilan church which I attended with my family until we joined William Edwards the dissenting minister who had built his Independent chapel at Groes Wen,' said Henry, obviously wanting to move the conversation on. 'Do you know of William Edwards?' he asked.

'I remember an Edward Williams coming to Parc, but he was called "Iolo".'

'That would be Iolo Morganwg,' said Henry. 'A different man altogether.'

'So what about your William Edwards then?'

They had stopped on the brow of some hilly fields, and Henry pointed to the west. 'Just over there, about three and a half miles away' he said, 'is the longest single span stone bridge in the world. And it was built by William Edwards our minister, who was also a stonemason and an architect.'

Catharine's admiration for Henry was growing as every minute passed. She felt she had learned more from him in half a day than she had ever learned in a month. As the esteem in which she held her partner increased so did her concern that her regard for him was more than mere infatuation. She wondered what she could do to seal her relationship with this exceptional human being and to establish a permanent mutual obligation.

Marriage had been referred to but they hadn't fully discussed matrimony. So far she had no reason to doubt the seriousness of his intentions but she was nonetheless apprehensive about

147

whether or not she could live up to his expectations. She knew that some would consider what she had done this day to be foolhardy and that if her dream suddenly turned into a nightmare she would have only herself to blame.

Soon she would have to start asking questions with regard to how and where they were going to live together; how they would earn enough to feed and clothe themselves. These matters would have to wait; for the moment she would let herself wallow in the unrestrained sensuality made possible by his walking into her life.

They arrived at a thatch-roofed cottage at the edge of some woodland and to Catharine's surprise, Henry went straight to the door and opened it. '*Susannah!*' he called loudly. '*Wyt ti 'ma?*' ('Susannah, are you here?')

There was no response from inside the cottage but a voice could be heard coming from the yard behind. Henry indicated that Catharine should follow him and they went to the rear of the house.

'This is my sister, Susannah,' said Henry, and Catharine could see the resemblance immediately. Unsurprisingly, Susannah was a good-looking woman of about thirty. When they arrived, she had been scattering corn for some noisy hens.

'Actually,' Henry went on, 'she's my older sister.' Putting his arm around Catharine he introduced her to Susannah as his best friend in the whole world and that they were going to be together for ever.

'*O's isha bwyd arnoch chi?*' ('are you hungry?') asked Susannah. A nod from Henry was enough. Susannah took just a few moments to scatter the rest of the corn from her dish and the hens cackled happily.

In minutes, Henry and Catharine were seated at a table in the kitchen and before them was a spread of cheeses, a large chunk of boiled ham which had been sliced ready, cold boiled potatoes, fresh bread, *teisen lap, bara brith* and tall mugs of fresh milk.

'Where's Owain?' asked Henry, with difficulty, for he was chewing a heavenly piece of cheese.

'He's up on the hill, counting late lambs,' said his sister, 'he won't be back before the sun goes down.'

'We'll miss him then,' said Henry. 'I think it will be a while before we can come back.'

'Be careful,' said Susannah, intriguingly, 'I told the last callers you were going down west.' Then, after a pause, 'I wish you'd see sense.'

Catharine chose not to even think about that last remark. She simply hoped it was not in reference to her partnership with Susannah's brother.

There were hugs and 'goodbyes' and soon Henry and his partner were on their way again.

They strode onwards and then paused to take a last look at the cottage.

'That's the house where I was born,' he said. 'After my parents died, I went out into the big wide world and my sister with her husband Owain took over the farm. There's a hundred and fifty acres so it's a big holding for around here.'

'So you didn't have a poor upbringing then?' said Catharine.

'No indeed,' answered Henry, emphatically. 'I was even sent away to school.'

'No wonder you are so clever,' said Catharine, looking at him adoringly.

'I'm not clever,' said Henry, 'just cunning . . . I'm an old fox really.'

'Well,' said Catharine, 'who were those callers your sister mentioned?'

'Just friends,' he said, looking up at the sky instead of at Catharine which was his normal way.

After taking a few rests, they stopped and sat on the grass once again. They had walked more than nine miles since they left Parc that morning and were tiring. Away below them was the town of Caerphilly and in the middle of it was the great fortress that had made the place famous. It wasn't just a huge ruin; it was still fearsome in appearance despite its fallen masonry here and there. Henry pointed out that this was only one of a phenomenal number of fortified buildings raised by Anglo/Norman invaders in Wales. He explained that these fortresses were whitewashed in their prime during the Middle Ages and this would have made them even more terrifying.

Catharine asked Henry why there were so many castles in Wales.

'Simple,' he said, 'it was a matter of – the stronger the servant, the bigger the stick!'

They headed for Caerphilly town and Catharine said she would love to take a closer look at the castle.

With the drawbridges and portcullises long out of use, it was easy to get into the heart of the fortress through one of the main entrances, access to which was a recently built causeway across the moat. They paused while Henry pointed out the intricate patterns in the masonry which evidenced the knowledge medieval builders had of structural strengths and so on. He went on to say that William Edwards had come here as a young man and after studying the stonework found the secrets which led to the construction of his successful single-span bridge over the Taff.

They walked hand in hand around the ruin and felt the inherent solemnity of a once mighty citadel. Its broken walls and gaunt towers now partly clad in ivy, emphasised the loss of the majesty it had enjoyed when it held the local populace in a grip of terror. All was silent there now, except for occasional squawks from quarrelling jackdaws. The grassy banks in the courtyard were kept trim by a dozen or so sheep who, after lifting their heads briefly to note the arrival of the two visitors, went on with their grazing.

The time had come for Catharine to ask one or two reasonable questions. Firstly, she felt she should be told where they were going – and why.

'We are bound for wherever the open road will take us,' said Henry, 'just think of it as an adventure.'

'I shall be happy wherever you take me,' said Catharine, 'I want to be with you every minute of every day.'

'And every night?' said Henry, with a pronounced chuckle.

'Of course,' said the young woman who was totally in thrall of the man.

In the cloudless sky a million stars twinkled their approval as the pair agreed to settle down for the hours of darkness in an enclosure, which, they had deduced, must have been the royal room during the castle's medieval days. As it was unlikely that they could sleep standing up, it was necessary to find some means of comfortably resting their bodies.

They found a makeshift barn which someone had built from scattered stones. With a timber roof on which had been laid clods of grassy turf, it was being used as a place to keep fodder dry. Thence they took some bundles of dry warm hay with which they made soft beds – or rather, one soft bed.

Whereas Catharine Griffith and Henry James had lain together that night as a pair, they awoke with the dawn as one. They were tightly embraced and when the crow of a far away cockerel brought them to consciousness, they released each other in a state of pure happiness. They were in love – and as far as the laws of nature were concerned, were as man and wife.

Leaving their castle in the morning they walked towards the rising sun. Henry still had Catharine's bag slung over his shoulder as they strode onwards, confident that they could face anything the new day would bring.

They left Caerphilly and soon the sounds of the waking town were well behind them. Out in the countryside again they came to the boundary wall of what was obviously an important property. They paused near an iron-gated doorway over which was framed a somewhat daunting notice in English.

Henry was aware of Catharine's illiteracy but not in the least disturbed by it.

'I'll read it to you,' he said, putting down the bag for a moment.

> *'If thou cometh in anger, begone – for on this side of ye wall*
> *we believeth in ye wisdom and justice of ye Almighty.'*

A voice from behind them said, 'In there is a big house they do call the Van. The family of this place do own everything for miles around and if you do take my advice stay out or they will own you as well.'

They turned to see a little bent old man with a stick who went on. 'Aye they do have mansions all around – from here to St Fagans.'

'That's where I come from, or thereabouts' said Catharine quickly. She found it curious that on hearing her remark, Henry put his finger to his lips indicating she should not elaborate.

As they resumed their walk, Catharine asked Henry why he had reacted in that way to what she had said.

'Oh, it's always safer not to tell people too much,' said Henry. 'Much safer.'

Although she was still puzzled, Catharine decided not to pursue the matter further.

Back at Parc Old Lewis was watering some hollyhocks at the front of the house when he heard the sound of trotting horses approaching. He stood up, and shading the morning sunshine from his eyes with the back of his hand, he saw three riders coming into the yard and dismounting almost before their horses had come to a halt.

He recognised one of them. It was Alexander Calder, the Cardiff Assistant Constable who had visited Parc many times for criminal hearings. The other two were younger men, both well-dressed – and wearing swords.

'Hello, Lewis,' said the constable, 'is Mrs Price here?'

'Indeed she is, Alex,' said the old man, and, sensing there was some urgency in the question he put down his watering can and disappeared into the house muttering 'I'll get her now.'

One of the armed men fumbled for his watch that was chained to his inner tunic and said to his colleagues, 'They have a twenty-four hour start on us and could be in Birmingham by now.'

'Aye,' said the other, 'we should have made our move yesterday.'

As he spoke, Madam Price emerged from the house and after a quick greeting to Alex, said, 'To what do I owe this singular pleasure?' and with a twinkle in her eye she added: 'Or have you come to arrest me?'

'No Ma'am, certainly not,' said the constable. 'I'll tell you straight. We've come for your labourer, Henry James. He's wanted by the Cowbridge House of Correction as well as the Sheriff of Carmarthen, not to mention the Dragoon Guards and the Kent Militia. When they've finished with him, the Thames Police at Holborn in London will want him handed over to them. These two gentlemen are Bow Street Runners and they have been on his trail for twelve months.'

Madam Price, keeping her composure said, 'I am sorry, gentlemen, I can't be of assistance to you. The labourer of whom you speak has gone away from here.'

'We know that, Ma'am!' he said. And, with a hint of impatience, 'we also know that he took a wench with him from here.' As he spoke, the horses were getting restless and the Runners had already remounted. The constable put his left foot in a stirrup and reaching up to grip the saddle pommel he pulled his big frame onto his mount. As he did so, he said to Madam Price, 'Perhaps you will be good enough to tell us where they intended going.'

'I do not know where they went,' said Madam Price, 'but if they are wanted in Carmarthen, Cowbridge and London, they would be well-advised to go to Brecon and far beyond. They will be safe up north. You'll never catch them up there!'

'By God's word, Catherine, I think you are right. Thank you for your help. Brecon it is then,' he said, and for the benefit of his two colleagues from London, he pointed his crop and said: 'turn right at the bottom of the lane. Brecon is only forty-five godforsaken miles from here!'

Madam Price went back into the house with a smile on her face, and Old Lewis went on watering the hollyhocks.

The elopers walked through the village of Bedwas and after a few miles more they were a long way from any evident human habitation when Catharine asked about the possibility of food.

'Forgive me,' said Henry, adopting a Thespian stance. 'Don't fret, there will be bounteous commons laid before this pair of starving pilgrims.'

Before slipping away, Henry asked his fellow-traveller to rest in the shade of some oak trees. Within twenty minutes he was back with a full-grown rabbit, which he then skinned and gutted for cooking. He asked Catharine to collect some kindling and she returned with an armful of twigs. Henry took from his pocket a little tinderbox and as if by magic produced a glowing ember of fabric which he applied to some dry grass he had put amid the dry tiny branches and assisted the combustion with expertly emitted breaths of air. Within moments the twigs were burning; then so were the thicker sticks – until a veritable small log fire was alight before them. Henry placed some flat stones in the fire making a cradle for the rabbit's carcass, which he had encased in clay taken from the bank of a nearby stream. Finally he formed a wigwam of bigger logs over the fire.

Then he shocked Catharine by telling her it would take two hours for the meat to cook!

'Never fear,' he said, 'there is something else we can do while we wait.' He indicated that she should hide her bag in some bracken and then follow him. With the acquiescence that had become her second nature, she did as he asked.

After trampling through bramble covered ground and over gorse covered banks they entered a wood and found a well-worn path weaving its way through birch, beech, hazel and blackthorn. Eventually, leaving the woodland, they heard voices and the tinkling of metal coming from a country tavern at the side of a road. Inside, Henry bought two mugs of ale and paid for them with two pennies he drew from a pocket.

'If you need more money,' whispered Catharine into his ear. 'I have some tucked away.'

'I know,' said Henry, who was about to make a joke about Catharine's 'hideaway' when he felt a tap on his shoulder.

A large, burly man in the faded uniform of a dragoon guard spoke to him in English:

'Aren't you Henry James?' he asked, brashly.

'Why do you ask?' said Henry, with a quick sideways glance at Catharine.

'Just answer my question, you toad!' The ex dragoon stood up to his full height and continued:

'Answer!' he shouted, even more loudly.

Another similarly-attired brutish-looking individual came close and asked the same question; this time in Welsh, continuing:

'Ateba, mae isha ateb arno!' ('he wants an answer!')

After a pause, Henry responded: 'If I am the man you named, how did you recognise me? – and what is it you want with me?'

'It's not what *we* want with you, it's more like what the Sheriff and the Constable want with you down in Cowbridge,' said the first man.

'Aye,' said the second man, 'there's a hundred whiplashes awaiting you down there. And I don't doubt you deserve every one of 'em.'

This time, Henry chose not to look at Catharine, but grabbed the first of the two men by his collar at the throat and said in a commanding voice:

'You are starting to irritate me, my friend. And by the way, I am not a toad.' He then gave the man a push and he went crashing into a table around which were sitting several local farmers. As the second man lunged at him, Henry stuck out a foot and his would-be assailant also went crashing into the group.

Instead of inciting the locals into acting on behalf of fallen heroes, Henry's deed had an altogether unexpected reaction from them. The farmers bundled the two big men off the premises, and then came back to congratulate Henry on his fearless performance.

Shaking Henry's hand vigorously, one explained that the pair had been causing trouble all day.

'They are obviously not serving dragoons,' said the farmer.

'I expect they are wearing stolen uniforms,' said another.

'Bounty hunters, that's what they are,' said a third farmer, 'bounty hunters.'

'Pleased to be of assistance,' said Henry to those in the bar-room as he took Catharine's hand and left the tavern. They found their way to the woodland path easily and Catharine lost no time in asking him the obvious question.

'Yes,' he replied. 'They *are* bounty hunters and they are after *me* . . . and many others I should think. That's how they make their living: chasing and running in wanted men.'

'Wanted for what?' asked Catharine, becoming a little uneasy.

'Crimes, or what *some* regard as crimes.'

'What sort of crimes? . . . Serious ones?'

'Murder, rape, violent unprovoked assault . . .'

Catharine cut him short. 'Have you done those things?'

'Indeed not. I am just a simple thief.'

Catharine was speechless, her state of mind confused some-where between admiration for her loved one and uncertainty that stealing could sometimes be justified. Her disordered thoughts were not helped by recalling that she herself had once entertained a willingness to steal for vengeance's sake. Hunger soon took over her mental processes and she watched, fascinated, as Henry removed the rabbit from the embers and after pulling it apart, laid each half of the meat on burdock leaves they had gathered.

He then took from inside his shirt a hunk of bread and, breaking it in two, gave half to Catharine.

'You took that from the tavern bar!' she said, with just a hint of a frown. 'How on earth did you do it?'

'Sleight of hand,' said Henry, 'I'll teach you the secrets one day.'

Catharine decided not to ask any more searching questions that night but felt there were still several answers she deserved to obtain from Henry James.

They slept together once more beneath a starry sky.

Chapter Twelve

They once again set out soon after dawn and, still travelling eastwards, were now approaching Newport.

The rigours of travelling light at the mercy of the weather and other natural hazards had not been a concern to any degree in the first few days of their adventure. However, both Catharine and her hero were now in need of attention to their appearance. Catharine had hardly noticed the muddy patches on her clothes, nor the effect on her hair of having no brush. Henry had not shaved for three days and this was evident from the dark shadow on his lower face. In *his* case the result of this neglect was to enhance his manliness, whereas it is unlikely in the history of womanhood that dirty clothes and bedraggled hair ever improved the attractiveness of a female. These points were important as they were now seriously going to seek some work as a temporary measure to obtain food.

As they walked hand in hand up the High Street in Newport, they were taken to be vagrants, which, of course, they were. There were many jobs available in town for passers-through, but the pair knew there would be an unwillingness to engage anyone whose appearance might reflect badly on their employers. Another problem as far as Henry was concerned was the risk of falling victim to one of the notorious press gangs that roamed the seaport town.

They stopped before a shop that had a full-length mirror built into its main door. Catharine had not used a looking-glass since she had left Parc, and she was shocked to see the reflection of a pathetic waif looking out at her. She could have cried, for one of the things Madam Price had engendered in her was self-respect and it was clear that it would play little part in the new life she had adopted. Whilst Catharine was looking at her mirror image, Henry had gone somewhere but by the time she pulled herself away he was back and thrusting something into her hand: a hairbrush.

Her conscience was now in turmoil. She knew Henry had purloined the brush, probably from a High Street shop, and knew it broke the rule of law, but her need to restore her appearance was felt equally strongly. The age-old arguments raged in her brain for a few seconds as she struggled to take the right course of action. She quickly came to a decision: she put her arm around her friend and said, 'thank you, Henry.' She fleetingly wondered if her previously strict code of behaviour was beginning to succumb to the forces of self-interest.

They sat on a wooden bench near the town stocks which looked forlorn in their emptiness. The couple felt relaxed and Catharine spent about half an hour brushing her hair, humming quietly to herself. She would have gone on longer if they hadn't heard the sounds of a large group they could now see snaking its way down the road. There was an unpleasantness about the continuous shouting and Henry, fearing it might have been a press gang, quickly looked for an escape route. It was in fact a posse of law officers bringing a minor transgressor to the stocks. The man was forced into the wooden frame which was then padlocked. Within seconds he was being bombarded with rotten fruit, cabbages and much worse. His wife and young family were standing in a huddle nearby, weeping.

Henry asked someone what had been the man's offence and was told it was stealing half a loaf of bread. Had it been a full loaf, he would have been whipped. Had it been two loaves, he could have been whipped and transported.

The jeering crowd eventually dispersed, and as soon as the law officers also departed, Henry went up calmly to the stocks, opened the locks and parted the timbers so that the man could escape.

To Henry's astonishment, the prisoner declined the offer and asked to be locked in again. Clearly he knew that if his escape was detected, his punishment would be even more severe. Henry accepted this and when the guard from whom he had expertly stolen the keys returned to the street, the master thief held up the bunch and said, 'You lost these I believe!'

Whilst Henry kept guard, Catharine disappeared into a cleft in a stone wall and changed into the dress which had been carried in the bag, discarding the no-longer-wanted garb she had worn the past couple of days When she emerged she looked fresher and certainly cleaner.

Catharine and Henry then seriously set about finding some work and an opportunity presented itself far more quickly than they had expected. It wasn't anything that required special skills but it would earn them a few pennies – enough for some cheese and bread.

Given the number of horses answering the call of nature on the streets, clearing dung was a major operation.

A man dressed in similar fashion to a town crier was slowly walking down the street threading his way past stationary wagons and dodging trotting horses. He was shouting alternately in Welsh and English, words they at first could not properly hear. As he got closer, it was clear he was offering temporary employment.

'Shit shovellers! Shit movers! *Carthwyr tail!* Come this way!'

It was customary to find shovels, brooms and rakes leaning against shop walls, placed there for the purpose. These were now being taken by a number who were in need of the price of a meal, including Catharine and Henry.

For an hour they shovelled and brushed, throwing large amounts of manure onto small hand carts which were being pulled along the road by young lads strapped between the shafts. The moment any of the shovellers relaxed they would be shouted at by the would-be town crier and another man who followed closely behind him carrying a leather satchel. The pair were told that the latter was the man to see to obtain the payment that would be due to them.

The end of the stint hardly came quickly enough for the dozen or so weary workers who now formed an orderly line to collect their pay. Some were given money, but when it was the turn of Catharine, Henry, and a few others to be paid, the man with the satchel held his hand up and stopped them as they approached. Glaring at them, he said, 'Who are you? I've not seen you before.' In the ensuing rush there was a lot of pushing and falling and in the confusion Henry caught Catharine's hand and dragged her away from the mêlée.

They were out into the countryside again when Catharine said: 'We wasted our time down there! Why couldn't we demand our money from those rogues? And why did you want to get away so quickly?'

Henry suggested that they rested for a while in the shade of a big beech tree. She could see from his expression that he wanted to talk more seriously than he had since they left Llanilltern.

I must ask you a question before we move further on.'

'You haven't answered *my* questions yet!' she said, with her voice raised a little more than usual.

'The question I want to ask is more important than yours,' said Henry, taking her hands as they stood up. He pointed to the east where they could just make out a line of water.

'We crossed the rushing Taff river when we were in Glamorgan,' said Henry, solemnly; 'then we went over the Rhymni. Today we saw the Usk at Newport. We will cross the beautiful

Wye at Chepstow – then ahead of us will be the really big one, the Severn.'

'Why are you telling me this?' asked Catharine, with a quizzical expression.

'Because,' said Henry, 'when we cross those rivers we'll be in England and a long way from home. So now is your chance to go back. I will take you home if you wish.'

'I've always wanted to go to England,' was her answer.

'Let me explain,' he said, as they sat down once more. 'What I want to know is this: are you truly willing to put up with the hardships that will come our way if you stay with me? You might think it's an exciting way of life but I must tell you it can be very hard on the road, very hard indeed.'

Henry was surprised at her answer. 'I have always craved adventure,' she said. 'As long as we get a little money now and again to keep us going we'll be all right. Which reminds me,' she added, 'why didn't we get our earnings back there?'

'We did,' said Henry, 'don't be shocked.' As he spoke he drew from his pocket a little leather pouch and shook it. 'We can get food in that tavern down there.' The unmistakable sound of coins being shaken fell on Catharine's ears as the latest challenge to the moral code which had guided her through her life. She now realised that her friend had picked the pocket of the money man.

'Come on then, let's go and eat,' she said, getting to her feet quickly.

Perhaps it was the fact that the money had been taken from someone who had wronged them that justified the theft in Catharine's mind, but she feared the future would bring fewer clear-cut dilemmas.

At the bottom of a lane past the church of St Pierre, they came to a country tavern from which emanated rowdy choruses and the laughter of the inebriated. As Catharine and Henry entered a bar-room the raucous noise ceased suddenly as the new arrivals were eyed up and down by the regulars. After about half a minute of comparative silence, broken only by a few burps, coughs and a sudden loud breaking of wind from an old man at the bar – at which occurrence everyone roared with laughter – the normal noise level was resumed.

Henry surveyed the place with that eagle-eyed look to which Catharine had now become accustomed. She was sure he was checking the place for bounty-hunters and press gangs. He was obviously satisfied that it was a safe haven for he was soon bringing from the bar two meat pies and two tankards of beer.

'Where are you heading for?' asked one of the regulars.

'We're going to visit Our Lost Land,' said Henry.

Someone else then piped up: 'Oh, would that be to do with enclosures then?'

'No,' said Henry, 'we're going to England. As I said, "Our Lost Land".'

They had been speaking English up to now, and a rather well-dressed man continued with an explanation.

'That's what these Welshies call England in their own tongue,' he said. 'Our Lost Land!' The laughter that followed that remark was ear-splitting.

'Not many Welsh around 'ere, see,' said an uncouth looking individual who kept spitting on the sawdust-covered floor. 'Don't like 'em myself . . . always singin' them buggers are. Aye, always singin'.'

'Do you sing?' asked the man behind the bar who was washing tankards in water as thick as gravy in a bowl.

'Only for money,' said Henry, and he immediately broke into an old comic Welsh song. No one understood the words but the lilting cadences of a happy tune clearly pleased them for when he came to the end of the piece a man collected coins –

mostly farthings, which were tossed into his tricorn hat as he went around.

Encouraged by this, Henry called Catharine to join him and between them they entertained the drinkers so well that more joined them from the other bars. When Henry finished the show with an extemporary clogless dance there was a shower of so much money they had to ask the landlord to put it aside for them. The owner of the tavern insisted they stayed the night with no charge so when Catharine and Henry eventually retired to the room and bed provided for them, they felt it had been a most successful evening and were very glad they had called there.

The comfort of the feather bed sent Catharine into dreams of heaven but only after she had recounted the experiences on the road to date. Although she was dirty, tired, also a little afraid, she felt that, on the whole, leaving the ordered everyday life of Parc was an escape from boredom. She didn't know it but it would take a lot more of the roughs and tumbles of life before she would appreciate her memories of her early years.

Henry and Catharine sat at a table in the window of the bar-room and were given a breakfast that would have pleased a monarch. Thick slices of bacon, kidneys and fried eggs were served on large pewter plates. Henry muttered something about it comparing almost favourably with a morning meal he had had in Valencia one time, so he too was obviously impressed. If there was a problem with the excellence of their treatment whilst at the Traveller's Inn, it was that it lured Catharine's thoughts into imagining it could happen all the time.

In fact there was yet another kindness to come from the taverner. He was going to Chepstow by cart and said he would be pleased for them to join him on his journey. It was a wobbly ride but the pair were very happy when they were put down on the far side of the medieval bridge that spanned the Wye at the border town. As they crossed the river they surveyed the magnificent Anglo Norman fortress the ramparts of which towered up from the river bank.

'I suppose we could sleep there tonight,' said Catharine with a smile – 'then I *will* feel like a princess!'

Henry grinned back at her and said 'no, we must move on.'

They walked for a further hour or so and arrived at the mighty Severn near a place called Black Rock. There were solid jetties and firm looking piers extending from the muddy bank and a few of the men who were bustling about were recognised by the pair as having been among those in the tavern the previous night. The Severn estuary was still quite wide here and the battle of the currents made it one of the most dangerous crossings in the world. An ambitious operation, 'New Passage', had commenced some time back at Black Rock in competition with the 'Old Passage', which was further up river crossing from Beachley to Aust. The man taking the fares at the ferry recognised the Welsh pair and refused to take any money from them.

'Oh, my friends,' he said, 'you were wonderful last night. I hope you'll be back soon.'

'I doubt it,' said Henry, but Catharine didn't hear him.

Chapter Thirteen

The crossing was shared with a detachment of the Gloucester Militia whose bawdy songs were a far cry from the entertainment the Glamorgan duettists had provided the night before. The soldiers' singing was accompanied by loud creaking noises from the boat's timbers as it crabbed its way across the treacherous river. The two travellers wisely ignored them and held on to the handrail on the deck whilst they watched the boat's battle with the swirling waters. There was also incessant grunting from six muscular oarsmen and the flap-flap of a huge square sail beginning to come apart from its attachment to the single mast. Fortunately the vessel neither fell apart nor toppled and within twenty minutes the passengers were stepping onto a short pier at New Passage.

'Are we are in England now?' asked Catharine.

'Yes, and don't forget we are foreigners here,' answered Henry.

An Englishman who told them he had heard their performance the night before, disembarked the same time as them. On the way to the road, he asked in his own language, 'Where are you travelling folk going next?'

'I thought we'd walk to Bristol and then Bath,' said Henry, squeezing Catharine's arm slightly at the same time.

When they were on their own again, Catharine's next words surprised him.

'I've already been to Bristol and I don't see why I should have a wash all over,' she said, without a hint of deliberate irony.

This time using the Welsh name for Bath, *'Caerfaddon'*, he explained that it was an ancient city and most importantly, it was on the road to London.

'Oh,' said Catharine, '*that* Bath!'

'Forget Bristol,' said Henry. 'That was false information I gave the *Sais!*' (Saxon).

Twelve hours later they were walking down a long hill into Bath. They had been given a lift for part of the way on a rickety old cart pulled by a rickety old horse and driven by a rickety old rustic who kept swearing about everything under the sun. He complained about the price of barley seed, the scarceness of good wheatflour, the behaviour of young people, the poor quality of cider compared with the old days, and the immorality of the French prisoners of war who had been sent to work for him. The only thing he said that pleased his passengers was 'this is as far as I go,' whilst disgorging the pair unceremoniously onto the side of the road before turning into a lane and heading for his farm. They could have walked more quickly but were, in fact, glad of the chance to rest tiring legs.

Catharine had never seen such buildings as the ones which adorned the streets of Bath. They were stately and imposing, but they also had elegance and charm in abundance. As much as she loved the homely houses and quaint shops of towns like Cowbridge, they could not compare with these tall majestic structures which looked as if they had been built to last forever.

The next surprise for Catharine was seeing Henry opening the door of a house and, taking her by the hand, entering. Before them, inside, was a fine staircase with marble steps and a wrought-iron rail. Still holding Catharine's hand, Henry stood at a door which had a sign declaring it was the office of Jeremiah Moses, Moneylender. He gently tapped the brass doorknocker.

'Come in,' said a voice, and Henry gave a little tug on Catharine's hand as they both entered. The room had oak-panelled walls and sitting behind a huge desk was a dark diminutive man with a broad smile on his face. On seeing his visitors he quickly got to his feet and greeted Henry like a long-lost debtor.

The thoughts that raced through Catharine's mind were out of control as she was introduced to the little man. Surely, she thought, they hadn't come here to borrow money. That would have been a most disappointing start to their career as a pair of 'roadsters'. What happened next both shocked and delighted Catharine.

Henry withdrew from his pocket, a bag of money, not dissimilar to the one he had filched from the bullying horse-dung foreman.

'There it is,' said Henry, 'count it if you wish.'

'No, Mr James,' said the moneylender, who quickly put the bag into a drawer which he immediately locked, then stuffed the key into the inner confines of his shirt. 'No, sir, you are one of the few people on this earth that I trust.'

Once more out on the street, Catharine could hardly wait to ask Henry to explain the reason for their visit to a moneylender. She felt somewhat disappointed by his uninspiring answer.

When he said: 'I had simply collected some money owed him by someone in South Wales, that's all,' it didn't fit in with her usual association of her lover with daring and adventure. If he had told her the whole story she would have learned that he had risked his life tracking down two of the most dangerous villains in Glamorgan to retrieve the twenty sovereigns they had stolen from his old friend Jeremiah.

Living 'on the road' Henry had come to know a large number of persons on both sides of the law and was fully aware of the often thin line between legitimate commerce and felonious activity. He operated in an underworld of intrigue and counter intrigue. In the case of the repaying of Jeremiah Moses, he found that the brigands who had robbed his Jewish friend had been acting on behalf of a company offering shares to investors in the slavery trade. Moses had refused to co-operate at first but the money was taken from him under the threat of blackmail, resulting from a trumped up charge against him concerning alleged extreme usury some years before.

It was during the time that he was at Parc that Henry was made aware of a request from the Jew of Bath, as Jeremiah was known from London to Carmarthen, to recover his sovereigns for him. The message had been sent westwards along a line of roadsters and was eventually given to a returning drover who knew where he could find Henry James.

Henry had lost no time for he knew where to find the pair who had abused his kind friend. It was night time and they would be drinking at the Red Lion in Groes Faen, just a short pony ride away from Parc.

When he arrived there he peered through the mullioned window and saw them in all their obvious malignancy. He entered through the swing door and saw that they were standing at the bar, each with a pistol stuck into his belt, regaling the regulars with their ribald yarns. Henry caught the eye of a young local farmer, Cadwgan, whom he knew, and indicated that he would like him to come outside. He hadn't been noticed by the two rogues so it was safe for Henry to proceed with his plan and he asked the young man for his help.

Politely waiting for a break in the story-telling, Cadwgan went up to the two men and said, 'which one of you is Glanville Bowring?'

'That's me,' said the slightly smaller of the two men. 'Why are you asking?'

'There's a little girl out the back with a message from an old friend who won't come himself for he don't enter drinking establishments like this.'

'Bloody Methodists!' cursed the knave, as he made his way out to the rear of the tavern. His colleague, feeling there was no threat if the messenger was only a child, simply ordered another schooner of rum.

Glanville Bowring didn't see the rope across the doorway. As he tripped and hurtled forward, Henry jumped on him, at the same time wrenching the pistol from the man's belt and flinging it away to the trees. With his knee in his back he pulled the man's arms suddenly together and slipped the prepared noose of a rope around them. There was sufficient rope to then lash his legs together at the ankles. His victim's shouts ceased when Henry jammed a large kerchief into his mouth, tying the ends around the back of his neck. Totally immobilised and silenced, the villain was dragged and left behind a wall about fifteen paces away. Henry then calmly walked into the bar just as Glanville Bowring's partner was beginning to wonder if anything could be wrong. As the ruffian turned from the bar to walk out he came face to face with Henry, who spoke calmly but firmly.

'Jim Penybont,' said Henry, 'I am so pleased to meet you.'

The big man put his hand on the butt of his pistol and said, 'And who the hell are you?'

'I'm Dick Turpin,' said Henry, 'and I want your money.'

'Dick Turpin, my arse,' screeched Jim, taking out his pistol and pointing it at Henry's heart. A deft kick from Henry sent the gun flying from his hand and as it flew towards the ceiling, he lunged forward and sent his head crashing into Big Jim's stomach. Henry brought his clenched fist down onto the top of the villain's head and there was a loud dull thud as the man's big frame fell to the floor. As the pistol came down from its aerial trip it had been caught by one of the regulars and now an unseen hand passed it to Henry.

When Jim Penybont came to his senses the coward started shouting abuse, alternating each phrase with a call to his missing friend.

'Glanville! . . . where are you for God's sake? . . . Help me, Glanville!'

'Get up, you brute,' said Henry, now pointing the pistol at his adversary's head.

As no-one moved to help the stricken blackguard, Henry knew he was among friends. He pulled back the hammer on the flintlock and wrapped his forefinger around the trigger, moving the weapon ever closer to the scoundrel's head. With his other hand he took from his pocket a leather pouch and placed it on the bar.

'Put your coins in there, one by one, and gold sovereigns only' said Henry, nodding towards the pouch.

Realising he had no choice, Jim Penybont slowly got to his feet and started removing coins from his deep pockets and putting them one after the other into the little leather bag as ordered.

When the figure had reached a score, Henry held up his hand.

'That's what I came for,' he said – and in seconds he was gone and galloping homewards through the darkness.

Catharine felt she knew there was more behind the story of the twenty sovereigns than Henry's simple statement, but she decided not to pursue the matter.

They were now away from the centre of Bath but before they left the eastern boundary of the city they became aware of loud shouting. If Catharine was enjoying up to this point what she might have described as a new exciting life, she had some shocks ahead of her for there were experiences to come that her naturally compassionate nature was hardly equipped to deal with.

The suburban road along which they walked with increasing pace since they heard the noise ahead of them opened out into a square. The incongruous sight of figures sitting on the eves of thatched cottages immediately ignited their curiosity, as did the tumult at ground level. There, a restless human throng of all ages was moving like maggots in a pot, jostling for position to observe something that was clearly on the brink of happening. Everyone seemed excited with anticipation and their patience was about to be rewarded.

Outside a blacksmith's forge, Henry and Catharine stood on a mounting block from which they had a view of the whole square. The noise had not subsided in the least since their arrival. In fact it increased as the crowd parted to allow men with tightly-leashed dogs with frothing mouths and bared teeth to come through. The noise by now could have raised the dead for, added to the demonic squeals of allegedly human creatures, some of whom were also frothing at the mouth, there were blasts from hunting horns, post horns and bugles. Everyone, it seemed, was eager for the entertainment to commence.

Catharine became faintly aware of something at the other side of the square. It seemed at first to be a mound of some sort – earth, maybe, or even a clump of dark foliage. It was only when there was frantic movement from within the dark shape that it was obvious it was a large cloth sheet covering a live object. When half a dozen or more of the barking and snarling dogs began moving towards the hulk it started to move. There were grunts coming from that direction, so loud that they were audible even above the maniacal chants of the crowd.

It could then be seen that a rope was strung around the shape and trailing towards a big man who was clearly in charge of the event whatever it should prove to be. The line must have been tied with a slip-knot for when he gave it a tug both the rope and the sheet fell away to reveal a monstrous grizzly bear. The animal must have been crouching during its concealment for now, standing at its full height it must have been eight feet from the ground to the top of its head. The expression on the bear's face carried a message to all present that he was not the happiest he had ever been. There was an iron collar around the animal's neck and shackles around its rear legs which were connected by a chain to a stout wooden post.

The only free movement the trapped bear had involved his front legs, which, because of his standing position were, in effect, his arms. He used these with deft accuracy to bring down over-ambitious curs who leapt at him suicidally. As the dogs swiftly flung themselves at the bear they were equally quickly sent to the ground with vertical chopping actions or sideways swipes, each defensive blow carrying not only the raw power of an enraged beast but also the sting of revenge that now guided the actions of the cornered creature.

Had Catharine the ability to put all her thoughts into words she would have described the behaviour of the dogs, the spectators and indeed the bear as a demonstration of animal mayhem at its crudest and of these three participating groups, the supposed humans were the most reprehensible. The dogs were simply enacting the role for which they had been bred; the bear was acting in enforced self-defence. The humans were satisfying a lust for violence and bloodshed which was neither edifying nor necessary. It made her feel sick. She had a dim memory of her mother telling her she had experienced something similar at Llantrisant years before, involving a bull rather than a bear.

Henry came off the mounting stone and helped Catharine step down. He asked her if she had seen enough. Her reply was blunt:

'Enough of that,' she said, with a wild look on her face. 'I felt I could have killed that man just in front of us – the one in the expensive clothes who was shouting what I think were obscenities all the time.'

'I didn't like him either,' said Henry, standing on his toes to see if he could locate the man who had earned their disapproval. Satisfied he could see him, Henry asked Catharine if she would excuse him for a moment, and in a twinkling, he was gone.

Catharine didn't have to wait long for her lover's return, for Henry was soon back with her and indicating that they should be on their way once more.

They crossed the county border into Wiltshire and after a strenuous long walk arrived at a picturesque village called Combe Acton. Henry pointed out that the name Combe, meaning valley, was one that had survived from their own tongue, the British language. In Wales it was 'Cwm' but it was the same word.

Catharine decided to ask about the state of their finances.

'Very healthy, and better still since I went up to that uncouth fellow back there. His pocket is a little lighter now.'

Catharine retorted: 'When I said I didn't like him I didn't mean you should steal from him!' She declined to add anything for she was inwardly pleased that the man had, in a way, been 'punished'. In fact she was slowly, very slowly, beginning to feel that whilst thievery as such was mostly a bad crime, it was nevertheless often a way of exacting sweet revenge – not to say a convenient means of paying one's way. It seemed acceptable if the 'victim', for one reason or another, deserved to be robbed. Her memories of all those sermons were fading fast.

A little weary from walking and still feeling uneasy about what she had witnessed, Catharine longed for something pleasant to happen to ease her doubts about the righteousness of mankind.

They entered a village that appeared timeless – engendering an all-pervading feeling of peace. The thatched cottages, all different, were obviously real homes, with real people going about their daily routine. A man was drawing water from the nearby village pump whilst whistling a bright tune; a woman carrying duck eggs in her apron was followed down the road by half a dozen of the quacking birds; two carefree little boys were sitting on the bank of the nearby brook fishing. The smell of freshly-baked bread wafted from a building out of which a man came and shook himself, causing a cloud of white flour to hang in the air for a few moments before falling like snowflakes to the ground. Catharine was enchanted: the tranquility and sheer loveliness of everything was so different from her recent experience of that hideous mob.

It wasn't a dream, for Henry, as real as ever, was still beside her and now talking to the baker. After congratulating the man on the heavenly odour for which he was responsible, he went on to ask him questions about his methods of making bread. The baker was clearly taken aback by the stranger's words. Henry explained that he had been a miller at one time and he had learned about the nature of grain and flour, also the technicalities of baking. Impressed by Henry's knowledge and delighted to receive praise from someone so experienced, he called them both inside to show them his workplace.

Henry was not slow in respectfully offering advice with regard to improving even further, the already excellent texture and taste of the baker's products. Ten minutes later the pair left with two loaves of the freshest bread given to them by a grateful practitioner of an ancient craft. Before they left the village for the open road again, they acted out of character for a moment. They went into a little shop and *bought* some cheese which, with the bread, they consumed whilst sitting under a hawthorn tree in full blossom. Catharine was enjoying the outdoor life with the man she idolised. To her it was still a glorious adventure.

'How do you know so much about everything?' Catharine asked Henry.

'I don't,' he replied. 'Only *nearly* everything!'

175

'But where did you learn about bakeries?'

'I didn't,' said Henry. 'I just guess these things.'

'You are a crooked man.'

'And so I am.'

Catharine gave him one of her friendly slaps and soon they were on their way again.

They cut bracken, made bundles of it for pillows and another night was spent in the open air. In the morning they made a small fire and toasted what was left of the bread and cheese. They drank copiously from a nearby stream of clear water and freshened up their faces and hair before moving off once again in an easterly direction.

Among the joys of an unplanned journey is the excitement of not knowing what might happen next. One morning, the pair heard sounds that were somewhat alien yet strangely familiar too. The lowing of Welsh Black cattle on the move is not dissimilar to that of cows of other breeds. When, however, the animals are being driven along by commands in the ancient British tongue, the combined sound is distinctively reminiscent of life in the Cambrian hills. The sounds were coming from high ground to the couple's left and they went off course to take a look. Upon reaching a grassy ridge they were confronted by a slow-moving black mass of beef and horn going in the same direction as they were. Besides the snorting and mooing there were barks from attendant dogs, but it was hearing the drovers' calls that caused a little burst of homesickness.

'*Ymlaen! Ymlaen!*' ('Onwards! Onwards!')

Catharine was astonished to see Henry and one of the cattle men shaking hands and talking animatedly to each other.

'This is Pyrs y Porthmon,' said Henry, as Catharine joined them. 'He's known as "Dick Drover" this side of the border. Known him for years. Used to be a thief like me and we met when I once visited the Cowbridge House of Correction.'

'Aye, that's where they teach you the correct way to steal things!' said Pyrs, and he and Henry laughed loudly.

Then the drover said, 'That's where they did this,' holding up a hand with three missing fingers.

'You mean they cut them off?' said Catharine, aghast at the idea.

'Yes, but not as punishment!'

'He had frostbite,' said Henry, 'and they removed five of his toes as well. It's a wonder he can walk ten paces without falling over!'

'After a few tankards tonight in the Drovers Arms in Gresham I won't manage three paces!' Again they laughed and then they said their farewells before going on their way.

Out of earshot, Henry said that to his knowledge his old pal had made London twelve times. 'Not bad for an ex pilferer with half his toes gone!'

As they proceeded Catharine thought about that meeting with the drover. It had sparked a brief sensation that she was a long way from home and all those things which had been part of her upbringing. She had heard of the pull of intense longing called *hiraeth* which troubled Cymric travellers, but it had yet to manifest itself strongly. Nevertheless she had had a slight but very real taste of it, and she wasn't sure she would welcome it were it to happen again.

Chapter Fourteen

Catharine's happiness was heightened as each new day came – as did her adoration of Henry. There was little he could do wrong in her eyes for there seemed to be a noble purpose in all his actions. She was impressed by his vast knowledge and his manifold skills but more than anything she loved him for his kindness and his sense of fairness in all matters. She no longer questioned Henry's chosen path in life; for the time being she would not trouble her mind with questions about the immorality of stealing other people's possessions. That could all be explained later. For the present she felt ecstatically privileged to be able to observe this otherwise faultless human being from close quarters. For his part, Henry James was deeply infatuated with this young woman and he vowed to be true to her for the rest of his days.

As the intrepid pair walked along lanes they were musically accompanied by a chorus of linnets, thrushes, blackbirds, tits and dunnocks among other birds of the hedgerows. Catharine wondered if there might be a nest or two where fat young cuckoos were being nurtured by adoptive mothers. Not for the first time, Henry seemed to read Catharine's thoughts:

'They always return you know,' he said, looking straight at his partner.

'Who?' said Catharine quickly.

'Cuckoos. Weren't you thinking about cuckoos?'

'Yes, I was, but how did you know?'

'By the expression on your beautiful face,' said Henry, ducking sharply to dodge a playful slap from his beloved.

It was time to eat again. Catharine lay on her back on a grassy bank and looked up at a blue sky that was broken only by an occasional wisp of white cloud. She knew Henry was down near a stream which she could hear bubbling along. Without looking she knew that he would be lying prone and probing under bankside boulders with an outstretched arm. When it came to tickling trout, her man was a master of the craft. Soon two or three plump fish would be gutted and held over another campfire on makeshift forks and then consumed with the usual heartiness.

Their meal was, as usual, washed down with water – scooped this time from the cool Wiltshire stream which had provided their recent delicious repast.

The couple lingered for a while, lying together and listening to the sounds of summer. Bees came and went; a dragonfly hovered above them and quickly losing interest it swung away to some nearby gorse bushes. On the far side of the brook, a flock of ewes dotted a large field like pieces of white fluff whilst their three-month old gambolling lambs butted each other like rutting stags. It was altogether an idyllic moment of a kind Catharine had experienced countless times since her exciting excursion had begun. She was beginning to feel she had already lived three lifetimes and there couldn't possibly be more delights, or indeed excitement, to come. She was wrong.

Three days later they were making their way down the wide main street of Malborough in a dogcart pulled by a black pony. They had acquired this means of transport by the most economical method known to mankind. They had stolen it.

The pair had paused by the roadside to observe a gang of men and women hoeing in a turnip field. The way in which the workers' backs were bent, and the frequent groans coming from their direction confirmed that they were engaged in very hard toil. It appeared, however, that their efforts were not strenuous enough for a foreman who had just arrived.

After getting down from his dogcart the overseer strolled the headland of the field demanding that they move faster. From time to time he would walk down one of the rows and cuff the head of a male planter or give a stinging swipe to the bottom of a female with the stick which he drew from his belt each time as if it were a sword from its scabbard. A passer-by stopped, and, noticing that Henry and Catharine were regarding the turnip foreman with a look of disdain, he ventured:

'He's a bad 'un that 'un. 'E were a sergeant in the Wiltshire Militia for years till he killed a youngster in a fight and were chucked out. Aye, 'e's a bad un orlright, that sergeant Tomlinson.' The man went on his way.

'Don't like that man down there,' said Catharine without taking her eyes off the foreman.

'Nor do I,' said Henry. 'Let's go then.'

Without further discussion they unhitched the pony's reins from the gatepost and in minutes were trotting down a Wiltshire lane as happy as could be. Wisely they felt they should abandon the pony and cart as soon as they could. Out of concern for the animal they devised a plan. In Marlborough, Catharine held the pony and cart whilst Henry entered the King George Hotel and quickly came out with the names of the counter clerk and the stable manager, information that would be crucial for their next move. He took the reins from Catharine and drove under an archway into the hotel's back yard. Approached by a tough-looking side-whiskered individual wearing a tall box hat, Henry simply handed him the reins as they jumped down from the dogcart.

'Mr Hutchinson said you were the best horse man in the county. You *are* Mr Bingley, aren't you?'

'Why, yes, that's right sir, what shall we do for you?'

'Oh, the usual, Mr Bingley, please. Best hay for Dobbin and stabling for three nights.'

'And what would the name be, sir?'

'Tomlinson,' said Henry, 'of Church Pews farm, Stop Blinking.'

'Thank you, sir,' said Bingley as the pair walked slowly out through the arch. As soon as they were on the street once more they quickened their pace and left the town, laughing at their little jape.

Life for Catharine Griffith and Henry James followed no pattern except that it was clear they were going towards London. They met every challenge connected with travelling, sleeping accommodation, food and drink, also clothing, with ingenious solutions conjured by Henry and they proceeded through the summer with confidence. They idolised each other and nothing troubled Catharine's conscience, even though by now not all of the robberies were clear-cut examples of the righting of wrongs.

Time flew by for the couple and it was already late autumn. The outdoor life suited Catharine Griffith for she continued to bloom with health. She brushed her waist-length hair daily and tried not to let her clothes become soiled. Both she and Henry had re-attired themselves from the wardrobes of the well-off. Henry James was no less handsome because he now had a thick black beard. If anything, it enhanced his white-toothed smile.

Nothing seemed to be new to Henry James but Catharine was learning things daily. For one thing, whilst she and Henry conversed in their own language when alone together, she was hearing different English accents as they proceeded eastwards and her partner had to translate those words she didn't understand.

They entered a place called Newbury and sat on a bench in the main street listening to the town crier acquainting the locals with the latest news. Passers-by often greeted some items with rude gestures at the crier and shouted willful criticism doubting the veracity of what he was saying.

The man making public announcements might as well have been speaking Chinese as far as Catharine was concerned, so Henry had to translate his words too. The crier didn't waste much time on items of news from the monarchy or reports from the East India Company; less still on stories from America, apart from some which were designed to foretell the imminent failure of the colonists' new regime. There was virtually no news of developments in Paris; all that would come later. Henry passed on to Catharine details of the one item which seemed to have priority that day. It was, apparently, 'The Event of the Year'. She had misgivings about it since Henry said it was another example of an activity that appealed to man's innate blood-lust. She eventually agreed that it would be another 'life-experience' that would help shape her character.

Henry read from the poster on the wall of the town hall. It confirmed what the town crier had been promoting: 'The Biggest Cock-Fight in the History of the Great Diversion.'

They went to the arena down at a racecourse on the outskirts of the town. A procession six or seven abreast was making its way to the little stadium known as the 'Blood and Talons Cockpit'. That should have been enough to put Catharine off but she continued, holding Henry's arm.

Even before they arrived at the cockpit itself, they were waylaid by bookmakers lining the approach path. 'Best odds here!' . . . 'Make your fortune here!' . . . 'Come here poor, go home rich!'

It was clear though that the betting odds were very close in each event for, as Henry explained to Catharine, the emergence of an outright winner depended not so much on the fighting prowess of one gamecock or the other as on the extent to which an owner had equipped his bird with razors attached to its legs as 'illegal' spurs, sharpened its talons, or indeed the extent to which one bird or another had been given doses variously of gin or even laudanum!

The arena was a kind of round barn with some seating at ground level and the rest in a circular gallery. These were quickly filled – with Henry and Catharine choosing to go upstairs.

As in the case of the bear-baiting, the spectators were from various strands of society but with a common predilection for watching suffering. Their faces had grotesque expressions even before the combatants were released into the arena. Strangely, there was less pre-contest noise at the cockpit than had been the case in Bath. Henry explained that the reason for those ear-splitting shouts at the other place had been to get the bear agitated. Fighting cockerels needed no such incitement.

Before the first contest began there was entertainment for the mob. Two men, dressed as gamecocks, entered the arena to cheers and weird laughing. They stalked each other around the ring for half a minute, occasionally scraping the ground with their feet, as cockerels do – and then began their sham battle. Whilst emitting chicken like sounds, they approached each other and offered gentle taps with their outstretched mock-feather covered arms. The very mildness of their affray was regarded as hilarious by spectators who were aware of the horrors of the real contest that would follow. The two performers left the arena to cheers and loud laughter. Then there were few sounds apart from the calling of moneymen walking among the rows of benches.

Catharine whispered in Henry's ear: 'How did we get in here without paying?'

'Easy,' said Henry. 'It's an old trick. I put nothing into the doorman's hand . . . and the fool gave me change!'

As Catharine punched him gently in the ribs, there was a call from the Master of Ceremonies, now standing in the middle of the earthen floor of the arena.

'Silence, please!' he cried. 'You have five more minutes to place your wagers. Hurry to it!'

'Are we going to have a gamble?' asked Catharine, as quietly as she could when a man went by with a box of betting tickets in two colours.

'No fear!' said Henry, with feigned indignation. 'Those men are common robbers!'

A fanfare of trumpets launched the real business of the day and a dozen fighting-bird owners paraded around the inner floor of the arena each carrying his gamecock in a glass-panelled box. The birds were unruffled, obviously unaware of the do-or-die confrontations ahead.

When the trumpeting was over, two owners faced each other across the trodden clay floor. They held firmly their respective contenders for the title of 'Newbury Fighting Bird of the Century'. The records of both gamecocks were announced by the MC who had no more to say apart from asking all present to sit back and enjoy the finest sport in the world. In fact no-one sat back, for as soon as the bell was struck for the contest to start, everyone stood to their feet issuing the deafening screams and howls of what in another age would be considered to be demented low-life humanity. The savagery that followed left Catharine Griffith in a daze of displeasure that would take some time to fade. Henry James, too, came away from the arena with a feeling of deep disapproval. They spoke but little as they went off again.

The bear-baiting and the cockfighting had done nothing to assuage Catharine's worsening regard for humankind in general.

Seeing her fellow creatures behaving so badly had made her feel that her *own* misdemeanors were trifling in comparison. She once more held the view that stealing another's property was probably not sinful provided it could be regarded as justifiable revenge. There were signs though that this proviso was becoming even more open to her personal interpretation – or rather that of her man, for it was he who led the way in all matters.

'How far is London?' was Catharine's much repeated question as they plodded onwards. She hoped that the big city would add even more excitement to her already transformed life but also that she would see less of man at his cruellest there.

'About twenty days if all goes well,' was Henry's answer. 'We should be there by Christmas.'

As they moved ever eastwards, the more Catharine became aware of a level of wealth far beyond anything she had ever known. From time to time she had a fleeting glimpse of a class of society that she had been told about but could not bring herself to believe, existed.

One day as she and Henry trudged along a country lane near Theale they were forced into taking evasive action by a cantering horse ridden by a red-coated flunkey.

'Aside there,' the rider shouted, as he went by flailing the air with his hunting crop. 'The Duke and Duchess are coming by!'

Henry and an alarmed Catharine pressed their backs into the grassy bank of the hedgerow as a procession of vehicles went by. First it was a cabriolet drawn by two trotters nodding their heads proudly, their driver holding his head high in a disdainful pose. Then came a brougham, its four horses straining at their tug chains so much the whole harness appeared to be ready to burst apart.

Next half a dozen youngsters dressed in what must have been the latest fashions – certainly Catharine had never seen the like before – their tall narrowing hats bobbing as they rose in the saddle in perfect rhythm with their trotting mounts; their calfskin breeches of a quality also never before seen by Catharine.

They were followed by the main item in the procession: a coach that must have been carrying the Duke and Duchess – although they couldn't be seen because of the veiled windows. Sundry outriders brought up the rear, the last of them a big man again wearing red livery who turned his horse around upon seeing the pair.

'Be off with you. Keep away from here,' he said. 'Go back where you came from, or you'll feel the sting of this,' he said, holding up his riding crop before spurring his horse and riding off to catch up with the others.

'I do believe he thinks he has scared us,' said Henry.

'I wonder what's their hurry,' said Catharine.

This was overheard by an old woman who walking past, carrying a bundle of firewood. 'Late for church again, that's what they be,' she said. 'I'm supposin' you know who they be?'

Catharine didn't understand her, but Henry quickly said, 'Who are they? Pray tell us.'

'Why the Duchess and his Royal Highness the Duke of Cumberland, that's who they be. They're stayin' with relatives in that big 'ouse over there, up that drive.'

'Of course,' said Henry. 'Thank you, Ma'am.' They quickly made their way to the country seat and whilst Catharine kept a look-out, Henry broke in.

It wasn't easy to carry the things they had newly acquired but the length of dimity was folded nicely and carried beneath Catharine's dress. The silver spoons and a pair of slippers were tucked into the pocket of a greatcoat which Henry had lifted from the same source.

They entered a village about ten miles on and found for-tuitously that a market was being held. Within minutes, Henry was standing amidst the crowd advertising the items he had for sale. No-one questioned the provenance of what he was offering and they were quickly on their way again, a sovereign and several shillings better off.

One day when they were consuming one of their 'campfire meals' in a clearing amidst some Berkshire woodland, Catharine reminded Henry of his promise to teach her some skills of the street-thief. She had told him it was time she shared their work.

'Well,' he said, giving the fire a little poke of encouragement, 'it's not an ability people are usually born with – but most can be taught.' He gave the stew in the saucepan a stir and, looking at Catharine, said: 'Do you know what the first requirement is?'

'Er, no,' she said, shaking her head.

'Well,' said Henry, 'it's the *desire* to steal . . . it is essential not to feel guilt when you are thieving.'

'I think I understand that very well,' said Catharine, who was only now coming to regard basic pilferage as acceptable. It had also helped that she hadn't been to church for a long time.

'The second thing,' said Henry, sprinkling salt onto the bubbling broth, 'is planning.'

'In what way?' asked Catharine, pausing in her attempts to cut a loaf of bread in half with a blunt knife. 'Do you mean making sure that stolen cutlery works?' She went on gouging the bread.

'No, I mean there must be absolutely no risk of apprehension so it means thinking through what you intend doing until you feel sure it won't fail.'

'And what if you don't feel sure?'

'Then you don't do it.'

'Have you ever failed?' asked Catharine, immediately thinking she shouldn't have asked such a question of a perfect man. His answer surprised her a little.

'Why then do you think I was at the Cowbridge House of Correction . . . or in gaol in London? It wasn't because I was in need of a rest! It was because I had slipped up on my preparation and the buggers caught me.'

'Alright then, what's the third important thing?'

'Distraction.' Catharine gave him a blank look.

'The attention of an intended victim must be diverted,' said Henry. 'It's difficult when you work alone, but there's nothing easier if you work as a pair.'

'So from now on are we a team?' asked Catharine.

'Yes, but remember this,' said her mentor. 'Before, you were just a receiver . . . now you'll be a full-blown wicked felon.'

'I can't wait,' said Catharine, the novice.

Chapter Fifteen

The following morning they stayed in the clearing where they had slept overnight and didn't leave until Henry had given Catharine her first lessons in distraction. He went through a series of visual and audio examples of deceptive manoeuvres. Catharine even learned how to cough in a certain way and to make movements that would catch the eye of a guard without revealing herself. They swapped their roles of victim and thief over and over again. By the time they were on their way, Catharine felt she had learned a lot about finesse and dexterity.

As they were looking rather dirty and dishevelled they decided to have a wash and brushing down at the first opportunity. Their hopes that this might come soon were raised when they saw a cluster of tents of various faded colours ahead.

'Gypsies,' said Henry. 'Our luck is in.'

Catharine's jaw dropped slightly. 'Will it be safe?' she said, with a hint of alarm.

'Nowhere safer,' said Henry. 'Just leave it to me.'

Catharine moved a little closer to her man as they walked into the encampment.

A swarthy fellow of about 40 years of age wearing a red and white spotted neckerchief got up from a stool as the pair approached. He raised his hand to shade his squinting eyes and shocked Catharine by uttering a stream of words – not because they were in a tongue she didn't recognise, but because they included the name 'Henry'.

The two men, now embracing, were obviously well known to each other. Catharine was introduced to Ephrem and shook his gnarled hand.

'We are old friends,' said Henry, as the man went to a tent nearby and brought out three others: a man in his thirties, a girl of about Catharine's age, and a woman in her sixties.

'Latcho dives,' (Good-day) said Henry, *'Latcho dives.'*

'My God,' thought Catharine, 'is there anything this man can't do? – he's now speaking Gypsy language!'

'Latcho dives,' said the Romanies in unison.

'Everilda!' said Henry as he moved towards the older woman. She flung her bangled bare arms around him, and was so overcome with emotion she burst into tearful laughter before turning to Catharine. *'Yang womaan,'* she said, *'yoo are very lacky to 'ave theese maan.'*

Catharine was then introduced to Ephrem's brother Nicolao and his sister Talaitha.

The lady then made circular motions with her hand on her stomach region and pointed to one of the larger tents.

'We have to eat with them,' said Henry, 'Everilda says so,' and led the way holding Catharine's hand.

Catharine was still rather perplexed as they entered the tent to partake of the food that was being brought in by other gypsies. As there was no table, they stood and ate from large wooden plates onto which various foods were placed with regularity. Catharine's bewilderment was short-lived for she quickly decided that these were good people. Her prejudices, born of tales she had heard long ago quickly vanished.

Henry continued to impress Catharine with his use of the Romany language. When they were served *'Gushwara pie'* he kept saying *'cooshtie, cooshtie!'* 'Very good, very good.'

In another tent they were each given a tub of hot water, a bar of soap, and towel cloth. Henry was also handed a razor and mirror and in no time he was bare-faced once more. When they had washed and dried a gypsy girl came around to brush Catharine's long hair.

They were fresh again and eventually left the camp thanking the gypsies for their kindness.

'*Nais tuke*,' ('Thank you,') said Henry. '*Nais tuke*,' said Catharine. They looked back towards the camp when they got to the brow of the next hill and saw that the Gypsies were still waving.

Out on the open road again, Catharine asked the astounding man alongside her where he had known the Romanies.

'I lived with them for a year up in the English Midlands. Parliament had made them outlaws and were tracking them down and moving them on. Then they started falsely accusing them of theft – even murder. With another Welshman who was with me at the time we said it was we who had done a certain burglary that they'd been accused of. We knew we'd get out of that gaol so we let it all happen. The Gypsies were very grateful to us for they were left alone for a while. We escaped within a month but we heard that later on five young gypsies were hanged – all innocent.

As they had eaten well, food would not be a priority for a while. It was turning out to be a nice day and still warm when they entered a village called Oakingham.

They went into the Queen Elizabeth Arms for a cooling drink and sat outside on a bench at a wooden table, gradually becoming aware of an increasing number of horse-drawn vehicles going past. Some riders too went by, mostly on horses and ponies but also some on donkeys. Then groups of pedestrians, some of them quickening their steps as they arrived in the main street.

Two men came out of the inn and paused nearby, arguing volubly about the likely outcome of some event or other. The bigger of the pair was most insistent that his view was the right one and he calmly made his point whilst the smaller man was much more aggressive in making his opinion known.

It was only when he adopted the typical stance of prize-fighters of the day and demonstrated a slow punching movement, that it all became clear. A bare-knuckle contest was due to take place in the locality. The two men stopped on their way to the road and the short one, addressing Henry, said, 'who's your money on, Tom or Jules?'

'With respect, sir, I'm not a gambler,' said Henry.

'Ah, very droll,' said the man, 'very droll . . . as if anyone would come here if he weren't a betting man!' and he and his friend went off to join the walking crowd.

Catharine and Henry found that the match involved the greatest prizefighter of his day in England, the gentlemanly Yorkshireman, Tom Johnson, who was backed by the Earl Bullock of Surrey. His opponent, four stones heavier, was Jules D'Art who hailed from Calais and was a contender for the French championship.

It appeared that Oakingham was the location for many of the important prizefighting matches of the time and thousands attended them.

After the bear-baiting and cockfighting, Catharine had no enthusiasm for watching two men drawing blood from each other and would have happily walked on. She agreed to go to the prizefight only when Henry said this too would add to her life's experience and she could tell her grandchildren about it sometime in the future. That remark was meant to cause a smile but it didn't.

They had a good view of the proceedings and Catharine was intrigued to see so many females among the spectators. The fight went on in a square clearing which had a wooden platform about a foot in height. There were no ropes and the only objects in the area were buckets of water used by the fighters' seconds at the end of each round. There was a lot of grunting from the two contestants who belted each other with infrequent but devastating blows with their bare fists to the head and the midriff.

The awful sounds of fists hitting their targets would have been enough to upset Catharine had they been audible above the sickening sounds that came from the crowd. Catharine found the whole thing hideous and said so. Henry did not hesitate to take her by the arm and lead her away from the place. As they walked out of the village they could still hear the voices of degraded humanity in the distance.

Four hours later they settled down for the night on the banks of the Thames near Maidenhead. They had been helped on their way by a friendly driver who was taking an empty cart to Twyford. He needed ballast to give his vehicle stability so that he could trot along at a good speed. Two Irish vagrants were also taken aboard and with Catharine and Henry they sang all the way to Twyford.

The couple had walked to Maidenhead and were now ready for a good night's slumber. It was a balmy evening and before dropping off to sleep, Catharine listened intently to the sounds of the river which were new to her. Boats were still being rowed up and down after dark and as each one went past where they were lying, disturbed water slapping against the bank made a lovely sound. The last bird she heard announcing its presence was an owl in some nearby woodland.

The pair awoke in the morning to different birdsounds and sights. A kingfisher flashed past in a dazzle of brilliant blue, giving a whistle and a warble as it flew. Moorhens chirricked and quarked; coots followed with their mellow rings and metallic chic chics. Mallards wove their way around clumps of river grasses followed by miniature ducklings in symmetrical formation. When Catharine fully opened her eyes she was delighted by something so beautiful she at once felt she was experiencing visual heaven. It had happened to her once before. Her mind was called back to that day she went to Aberthaw. She had seen a ship on the Channel being powered along by the wind, its white sails set against the blue of the summer sky. It was moving gracefully and utterly beautifully.

She now had the same feeling when she saw a family of swans. A most comely picture. They too were moving with elegant grace, perfectly reminiscent of that sailing ship gliding decorously in a dimension of unsurpassed beauty.

'How far is London?' Catharine asked once more as she got to her feet stretching her arms and yawning the night out of her body.

'It depends on how many lifts we get,' said Henry. 'Could be there in a week.'

In fact they were there in less than a day for they were lucky to overhear a conversation at an inn about some experimental coach runs that were taking place. They heard that before long there would be a passenger service by coach from London to Bath and after that London to Bristol might be considered as well. Stages were being timed and the availability of livery and stabling along the route was being catalogued.

Here at Maidenhead was as far as the experimental coaches were going at present and they welcomed travellers to join them free of charge for the return journey into London. On average they stopped every ten or twelve miles to change horses but that exercise hardly slowed the journey because the new facilities were quite efficient.

For Henry and Catharine it was a perfect arrangement for it saved their legs and their shoe leather.

'They call this place Hammersmith,' said Henry.

'I thought you said we were in London,' answered Catharine.

'Well, we are and yet we are not,' said Henry. 'I don't know why they call this Hammersmith.'

'So you don't know everything,' retorted Catharine.'

'Oh no, no, no . . . as I keep telling you, just *nearly* everything!'

She gave him one of her usual friendly slaps, and they went on their way even further eastwards.

Catharine was impressed with the size of everything in what Henry said was Kensington. She had not seen such tall buildings since they had left Bath. They were tucked tightly together and seemed to reach to the sky. There was an occasional field with grazing cows, and a few signs of industry such as a timber yard and a big grain store, but most of the area was residential.

Pointing out the roof and chimneys of a large building in the distance, Henry said, 'That's Kensington Palace. King George the Second lived there.'

'Where does the King of England live now then?' asked Catharine.

'Oh, the third George. He's in Windsor Castle.'

'Where's that?'

'You could have seen it if you'd stayed awake on that coach ride from Maidenhead. I pointed it out to you as we were passing, but you were snoring like a gin-soak.'

'Old Lewis told us about the gin palaces and drunk people everywhere in London,' said Catharine. 'You had to step over them in the street. He came up here with Samuel Price years ago.'

'Parliament put a stop to all that,' said Henry. 'Well, mostly anyway . . . they drink other poisons now . . . and you still have to step over them.'

'You never drink much do you.' It was more of a statement than a question from Catharine for she knew his answer before he spoke.

Henry shook his head and said, 'There's never been a successful thief who drinks a lot of alcohol.'

They continued walking up the Thames Embankment and it seemed to have taken no time at all to reach Westminster.

'This is the real centre of London,' said Henry, pausing to rest against the river wall.

'Centre of the whole world then!' suggested Catharine.

'I suppose so,' said Henry, 'the English certainly think so.'

The river was very wide at this point and busy with water traffic. Henry pointed out nearby buildings.

'The palace of Westminster there,' he said, 'and down there, the Abbey.'

'If we were to follow the river down the next embankment,' said Henry, 'we'd be close to St Paul's Cathedral. But we need to go a little to the north tonight. I know a place where we can stay.'

'Indoors?' said Catharine.

'Yes, in a warm bed with clean sheets and food to make your mouth water,' said Henry, 'unless you want to sleep under a bridge with the dregs.'

'No, no, a warm bed, please,' she said quickly.

They zig-zagged their way northwards before Henry paused at the side of a wide street.

'They say if you close your eyes you can hear the ghosts on the move here,' said Henry, 'hundreds of them with their pitiful sounds.'

'What ghosts?' said Catharine, instinctively moving closer to Henry.

'The spirits of condemned prisoners, men and women, on their way from Newgate Prison to the gallows at Tyburn just down the road from here. Some call this Tyburn Road – others call it Tyburn Street; others say Uxbridge Road; yet others, Worcester Road. Anyway, it's the old route from Newgate to Oxford and for those poor devils Tyburn was the end of *their* road.'

'Can we move on?' asked Catharine, feeling a little uneasy, and Henry took her hand as they crossed the wide thoroughfare on which a variety of vehicles were travelling in both directions.

When they were on a quieter street which opened out onto green fields, she asked Henry a question that she had been planning for a long time:

'You told me you were in gaol in London. Were you at Newgate?'

'Yes, there were three of us, two boys from Caerphilly and me. We'd been working Fleet Market and doing quite well, when Rhys and Emlyn were apprehended by law officers acting for the Under Sheriff of Holborn. They were both seen 'switching'.'

Catharine interrupted him: 'What is that?'

'Well,' said Henry, 'it's when you go up to someone, hand them an article, and say, "I think you dropped this." The person is distracted and you fleece them while they are still confused. It's all over in a flash. That's another lesson in distraction for you!'

'You weren't caught yourself?'

'No, but I tried to remonstrate with the street watchmen who arrested my two pals.'

'Who were those watchmen?'

'Well, the whole area was awash with men looking out for villains like us. These were called the Thames River Police . . . although we were quite a way from that waterway. I had told the boys to be careful because if these bumbling law officers didn't get us, the Bow Street patrols would. Bow Street Runners are the experts. They'll chase you across the world and won't give up until they've caught you.'

'So what did they do to you?'

'I was obviously an accomplice so they took me in with them. Firstly it was to the Fleet Prison and then to Newgate to await trial.'

'How did you get away?'

'I told them a half-truth. I made it known to the warders that the three of us were deserters from the Militia. I let them think it was the Kent County Militia and not the Glamorgan!'

'What was the point of that?' asked Catharine, finding it all very exciting.

'Because,' said Henry, 'they were then obliged to hand us over to the nearest military authority. This would mean that we would eventually be taken out of Newgate.'

'So?'

'It was almost impossible to escape from "Fortress Newgate", but once outside we had all sorts of options.'

'How did you get free in the end?'

'They sent us to a Barracks at Richmond but with only three guards. No match I'm afraid for three strong farmers' sons from Eglwys Ilan!'

'I've heard enough,' said Catharine, adding a yawn.

'Alright, let's go to see Gwenllian then,' said Henry, and taking Catharine's hand again broke into a brisk walk.

'This,' said Henry, 'is a district called Camden. It's an area of Hamstead Heath. That rising ground you see is Parliament Hill and you'll always find Welshmen around there.'

'And Welsh women?'

'No, not very many.'

'What sort of Welsh people come here? . . . thieves like us?'

'No, no,' said Henry, dismissively. 'Certainly not!'

'Who then?'

'Writers and poets mostly. They come here to compare their works. Also they collect old manuscripts.'

They soon arrived at a house from which came the sound of a female singing.

'That's a Welsh song!' said Catharine, excitedly. 'I know it!'

'It's Gwenllian,' said Henry. 'She'll want you to sing with her.'

'Who is Gwenllian?' asked Catharine. Henry held a fore-finger to his lips as he guided her through the open front door. Still out of sight of Gwenllian they spontaneously joined in with the woman's song, Catharine offering her perfect contralto and Henry also harmonising beautifully, taking the treble above Gwenllian's melody.

Gwenllian's face was a delight as she came from behind a door and threw her arms around Henry. Then she turned to Catharine and hugged her too.

'You still sing of sheep and shepherds then, Gwen,' said Henry. 'Even in this God-forsaken place!'

'Yes,' said Gwenllian, whose eyes were moist.

'By the way, this is Catharine, she's a thief like me,' said Henry, so casually that it made Catharine wince a little.

'Teaching her the ropes are you? . . . well, she couldn't have a better tutor.' Then, leading the way, she said, 'Come into the kitchen, I've made some treats this morning.'

Henry and Catharine sat at a scrubbed pine table to await the return of their host who had disappeared to some back room.

'Gwenllian speaks very little English and most people around here think she's Spanish or Portuguese!' She's very helpful to the Welsh who come here for some of *them* have no English either.'

Gwenllian was a woman of about fifty years, still good-looking and sprightly. She was also obviously a good cook for she walked in now with a tureen of steaming broth that had an aroma worthy of a Welsh farmhouse kitchen.

'*Y cawl gorau yn y byd,*' said Henry, 'The best broth in the world . . . I've had it here many times.'

The talk whilst they ate was illuminating. Gwenllian was a knowledgeable woman with regard to historical facts, most of which meant nothing to Catharine who was content just to listen to the others.

'Have you heard of Guto Ffowc?' asked Gwenllian, looking at Catharine.

It was Henry who responded, to save Catharine revealing her ignorance of history:

'Over a hundred and seventy years ago Guto and his cohorts planned to blow up the Houses of Parliament but they were caught and executed. Had they succeeded they were going to watch the explosion from up here on the hill.'

'Some still say it is a pity they failed!' said Gwenllian with a smile as she went out of the room again.

Catharine took advantage of the lady's absence to ask Henry to tell her exactly what they were doing there.

'It's a lodging house,' he said. 'She doesn't charge much. In fact, in our case she won't ask for anything.'

Before Catharine could ask for an explanation, Gwenllian was coming back with a tray of slices of *bara brith* layered thickly with butter.

The conversation that then ensued raised a few questions for which Catharine would need answers in due course from her man.

'Your room is clear,' said Gwenllian, 'Dewi ap Robert went away this morning. He was here three weeks, meeting Iago, Penri and the others. He left some papers though. They have big plans.'

'Are they planning to blow up Parliament?' Asked Catharine.

'No, unfortunately,' said Gwenllian. 'What they are doing is very peaceful. They are going to help Iolo revive the bardic tradition . . . there's strong feeling about it at the moment. Iolo himself stayed here for two weeks when he was last in London.'

'You met the man of whom Gwenllian speaks,' said Henry, turning to Catharine. 'I remember you telling me about the conversation the scholar was having with Dr Richard Price at Parc.'

'I didn't understand the points they were making,' said Catharine.

She would have continued but Gwenllian suddenly broke in, saying, 'You were at Parc, with Catherine and Samuel Price?'

She reached out and held Catharine's hand and went on: 'Then you must have known Shencyn Lewis . . . Old Lewis they called him.'

'Yes, indeed,' said Catharine, getting to her feet. 'You have bad news?'

'Please break it gently,' interjected Henry, fearing the worst.

'I have all the news from home. My friends are so regular and I hear things within days of their happening.'

'Please,' said Catharine. 'Old Lewis was my friend.'

'Sit down, my dear,' said Gwenllian, her eyes full of pity. 'Perhaps I should spare you the details.'

Catharine sat down alongside Henry and he took one of her hands. 'I think Catharine would prefer you to tell the whole story,' he said.

'Well,' said Gwenllian, 'this is what I was told.'

Henry squeezed Catharine's hand tighter and held her head softly to his chest as Gwenllian spoke.

'Old Lewis went to untether Hadrian the big Welsh Black bull to let him out of his pen and into the enclosure near the stables. As he reached over in the usual way with the hooked pole, he slipped on the mucky slabs and fell under the animal's body. Seconds later he was skewered on one of Hadrian's horns and lifted in the air. With a shake of the bull's head he was flung over the wall and onto the dung heap. The old man had died instantly, thank God.'

There was silence for a short while and then Catharine burst into tears and wails.

Little could be done to mollify her feelings; nevertheless, Gwenllian and Henry went out of their way to allow her to come to terms with the sad news.

After about a week of being fussed over by Gwenllian, and having the benefit of her exceptional cuisine, Catharine began to feel a lot better. Also sleeping in a real bed helped her regain her composure and the strength to once again face life on the open road where there were no such comforts.

Henry showed her many of the sights of London and she was impressed with the size and grandeur of St Paul's Cathedral. She liked other churches of various sizes and styles as well . . . but was never tempted to enter any of them. It was a long time since she had heard a sermon. She no longer wasted her time fretting over the Ten Commandments. She was a thief now and that was that. In any case she had total faith in Henry and was certain that he could find a moral argument to justify what they were doing. He was not only her lover, but also her mentor in all things that mattered. In other words – she was still totally in his thrall.

It was on the streets of London that Henry taught Catharine the finer skills of robbing directly from persons and on his own admission, after six months she had become as proficient as anyone he had ever known. She had firstly practiced the business of distraction over and over again and was not allowed by Henry to carry out a 'take' until he was satisfied she had reached the required level of skill. As important as anything else was the exercise, usually involving eavesdropping, that helped them select 'worthy' victims.

One of the best times Catharine would remember of their time in London was that Christmas of 1787. It snowed heavily two days before the festival and groups went around London at night under the light of flaming torches singing about the birth of Jesus and the presence at the event of asses, cattle, and lambs. They also sang of the star that guided wise kings to the manger where the event took place.

Although not altogether in the religious sense, it was an enjoyable time for Catharine and Henry who were protected from the cold by warm clothing they had removed from some unsuspecting party's ample wardrobe. It should be recorded too that several of the local poor were similarly well clothed against the pains of freezing weather due to the generosity of this skilful partnership.

It wasn't in Catharine's nature to be sentimental about life, but she could not resist revelling in these moments of seasonal joy. Using a roaring fire in a makeshift iron-framed brazier, an old man was roasting chestnuts and selling them in pewter bowls which were dutifully returned to him when the nuts had been consumed. Henry bought several helpings and fed the heavenly chestnuts to eager young waifs who had gathered.

Chapter Sixteen

Before Catharine and Henry left London they had seen the city at its beautiful best and at its awful worst. For over a year they went up and down the Thames on barges, skiffs, and dinghies. They had seen sailing ships of all sizes coming up river laden with untold quantities of exotic goods from far-flung places. They had seen a huge pouring of pathetic human cargo onto the streets of the world's largest city.

Away from the river they had watched parades of all kinds and observed ceremonies both of celebration and of mourning. They had experienced the relentless throb of humans going about their business in streets where there was hardly enough room for pedestrians to pass. A regular sight was of horse-buses disgorging shoppers who had come into town for the day and private coaches out of which fashionably dressed ladies were helped to the pavement by ornately attired flunkeys. For a thief, especially a selective one who targeted the mean, the cruel and the undeservedly rich, London was Heaven on earth.

It was now in the spring of 1788. The intrepid pair had discussed the possibility of giving up their way of life, heading back to Wales and settling down to bring up a family. They were not troubled in any way by matters of conscience. On the contrary, they felt that they had been performing a vital role in society.

Catharine could never be entirely sure that the lady who had been so kind to them was aware of what she and her accomplice actually did. However, there was a little hint that almost passed unnoticed in the middle of one discussion. Gwenllian, looking at Catharine said: 'The English have their Robin Hood . . . we have Henry James!'

They had returned regularly to sample Gwenllian's incomparable hospitality and there had been some memorable evenings at the lodging house. When other Welsh folk stayed there at the same time, it took little effort to persuade Gwenllian to bring out her harp. Henry would then give a recital or two on the strings before the night ended in a riot of songs, ballads and short choral pieces in which all present joined in, singing sometimes in up to six part harmony.

It wasn't until they had said their farewells for the last time that Catharine learned the full story of Gwenllian.

When living at *Tresimwn* (Bonvilstone), in the Vale of Glamorgan, Gwenllian James had been enjoying a lifestyle equal to that of minor gentry. Unlike the majority of her social class, however, her family spoke the native tongue almost exclusively and were consequently regarded as a little odd among the prosperous in the Vale community. Life was going well before her wealthy farmer husband Meurig, her son and her daughter all died after an outbreak of smallpox. Distraught, but full of courage and also rich, she decided to go to London to start a completely new life.

She bought the house in Camden Town and immediately made it known that all Welsh persons in London were welcome there. She didn't restrict bookings to people of Cambrian origin but it was mostly the Welsh who went there. Inevitably, the Cymric literati became regular visitors. Soon it was a well-known haven for troubled souls as well as those without a care.

Catharine was sorry to be leaving Gwenllian for she had come to like her in the same way as she had become fond of Madam Price at Parc. Whenever her thoughts drifted back to Llanilltern and Parc, Catharine felt a pang of nostalgia.

Nothing induced this feeling more strongly than hearing the cuckoo and she heard that herald once as they walked at Hampstead Heath. They had been away from home for two years. She did not entirely dismiss the possibility of going back home one day but as Old Lewis had gone, perhaps Madam Price too, for the time being she would put those ideas to the back of her mind.

Henry and Catharine did not find it easy to drag themselves away from the big city. Although they continued to make regular forays into the heavily congested districts, each one a pick-pocketing paradise, they also took jobs in the fish market and other places where work could be found to help them over the winter.

One of the pleasing things about getting away from the big metropolis would be a sense of freedom gained from being on the open road again. There were pleasanter smells and sounds to accompany journeys down country lanes; the skies above were broader and there was some relief too from leaving that clinging throng of human bodies. However, one problem which did not obtain so often in the city was a daily hazard in the countryside.

Mounted robbers known as 'highwaymen' had an aura about them resulting from what some would say was misplaced romanticism. These thieves had enjoyed for many years an heroic status and were admired for their courage and devil-may-care approach to their profession. People seemed to ignore the fact that they were ruthless, indiscriminate criminals who would kill if necessary to achieve their aims.

Henry had little time for these 'knights of the road', whom he described as 'ruffians without a scrap of morality'. To him, there was something dignified about the methods he and Catharine adopted to purloin another person's property. There was only one thing more important than the finesse involved: it was the belief that their own actions, seen against the whole spectrum of crime that defined eighteenth century society, were morally justifiable. Few would have agreed with Henry but there was no denying his sincerity.

When they were walking along country lanes Catharine liked nothing better than to be told stories from Henry's vast experience of life. By now, she felt she could differentiate between his truthful tales and tales which were fantasy. Henry was able to switch from serious comment to a light-hearted description to make a tale all the more poignant or hilarious as required. Catharine particularly enjoyed his recall of an incident when he was a member of a company of Dragoons.

Henry had been one of ten militiamen armed with swords and loaded muskets hiding themselves in a covered wagon that contained the pay for five hundred soldiers based at Bridgend. The vehicle was drawn by two horses which were lazily plodding along the Cowbridge turnpike. The dragoons felt the cart suddenly come to a halt. Their training told them they should not move until called by the officer who was sitting up front with the driver.

Henry continued the tale: 'After about five seconds of silence, a voice was heard coming from a spot a little ahead of the cart:'

'*"Sefwch!"* somebody squeaked. *"Eich arian neu eich einioes"* (Your money or your life!)

'"Have you quite finished, Twm?" said Captain Roberts, grinning. "Put that gun away before you hurt yourself." He could see that it was Twm Twpsyn a local simpleton who had done all this several times before.'

'Then, on the captain's command,' said Henry, 'we, the ten militiamen, hurtled ourselves out of the cart and surrounded poor Twm who was now all maniacal smiles.'

'So that was the end of that?' asked Catharine.

'Oh no,' said Henry, 'I took his gun from him and thinking it was all a sham I pulled the trigger.'

'And?'

'It blew a hole in the roof of a nearby house and set the thatch on fire!'

In the summer of 1789 they were striding towards Oxford where the pair expected there would be 'rich pickings' for skillful thieves. But there was to be a change in their activities. Satisfied that Catharine could learn no more about sleight of hand and distracting street victims, Henry decided to begin a course of instruction in what was regarded as one of the most heinous of crimes – that of burglary.

Catharine had no idea of the complex skills involved in breaking into a property undetected. It would not be easy to learn to become a burglar for there were few opportunities to have a 'dry run'. She would have to rely on Henry's expertise.

Whenever there was a suitable building, Henry showed the best ways of secreting oneself behind a door, or using light and shade as camouflage, also how to open locked windows and doors from the outside. More than anything, Henry insisted that she should understand the importance of being patient. He explained that it was sometimes necessary to wait hours before making the decisive move to enter premises. Equally, the dangers associated with the urge to vacate premises too quickly were drummed into Catharine. She was also taught various methods of stifling incriminating sounds by using cushions and pillows.

Before they embarked on their first serious action they changed their shoes for more suitable footwear. Then they made masks, hoods and other items to help them disguise their identity. Another aspect of successful burglary was the advisability of knowing what items were to be taken before entering. If this was not possible, the temptation to make decisions based on assumptions must *always* be avoided.

One more crucial element of a successful 'break and go' was to ensure that the choice of egress was not in any way ambiguous. Changing an escape route must be made only when it is certain that there is absolutely no alternative to doing so. 'Our motto must be,' said Henry, 'don't get caught!'

At Oxford, Catharine and Henry visited inns, taverns, coffee shops and other establishments, vainly looking for persons who might deserve closer attention from the pair. It came as a shock to them that almost everyone seemed to behave well and were friendly to a degree. A less astute person than Henry might have given up and moved on to places where the locals were not so conspicuously honourable as the good people of the city of dreamy spires. He knew, however, that this place would attract the dregs as well as the healthy froth of society so he waited for his chance.

Moving around tables in the smoking rooms of the taverns he eventually came upon a conversation that demanded further listening. Four men were extolling the virtues of the business-men of Bristol and elsewhere who were, they said, responsible for the wealth of the country. This, in itself, was not a fact that Henry would have disputed for he was fully aware of all aspects of the slave trade.

The most outspoken of the quartet had said he was shipping money to Bristol in two days. The bank wouldn't perform the transportation of such an amount of cash without more notice; therefore he was assigning the exercise to a trusted company who could demand a military escort. He had even been foolish enough to say that he had the sovereigns locked in an oaken box. Finding his address was easy work, for he was a well-known figure in Oxford society. Henry and Catharine planned the escapade right down to the last detail.

Firstly, they heard that he spent every evening at the Bulldog Tavern which is where they had encountered him. This meant that he would not be home the next night and they still had a day clear.

They stood in the shadows of other buildings for a while before moving closer to the distinctive home of the Honourable Denton Fitzhammon. They waited and waited. There was no sign of life inside although an oil lamp shone in the kitchen area. They tried a door but it was fast. Henry tapped each window in turn for often householders did leave catches unclipped in the mistaken theory that no one would ever burgle their property. That, they thought, was something that happened to *other* people.

The burglars were not so foolish as to assume that the total absence of sounds from the house meant that there was no one on the premises. They would have to enter by the quietest means. Such an exercise meant ensuring that plans could be changed at any time.

Earlier, Henry had seen a carpenter's shop close to the Fitzhammon home. He needed a wad of glue so had walked in casually on the pretext of wanting some work done and under the very nose of the foreman, taken a scoopful of glue out of a cooling pot.

Now, half an hour later, the glue was still not fully set but Henry knew he had to work fast for fishbone glue is notoriously predictable.

Catharine watched with admiration as Henry dabbed the lump of glue onto the end of a short stick and then placed it strategically on a pane in one of the windows. He waited for about a quarter of an hour and, satisfied that the glue would hold firm, he took from his pocket a diamond glass cutter which, having been filched from somewhere, had earned its keep over half a lifetime. With the stick now firmly attached to the pane, he drew and cut a circle of about nine inches diameter around it. Then, after giving the stick a gentle tug to remove the circle of glass from the surrounding pane, he was able to reach through the hole and unhitch the catch that had held the window shut. Within half a minute they were in the house.

Caution was now essential for they were in, as it were, enemy territory. In military terms they might now have to beat a retreat at the first opportunity – but only after the basic aim had been accomplished.

Henry often said, 'You make your own luck.' There, on a table, as if it had been placed for their personal benefit, was the oaken box. Fortunately it had rope handles at each end, which made it fairly easy to carry. Even so, Henry insisted on a long pause whilst they listened for sounds which might lead to something that could impede their departure – but nothing came.

They gave most of the sovereigns away to the needy the next day, retaining on their persons no more than was necessary to sustain them for a week or so. The pair were soon on their way westwards again.

A village called Witney was their next experience. Nice, friendly people who never once questioned the small bulges in their apparel. They did a minor break-in at the home of a Beadle who had terrorised the villagers for twenty-five years.

They then moved on to Cheltenham, a place that rivalled Bath for the grandeur of its buildings.

The pair found several unlocked premises from which it was easy to take small items that they sold at the first opportunity. Wandering around the busy market they announced what they were selling and there were always ready buyers.

From Cheltenham the pair went north to work the lower west Midlands and then came down country again to the

Bristol area. They cut eastwards once more before turning back once again towards the Welsh border. Over a period of weeks they criss-crossed the country and entered many premises.

They broke into the court of her Grace the Dowager Duchess of Beaufort and took sheets, aprons, and stockings which they sold in Bristol to different people. They stole items from a house near Gloucester and doubled back to off-load *them* also in Bristol. These included a watch that was deposited at Alman's, a pawnbroker in Thomas Street. At Knowle they took from a house a number of silver cutlery items and sold them for five shillings in Clifton. They had rather a bigger haul from a property at Little Sodbury, taking a silver knife, two table spoons, a gold signet, an old fashioned case of a watch with a death's head upon it, two blankets and a quilt.

The pair crossed the Severn at New Passage near Pining and after a few hours arrived in Monmouthsire where they started work at Pontypool. They stole a horse with cropped ears and rode it over to Usk where they were happy to sell the animal for pennies to gypsies encamped on the river bank. Before they left that district, they stole some property of a Major Brown who lodged at the house of an eminent surgeon, Mr Davis. Among the items taken were boots, buckles, a hat and a waistcoat.

The pair frequently heard gossip about the spate of robberies that had taken place but remained free from suspicion mainly because of Henry's ingenious planning. However, one day, upon hearing that law officers had been making enquiries that could seriously incriminate them they decided to return to the comparative safety of Gloucester.

Now, though, Gloucester would present a new challenge to them, for the town had lately formed a rearguard defence movement against the growing crime there, especially in the matter of breaking and entering. It was in this city one dark night that the redoubtable pair of pilferers came closest so far to being apprehended. In a moment of uncharacteristic care-lessness, Catharine had tripped over whilst hurrying away from a house out of which they had taken some china plates.

Henry, who had gone ahead carrying his share of the stolen crockery, heard the give-away noise from behind. China plates breaking into fragments when thrown down, however unintentionally, onto cobblestones, cause a sound that could raise the dead. Guard dogs suddenly awakened from sleep make an unpleasant sound too.

Catharine, with great agility, leaped a fence and ran for her life. Henry, who had wisely discarded his plates, was waiting for her, and linking arms, they walked slowly down the road while dogs, residents, and law officers raced by.

Catharine was full of apologies for her blunder but Henry uttered not a single word of reproach. They then took the safest action, which was to enter another house close by when all were out on the chase. They came out with some small trinkets.

Whilst they were still in the city of Gloucester the adventure of the intrepid pair took some unexpected turns. Their affection for each other had not lessened; if anything, it had strength-ened. There were, however, one or two trends in Catharine's recent behaviour that gave Henry cause for thought. It was essential that both of them worked at the highest rate of efficiency for the penalties for failure in their chosen business were extremely severe.

It wasn't that Catharine was losing any of her practical skills. Far from it; her sleight of hand was as good as ever, as was her understanding of all the conditions required for a successful burglary. It was simply that the vacant facial expression that Catharine sometimes adopted these days, however briefly, suggested that she was a changing person. From time to time Henry would say something to her and she would appear not to have heard him. She would seem to be in some sort of stupor and then she would suddenly snap out of it. He would now watch for further signs in case there was more to the problem than he had feared.

Henry felt he needed to talk to someone about Catharine's state of mind and help came from an unexpected quarter on the day they were leaving Gloucester. They were standing on a bridge just outside the town taking a last look at the waters of the Severn when they heard female voices from the river bank.

'Everyone a whore,' said Henry. 'You'll want nothing to do with them!' It was his turn to use the term *trwmpan,* and Catharine's mind was rocketed back a decade or more when she had first observed 'women of the street'. She had since seen them by the hundred in London, but today she thought of Cardiff Bridge and the story of the *trwmpan* who had been murdered and she suddenly felt sick again. Henry walked on with her and they had hardly crossed the river when a familiar voice from the distant past rang out into the Gloucestershire air.

'CATRIN!'

The owner of the loud voice was none other than Sarah Phillips who ran up and threw her arms around her old friend.

'This is Raglan Sal,' said Catharine, when she was able to break herself free.

'Pleased to meet you,' said Henry. 'Catharine has told me much about you,' he said, taking her hand and kissing the back of it. You are a whore, but I don't mind.'

'Well you are a thief, and I don't mind!' retorted Raglan Sal.

'I'm sure we'll get on well,' said Henry, 'but we are returning to Glamorgan. Why don't you come with us?'

Sal looked at Catharine obviously for approval and the nod she received was enough to send her off to say farewell to her companions.

'Are you happy about this?' asked Henry.

'Of course,' said Catharine, 'she is one of my favourite friends.'

Chapter Seventeen

The trio agreed they should take a circuitous route back to home territory for they were all tempted by what they heard was a new wave of prosperity that was washing over towns like Abergavenny, Usk and Monmouth. They would arrive at those places in due course, but first there was another place that they would regret not visiting if they didn't now take the opportunity. They were still near the Severn but it would not take long to reach the glorious Wye at Ross and then go on to beautiful Hereford.

Raglan Sal had willingly agreed that their surpluses should go to the needy wherever practicable but she placed one condition on her co-operation. It was simply that on no account would they go to the place after whom she was nicknamed. As far as she was concerned, despite Henry's description of it as a rural paradise, Raglan was the home of demons. For her part she said she would no longer pursue the profession that had been her livelihood for years. Henry made no comment but nodded sagely.

The trio now shared their duties in turn, that of look-out, hands-on purloiner and carrier. They successfully robbed three dwellings at Ross, as an exercise, just to keep their reactions sharp. Not needing to raise cash for a while, they left their loot just outside the front door of each of the houses they had robbed. The neighbours later discussed their bizarre common experience and decided it could not be rationally explained.

Catharine Griffith, Henry James and Sarah Phillips made an efficient team; so far, their ability to remain undetected had hardly been tested. Despite this, Henry was becoming increasingly aware of those changes in Catharine's demeanor. He had overheard her on more than one occasion talking to herself. Then there was that blank look which she now produced more frequently. There was no apparent reason for it. Sal had also noticed it and mentioned it to Henry. They agreed they would both watch out for further signs.

There was another thing. It could not be doubted that Catharine was beginning to take pleasure from stealing for its own sake which was something that Henry could never be rightly accused of. In Raglan Sal's case, she never tried to disguise the fact that she enjoyed pilfering other people's goods and had never moralised about it.

On they went to Hereford and began their activities there with an outrageous daylight raid at the home of a rich landowner. They took cutlery, pewter bowls, and rolls of cloth which they sold at a nearby market before the afternoon was out. They followed that with a similar exercise at the residence of a Justice of the Peace whose name they had heard mentioned complainingly at a tavern. This time they removed a copper kettle, a wooden bucket, two walking sticks and a wig.

Then it was Monmouth's turn to have the pleasure of their company. It took them about ten hours to walk the twenty miles from Hereford and they arrived in the hours of darkness. Opportunities for mischief came one after the other and so they started work immediately. Before dawn they had deprived one house of its lace curtains whilst in another, only a dull outline was left on a wall where an oil painting had hung for two generations.

After mostly sleeping rough throughout the warmer months, they thought they would base themselves in the friendly town of Abergavenny and see the coming winter through.

For a long period, Henry worked during the day at a flour mill on the outskirts of the town where his expertise was very much welcomed. Catharine and Sal toiled in a laundry. At night the trio went on the rampage. This was the pattern throughout the winter which, fortunately, was milder than usual. The spring of 1790 arrived and soon it would be time to plan their final return to south east Glamorgan which had always been their intention.

One morning just after dawn, as they were walking towards their respective places of employment, a cuckoo called from somewhere out of town. Henry and Sal were astonished to see Catharine suddenly open both her hands to show her ten fingers three times in quick succession. It wasn't that in itself which disturbed her friends: it was her staring face and her pathetic attempts, in the voice of a child, to mimic the bird. 'Cookoo! Cookoo! Cookoo!'

Henry James and Raglan Sal glanced at each other in a way that suggested a serious problem was developing which they would have to address before long. In fact though, a more urgent problem for the trio was developing as Fate was about to deliver its trump card.

The Kings Arms at Abergavenny was a substantial building and a gathering place for people from all levels of society, both those with criminal tendencies and upholders of the law. It was heaving when Henry and his two companions arrived. Farmers, tradesmen, and various artisans filled the bar, their loud and excited conversation suggesting there was much to be discussed.

Had they been aware of one of the subjects of this animated talk, the trio would have departed quicker than a hare in the line of a hunter's fire. If they hadn't been alerted by a sharp-eyed old friend who happened to be in the bar, they would have been rounded up and taken to Hereford Gaol before they could take another breath.

'*Harri ap Siôn!* It *is* you, Henry, is it not?' The words were murmured into Henry's ear by a man standing behind him.

Before he even turned around, Henry recognised the deep voice of *Wil y Porthmon* 'Wil Drover', who added: '*Paid â gweud dim!*' (Don't say anything). The two girls saw that he was showing them the flat of his hand in a gesture that could only have meant 'stay – don't advance.' He then took Henry aside and went on talking to him in whispers. Presently Henry was walking quickly past Catharine and Sal, saying as quietly as he could and still to be heard by the two girls above the din: 'Come out in two minutes and join me up the road.' Then, bending his head, he left the bar.

Once out on the road, he quickened his pace until he was a good two hundred yards away from the tavern. He hid behind a hedge until the two girls caught up with him and they had a quick meeting to plan their next move.

'What's happening?' Catharine was the first to speak.

'Yes, and who was that man?' added Raglan Sal.

'There's a pair of armed lawmen searching for me. They are going from tavern to tavern. When they were at the Kings Arms half an hour ago they told everyone to look out for a suspicious-looking man accompanied by two women. They have followed our trail since Gloucester. Fortunately, Will Drover, another old friend, realised who they were after. We must split now, we have no choice.'

'Don't leave us, please!' said Catharine, sharply. The sudden feeling she was losing the company of the man who had been her constant companion for six years was so overpowering she began to sob.

Henry held her close for a few seconds, and then, after emptying his pockets and handing them about ten coins each together with a small knife and the tinder box, he said: 'I am sure to be caught, but have no fear, I shall be back home at

July's very end. Think of the cuckoo. It won't be that bird's month but like him . . . I always come back!'

He waved and went.

In fact Henry's freedom came to an end less than half an hour after his parting from his female companions. He had heard the sound of galloping hooves from some way behind whilst he was walking through the village of Pontrilas on the Hereford road. He knew that he would be no match for two hardened Bow Street Runners who had probably first heard of him in London. They wouldn't have come all that way without the certainty of achieving his arrest. Even before they got near him, he turned to face them with his hands held high. The two officers, one in a blue great-coat, the other wearing grey, dismounted a yard or two from where he was standing.

'Yes,' said Henry.

'What do you mean "Yes"?' said the one in blue.

'"Yes", is the answer to your question,' said Henry

'We haven't asked a question, yet!' said the greycoat.

'But "yes" will be my answer when you ask it,' said Henry, thinking that every extra second would help the girls to get further away from trouble.

'Is your name Henry James?' said bluecoat, obviously losing patience.

'I've already answered that question,' said Henry, smiling.

'Alright, alright,' said greycoat, 'we are arresting you on suspicion of burglary and larceny.'

'What about pickpocketing?' said Henry. 'Surely you've got that on your list.'

The two muttered some words which Henry didn't quite hear except for 'magistrate' which, for him, had always had a certain unpleasant ring about it. 'Hereford Gaol' wasn't one of his favourite terms either and he heard them mention that at least once.

After Henry's hands were tied at the wrists he was made to mount greycoat's horse. The Runner got up behind and together with his blue-coated fellow officer who had already mounted, they made off in the direction of Hereford.

Catharine and Sal wandered Monmouthshire and south Herefordshire for months, stealing here and stealing there, whenever necessary. They heard not a whisper from Henry but were not worried about any personal danger he might be facing for they both considered him to be invincible. However, Catharine pined after the man who had been her mentor and her lover throughout the most exciting and enjoyable period of her life.

She liked Sal too, but nothing could replace Henry's ability to explain and find solutions for the complex questions that now arose, more frequently than ever, in her mind. She was getting more confused by the day and began to wonder why Sal kept looking at her in a strange way. 'Perhaps,' she said to herself one day, 'Sal is going mad.' She had no idea that her *own* grimacing, her staring and other idiosyncrasies, had for some time been of concern to her friend.

They survived a harsh winter by agreeing to work as living-in serving wenches at the Skirrid Inn, Llanfihangel Crucorney. Their pay was poor for working eighteen hours each day. However, their food and sleeping accommodation was provided and they would have been allowed to supplement their income by treating customers favourably. They didn't earn a penny that way for Sal kept to her word that she would never treat men favourably in that way again. Catharine still had eyes for only one man and she prayed nightly that he was well. Besides serving frothing ale they sang and danced and told stories about alleged hauntings at the Inn by victims of the notorious 'Hanging Judge Jefferies' who held court there at the end of the Monmouth Rebellion a hundred years previously. Neither Catharine nor Sal knew anything about the historical facts. They had both learned story-telling from the man who had the greatest facility for turning fiction into fact and they longed for him to be with them once more.

It was springtime again, and, one day, when Catharine was cleaning an upstairs room at the inn, she went to an open window and gazed at the Skirrid Mountain from which the place took its name. Just audible from the oak forest that flanked the lower slopes of the hill came the call of a cuckoo. A few seconds later a cuckoo clock heralded six o'clock from the bedroom wall. For a moment or two the sounds both natural and mechanical were simultaneous and Catharine wondered if this was some sort of omen.

By the time summer was back in business, so were the girls. They rampaged through the rural communities of the Black Mountains before working the town of Brecon. Then they went southwards to Merthyr, which they couldn't get out of quickly enough. They found that the grime, the smoke and the noise offended their sensibilities. Thus the pair of choosy robbers found themselves working their way to their ultimate destination: south east Glamorgan.

A great change in the thieves' approach was now taking place. It was happening gradually, but they no longer felt the need to ensure that the people they stole from were deserving victims. With Henry no longer there to debate the matter of moral justifiability, they fell into a habit of stealing from anyone, anytime. Raglan Sal was happily unscrupulous and Catharine had lost the mental ability to question why she now actually enjoyed stealing for its own sake.

At last they returned to Catharine's home patch. Little had changed outwardly at least. They walked down the valley of the Taff sometimes in the company of other vagrants, sometimes alongside endless donkey trains. As they approached the village of Portobello, Catharine pointed out the well of the Taff, recalling the day she had gone there with Henry. At that point she gave one of her crazy looks but Sal chose to ignore it.

They crossed the Taff river by means of the same rope and little boat that had sent Catharine and Henry on their eastward journey a while ago. The old woman who had made such a fuss of Henry on that occasion was nowhere to be seen. This time a lad hardly twelve years old pulled the rope and charged them a halfpenny.

Making their way around the Lesser Garth they found the path that would take them down to Trelai on the outskirts of Cardiff. They made the distance in under two hours, and on arrival found themselves drawn to the Dusty Forge Inn, for it was the first tavern they had visited together on that trip to Bristol fourteen years previously. The pair had changed appreciably from the last time they had entered its doors. They looked healthy with their smooth skin tanned by the sun and the wind. They were well-dressed and shod too, with money to spend. They bought a dandelion-and-burdock each and took their drinks to consume them outside.

In familiar surroundings once more their conversation inevitably brought out reminiscences. Sal's memory of the area went back no further than the time she arrived at Parc to work as a servant labourer. One of her friend's earliest recollections was losing her mother's grip and falling in the stream.

Now, more than ever, when Catharine spoke about her distant past she would frequently take on that child-like voice. This disconcerted Raglan Sal somewhat but as it didn't impede their progress in any way she put the problem out of her mind.

In any case, she convinced herself that the incomparable Henry James would soon be with them again and all would be well.

They worked Cardiff houses for a week or so and sometimes ventured into the Vale as well. They robbed residences in Wenvoe and St Andrews and also broke into Fonmon Castle before going down to Cowbridge and Llanblethian where they were cheeky enough to enter the Vicarage. They were stealing little but thoroughly enjoying the experience. They were always on the look-out for Henry, for they were sure he would be as good as his promise to be back before July's end.

Back at the Plymouth Arms in St Fagans, the regulars were in fine form. The ale was flowing and so were the insults.

'I hear that the traitor John Price is back home from France then,' said Gomer Thomas. 'Getting too hot for him now I should think. Won't be long before he starts drumming up trouble here. Pity he doesn't clear off to America. They'll take anybody over there!'

'Aye for sure, there's some other undesirables around here as well,' said Ben Treharne. 'That James fellow is out and about again they say. Those Bow Street Runners who were here yesterday seemed determined to get him. They said he was plundering the country.'

'I hear the Sheriff will pay twenty-five sovereigns for his head,' said Isaac Tŷ Du.

'He won't get caught,' said Dic Bassett, 'he's a clever devil and that's a fact.'

'What's he like?' asked a man with a curly black beard who walked over from the bar to join them with his glass of lemonade.

'Oh, in his thirties, they say, clean-shaven and a bit of a know-all,' said Richard Garnant, 'he's given the law a run-around for years. Can't miss him, we're told, because he'll most likely have two women attached to him.'

'Lucky fellow,' said the stranger, who put down his empty glass and bid those present farewell.

As the man left the bar, Gomer Thomas said: 'Who was that?' whilst reaching out his arm for a refill of his tankard.

'Never seen him before,' said Ben Treharne and the others also shook their heads.

Outside, Henry paused and stroked his black beard before smiling and walking away in the direction of *Llansantffraid ar Elai* – St Brides Super Ely.

Catharine and Raglan Sal racked their brains to think of the most likely place they would find Henry. They didn't doubt for a moment that he would have escaped from custody and would fulfill his promise to rejoin them. But where? . . . that was the question. They went over and over in their minds the last thing he had said and it was Catharine who recalled his exact words.

She smiled eerily and said:

'Think of the cuckoo!'

'What are you saying?'

'Think of the cuckoo!' repeated Catharine.

'But why think of the cuckoo?' said Sal, who felt now that her friend had really lost her mind.

'That's what he said and that's where he'll be – I'm sure of it?' said Catharine, her maniacal grin getting ever wider.

'Where for God's sake?' said Sal, in despair.

'Yn y fera wair i lawr yn y Gog.' (In the hayrick at the Cuckoo).

'You mean there's a farm here called "the Cuckoo"?' said Sal getting excited.

'Yes, in St Bride's, near the church,' said Catharine. 'It's not the real name but that's what they call it over there.'

No doubt, in excited anticipation of meeting up again with her man, Catharine began singing as they walked along the lane from St Fagans to St Bride's. It wasn't a song which Raglan Sal had ever heard – so sadly she couldn't join in. She was further disturbed to hear it being sung in that now familiar juvenile voice.

Chapter Eighteen

Since the Treaty of Paris, in 1783, there had been much less military presence in the area apart from occasional training exercises. By 1791, however, some nervousness had returned with regard to relations with France and once again men of the highly regarded Glamorgan Militia were mobilised together with units from established army regiments. They were billeted in Cardiff and gathered daily at the Castle. Whilst awaiting the call for embarkation abroad advantage was frequently taken of their availability by those responsible for law enforcement. Thus, it was not unusual for miscreants to be chased and arrested by both foot guards and cavalrymen.

Anthony Blythe-Smith, the Under-Sheriff for Cardiff, and officer Daniel Stephens, Cornet of the 16th Dragoons, were telling a gathering of the men in the castle grounds of a menace that needed to be put down once and for all.

'The man we are after has the cheek of old Nick and is as slippery as an eel,' said the Sheriff. 'He has been a wanted man for over fourteen years. He has escaped from custody seven times. He started off simply as a scourge of beadles but by now there isn't a magistrate, a Justice of the Peace or an assize judge who doesn't want him behind bars.'

'Permission to speak, Sir?' said a Dragoon sergeant, saluting.

'Speak,' said Cornet Stephens.

'Is this man a murderer, Sir?' asked the Sergeant.

'No, Sergeant, but he is no less dangerous for being a compulsive thief!' The Sheriff seemed taken aback by the question and was helped by the Dragoon cornet.

'Just bring him in and we'll deal with him,' said Stephens, adding, 'Oh, and we're told that he has two women with him. Bring them in as well.'

The last day of July was warm as Catharine and Raglan Sal went along the lane to St Brides from St Fagans. The air was still and so were the blades of the windmill that stood like a silent sentinel a field away. They paused from time to time to take wild strawberries that grew in profusion on grassy stretches of bank. The way in which some brambles were encroaching on the pathway suggested that it was a route hardly used currently. The fact that there was no evidence of anyone else having gone that way in the recent past brought a glum expression to Catharine's face. This pleased Sal because she was getting fed up with her friend's weird look.

Meanwhile, a hundred yards further on, lying on his back on a mound of hay, with a stalk of straw in his mouth and contemplating a cloudless blue sky, was a handsome black-bearded man looking every bit the countryman without a care in the world.

The reunion was blessed from above. Catharine and Henry embraced lovingly whilst Sal waited her turn to put her arms around him. It wasn't that she had the same feelings towards him as did Catharine, but she was sure she would soon need his help with regard to her friend's state of mind.

The girls brought Henry up to date with what they had been doing. They learned little from him about his arrest and incarceration. He simply said he had escaped using a combination of distraction, deception, bribery, power of mimicry, muscular strength and gift of the gab!

It was almost impossible for Sarah to get Henry on his own for long enough to be able to express her concerns about Catharine's mental condition. As it turned out she didn't need to do so, for Henry sat down with them on a grassy bank alongside the hayricks and said things she would not have had the nerve to utter. With conspicuous kindness he came out gently with what was by then an obvious truth about the woman he idolised. The thrust of his remarks was that they would have to end the lifestyle they had followed so diligently for so long; otherwise they would be quickly apprehended and parted forever.

Henry and Raglan Sal were anxious to have Catharine's reaction to this and at first they were not disappointed.

'Oh yes, said Catharine, 'I know my mind is not the same as it used to be and I'll do anything you say,' adding mysteriously: 'I'm so glad to be back where I belong.'

What she said next truly shocked her companions. Speaking once more in that child's voice she said she had been talking the previous day to her mother who had told her to do everything her friends should ask of her!

Henry and Sal exchanged despairing glances. The three talked until the sun went down and although Catharine was rational some of the time, suddenly there would be a relapse and she would speak utter nonsense. There was no doubt that for periods her mind was regressing to an earlier time in her life.

After they had gathered bracken for makeshift beds, they saw Catharine kneeling and praying. In itself this was not an unthinkable act; what unsettled them was that her devotions were delivered with that child's voice again.

Catharine was the first to fall asleep and it was an opportunity for Henry and Sarah to discuss what to do next. Talking in whispers, Henry made it clear he was aware of the finality of Catharine's illness.

'I love this woman with my whole being, and I shall be nothing without her.' If there had been light Sarah would have seen the tears on Henry's cheeks. He went on: 'I have destroyed her . . . now I shall look after her . . . and I know that means giving up the life I have enjoyed for many years. All this time I have also stolen for the sake of stealing . . . and I have always known in my heart that it is a sin and am now prepared to pay the price.'

Sarah was moved by Henry's obvious sincerity and she reached out and briefly touched his arm in a gesture of understanding. Then she turned over and went to sleep herself.

The regulars of every hostelry from Newport to Bridgend had heard of the chase. There was the usual exaggeration of the facts. They had come to believe that the wanted pair had ravaged the land from Scotland to Cornwall, plundering and looting all the way and even committing murder to satisfy Satanic desires. Not all, however, belonged to the vindictive fraternity; a few tried to make a case for a couple who were intrinsically good people but had succumbed to the pressures of an unfair and uncaring society.

The Plymouth Arms tankard brigade considered itself to be the main authority on the saga of the pair now being pursued so assiduously.

'Hey,' said Gomer Thomas, 'they tell me that pair from Parc shot two street-traders in London and ran off with three hundred sovereigns.'

'Oh aye,' said Ioan John, 'I heard as well that they skinned a vagrant on a country road just to take his rags!'

'If you ask me,' said Dic Garnant, 'I think they should be sent to Americee or Austrailee or that West Indee and made to work like slaves. If not, then just shoot 'em.'

'What's Catti Price got to say about it?' said Ben Treharne, 'They tell me she as good as brought up the wench.'

'And what about the fellow?' asked Dic Bassett, 'They say he's a bad 'un. Couldn't tell a truth if he tried.'

'I heard he could take your string purse from you, remove the coins and return the empty purse to your pocket without you knowing a thing about it!'

'And I'll tell you something else. I'll wager that John Price will come along and say that pair are innocent or something.'

At this point Dr Yorath ap Rhys entered the bar and said, 'I couldn't help overhearing your conversation and I must say that if you remove all the usual lies from this story, what's left is just a tale of petty thieves whose actions will have had not the slightest effect on society. Best ignored and forgotten about in my opinion.'

The milk of human kindness continued to flow from the majority who were quick to offer their solutions.

'Whip 'em!'

'Strangle 'em!'

'Transport 'em!'

'Shoot 'em!'

'Hang 'em!'

Raglan Sal awoke to the sounds of the night. A vixen was screeching her orders to her capering cubs who were being too noisy for their safety. There was, too, a repetitive 'crek – crek' from a corncrake that was obviously unaware of the proximity of humans. Sal looked at Henry who was snoring quietly and decided not to arouse him from what was clearly deep slumber. She then glanced to where Catharine should have been lying and was shocked to find she wasn't there. Now she had no choice but to awaken Henry, who, glancing at his watch, said it was approaching midnight.

They looked for tracks on the ground and any other evidence that would indicate the direction Catharine had taken. Henry closed his eyes and concentrated with all his considerable brain power on the question of where Catharine might have been heading. He summed up all the possibilities and after discarding most of the options that would have presented themselves to Catharine, he felt he knew where she might have gone.

In less than half an hour, they were at the gates of Llanilltern church. They crept furtively up to the church porch and as they slowly opened the door it creaked and scraped across the stone slab. The sounds did not in the least disturb Catharine, who was kneeling in a pew with her hands clasped firmly together. Light from the moon coming in through the eastern window isolated her in a dim glow.

They approached slowly and carefully sat near enough to hear the words of her prayer.

'*O Arglwydd,*' said Catharine, her eyes closed, but with a smile, '*Bendigedig yw Dy garedigrwydd Di*' (Blessed is Thy benevolence, O Lord) And then, with open eyes and looking upwards, she continued: '*Mi glywais lais yr Iesu'n gweud, "Tyrd ataf Fi" flinderus un*' (I heard the voice of Jesus say "Come to Me O weary one"). She continued, but not only did her prayer become confused, she also adopted that child-voice again.

Henry and Sal led her gently out of the church and into the moonlit night. Whilst her companions were now thoroughly disconsolate, Catharine was buoyant and bright. Such was her mood she might have danced had not her friends held her tightly as they walked away from the church.

Catharine's adult voice had returned and she was singing as they walked. After about a hundred yards she stopped and pointed to some rising ground, saying, 'I know that place. I know it well. May we go there?'

Her friends knew exactly where they were for they were equally familiar with Parc. Not sensing any immediate danger they agreed to take her, and soon they were walking up the long drive.

'Do you know of this place?' asked Catharine.

'Yes,' said Sal.

'Yes,' said Henry, adding, 'Why do you want to come here?'

'To see my friends of course.'

'And who would they be pray?'

'Well, Mr Price and Madam Price, Gwladys Harris the cook; Old Lewis as well – unless he's been sent on some errand.'

Henry shook his head before glancing quickly at Sal who also was aware that of the four named, three were known to be dead. Turning to Catharine, he said, 'Why do you want to see them?'

'I want to tell them about what I've been doing since I left.' Her remark brought a shudder from Raglan Sal who momentarily considered running into the trees. Henry, on the other hand, simply cupped Catharine's face in his hands and kissed her gently on her forehead.

Turning to Sal, he said: 'Are we all in this together or not?'

'Of course we are,' said Sal. 'I'm just realising the hopelessness of our plight, that's all.' Then the three walked up to the front of the house.

There were sounds coming from the stables but there seemed to be no-one in the environs of the house itself.

Henry pulled the handle of the door-knocker rod and the iron hammer hit the plate with a series of cracks, producing sounds that echoed around the yard. There was no response. If there was anyone at home they were heavy sleepers.

The windows were closed but not fastened. Before anyone could question the advisability of the move, Catharine, whose cognitive state was such that she acted with no self-awareness, opened a window and climbed in. She was followed by Sal but Henry stayed outside. After some initial difficulty the women opened a door from the inside. Henry still declined the offer to enter the house but agreed to share some drink and cakes which were passed to him through the window.

Catharine was now clearly acting without serious conscious thought. She picked up some pieces of silver cutlery and handed them to Raglan Sal who immediately tucked them into her apron. The two women then went out to rejoin Henry who, by now, was in a state of excitement.

'There's someone coming!' he said, sharply. 'I've heard voices!'

Raglan Sal looked alarmed. Catharine looked pleased.

'Move quickly!' he added, 'We must go in different directions!'

Sal was still carrying the silver as she sped away but she discarded it before she reached the other side of the big field near the lane to Pencoed House, a quarter of a mile from Parc. Henry and Catharine had taken a slightly different route and were now heading towards St Brides.

Catharine was by no means sure about why she was running but felt it had something to do with her recent visit to see her old friends at Parc. She felt it was a pity that there was no one home to greet her, for it had been so long since she had seen Madam Price, Old Lewis and the others.

Six cavalrymen armed with muskets, pistols, and swords were now milling about the yard at Parc, annoyed by the fact that their prey had got away. Eventually they went off in three different directions. They caught up with Raglan Sal within minutes. When caught she thought she recognised the Dragoon who arrested her from some previous liaison on Cardiff Bridge – but said nothing. Her concern now was firstly for her friend Catharine, but also for Henry, for she truly liked him. The dragoons were closing on her friends who were now running down a woodland pathway which was getting too narrow for the passage of horses. The runaways gained about a hundred yards advantage as the mounted soldiers declined to take their mounts into the thick undergrowth.

It was a short-lived gain however, for there were foot soldiers approaching from their left flank. Catching sight of them, the pair turned towards the right. As they went by, one of the soldiers fired his gun in their general direction and Henry fell to the ground. The musket ball had hit him in his left shoulder but failed to lodge itself. He felt himself losing consciousness but not before he had placed his hand on the wound. As he removed his hand he saw that it was covered in blood and holding some flesh that was torn away from his body. Before he passed out, he murmured, *'Dos Catrin, dos!'* 'Go, Catharine, Go!'

Catharine however, was kneeling over him when the soldiers arrived with ropes. She was crying and laughing alternately as the men securely tied the hands of her still unconscious friend. Then, suddenly, she was gone. With three soldiers in hot pursuit she went like the wind. She sped down St y Nill Lane with the sound of hoofbeats and shouting in her ears. She wondered where the riders were going and even considered stepping into the hedgebank to let them pass. Overcome by a mixture of misunderstanding and abject fear she simply acted upon Henry's words: 'Go! Go!'

She arrived at the bank of a brook and her confused state of mind was not helped in the least by what she experienced next. Even though the stepping-stones looked inviting enough, she felt some apprehension about crossing the stream. It was only when she heard the sound of galloping hooves again that she decided to take the first step. She was hardly half way across the rivulet when she slipped and fell up to her shoulders in the water. Never having bathed – clothed or unclothed – her bodily feelings were unfamiliar at that moment, but her mental processes were in even more serious turmoil.

She rolled about in the water, her now heavy waterlogged clothes hindering her attempts to get back onto the stone slabs.

She was till floundering when she saw a hand reach down to her and an image came flashing back of the time she lost grip of her mother's hand all those years ago. With delight she cried, *'Mam annwyl!'* 'Dear mother!' She took hold of the helping hand and with a heave, pulled herself onto one of the flat stones. It was only when she recovered her balance and stood upon the slab that she saw what was attached to the hand. It was not her mother with smiling face and loving words. It was a handsome man with a sword at his side. He carefully helped her over the stepping-stones, and when they reached the safety of the bank, he spoke gently to her.

'Surely you know who I am,' said John Price. 'You are Catharine and I know about you going away with Henry James. Where is he?'

Catharine's response was an unearthly smile. She was obviously very cold from her dip in the stream so John started rubbing her hands to bring warmth back to them.

'Thank you, sir,' she said, in the voice and style of a young child. 'But I shall be alright.'

John Price, shocked by her infantile tones, said simply, 'I will not trouble you with more questions except where do you wish to go from here?' Hearing approaching horses, he glanced behind him, suddenly feeling that the situation was more serious than he had first thought.

The three horses crossed the water a little way upstream and as they joined Catharine and John Price their riders dismounted.

'I am Philip Jenkins, Cornet 16th Dragoons. What are you doing here at this time of night, sir?' said the first soldier, pointing at John Price with his crop.

'It makes no matter why I am here, Cornet, but in fact I was on an errand for my mother who is currently staying with my wife and myself at our new home at Llandaff Court. I came to collect her snuff-box which she had left up at Parc.'

The soldier ignored what John said and turned his attention to Catharine. 'You, woman, are under arrest for burglary, larceny and petty theft. Hold your hands out so Sergeant Baines here can lash you to his horse.

John Price moved forward but the third soldier stopped him by poking his pistol into his chest. A few minutes later John witnessed the pitiful sight of the mounted soldiers going away while Catharine, with hands tied at the wrists, stumbled along with them.

Raglan Sal was already in a cart destined for Cardiff Gaol. As soon as Catharine was thrown in alongside her, the wheels turned and they were on their way. The guard who sat with the two women tormented them all the way to Cardiff with crude comments about their gender, also about the punishments they were likely to get which ranged from having their bare backs whipped to the ultimate penalty. Raglan Sal occasionally retorted with equally crude comments which resulted in hard knocks across the head from the soldier. Throughout the journey Catharine gazed at the sky with a faint smile, quite oblivious to the hurtful banter exchanged by her friend and the travelling sentry.

Meanwhile, Henry had fully recovered his senses but was in considerable pain as the soldier guarding him, at risk of reprimand from his seniors, was helping to staunch the bleeding with dock leaves. Eventually they moved him to the main track where a cart was waiting to take him away. Despite his agony, most of Henry's thoughts drifted towards Catharine and he offered a silent prayer to the Almighty to save her any of the undue hurt that the authorities were noted for inflicting on captives awaiting trial. He had been through it all before and knew what was coming.

Chapter Nineteen

John Price lost no time in telling his mother what was happening to Catharine Griffith. Madam Price was appalled by his description of the rough way she had been handled, but even moreso upon hearing of her deranged mind. She knew that Catharine had returned with Henry James from their tour of the country. She wasn't sure yet what to make of the report that they were caught after a felonious visit to Parc. She would think about that later. Her first priority was to ensure that the authorities, with which she was becoming less and less enamoured, must be prevented from inflicting unnecessary suffering on the prisoners.

Madam Price called for Siôn Bowen and soon he was driving her in the trap towards central Cardiff and its dreaded prison in the street of St Mary. On arrival, whilst Siôn looked after the pony and trap, she strode into the office in the outer wall of the prison and demanded to see the gaoler.

Thomas Morgan, the Gaol Governor, knew Madam Price mainly because her late husband had been such a prominent Justice of the Peace and that she owned Parc, which was still a local landmark in matters legal. She made her wishes known to Morgan and was soon taken on a walk through the centre of the women's section of the prison where a series of iron-barred structures contained pathetic examples of the species.

As she strode past, hands and arms were being waved at her through the bars, and faces disfigured by pain and fear stared at her out of the gloom. These images were accompanied by an incessant and wholly appropriate hum of human voices in torment, much like the howling of foxhounds before feeding time.

They came to a cell that had a single occupant: Catharine Griffith. There was a metallic jangling of big keys as a barred gate was opened and Madam Price was let into the little room. She found Catharine sitting on a stool in the corner. Her head was shaven to the scalp; her face and hands were grubby as indeed were her ragged clothes. It was well-known that gaolers earned a sizeable amount by depriving incoming prisoners of their clothes which they then sold on to willing buyers. The victim would then be provided with torn and dirty rags in their stead.

Catharine was wearing her fixed smile and looking at the ceiling when Madam Price arrived.

'Do you know who I am?' said Madam Price.

'Yes, I do,' said Catharine, making eye contact with her visitor for the first time. You are Madam Price who was so kind to me.'

The gaoler said sharply. 'You must speak English here! Turn to English this moment!'

He said no more as Madam Price gave him one of her disdainful looks and went on speaking in Welsh.

'What may I do for you?' she said, moving closer to Catharine. 'I so want to help you.'

'I believe my man is somewhere in this place. Please be sure they are gentle with him for it is my fault that we are here. I have been an evil influence on my Henry, my wonderful Henry.'

She broke down sobbing at that point. Madam Price was momentarily thrown by this for it was contrary to what she had considered to be Catharine's relationship with the man who had taken her away. It did not take long for the perceptive

Madam Price to realise that what her son had told her of Catharine's mental state was true. When not actually conversing, Catharine was staring at the ceiling and wearing the eerie grin often associated with those of troubled mind. When she did speak, she frequently reverted to the tones of a ten-year-old.

Madam Price turned to the gaoler, and said: 'We'll be back. But I shall see the authorities first.'

She gave a shudder as she left the cell, for she had been devastated to see her friend's transformation. Whilst she determined to provide Catharine with all possible moral support she felt disinclined to offer either Henry James or Sarah Phillips any assistance.

The three 'desperadoes', as they were described in a news-sheet, were subjected to all the usual indignities whilst awaiting trial. Raglan Sal too had her hair shaved off, whilst Henry had been given two black eyes; also a limp from being beaten repeatedly on the shin with an iron bar. They were kept apart whilst investigators took from them their versions of their escapades. For a week they were in single cells and a scribe on behalf of the legal authority went to each of them in turn to take down their stories.

For many miles around their notoriety earned them celebrity status, but when news of their capture had reached Caerphilly it had fallen with surprising results upon the ears of Henry's sister, Susannah James. Her reaction was cool and unemotional. She simply shrugged and considered the event to be just another highlight in the career of a brother who had chosen a vagabond's lifestyle. She had no doubt that Henry would soon be free again.

Tales of the exploits of the trio and particularly those of Henry James and Catharine Griffith were colourfully embellished by people who had nothing better to do. The know-alls continued to add incidents that could not possibly have happened and to suggest appropriate punishments. Most of these bar-room barristers simply exposed their prejudices by arguing aggressively. In truth, their knowledge of the outside world hardly went beyond the price of turnips.

There were exceptions though, such as Dr Yorath ap Rhys. He had several times tried to explain some of the new theories that were coming from the continent about such things as compulsive stealing.

'No doubt about it,' he said, 'it's an illness. They will put a medical name to it one day but as yet they don't know what to call it.'

'I'll tell you what *I* call it,' said Ioan John. 'It's an offence against the Ten Commandments. That's what it is!' Hearing noises of agreement from all around he went on: 'And that means offending God!'

'Very true, very true,' said Dic Bassett. 'Thou shalt not steal!'

The prison system towards the end of the 18th century was in need of reform. It had degenerated into almost a free-for-all where money could buy favours for the internees and achieve in some cases a high degree of mitigation. Almost anything was possible up to the day a prisoner had to appear at the Assize Court. The problem in this particular case was its very celebrity which had made the affair the talk of the county and beyond. It split opinion in society with regard to what penalties should be imposed. Although a large majority felt their punishment should be as severe as possible, there was also a sizeable number that favoured leniency.

Penalties for stealing were hardly ever based on the value of goods taken; there was a lack of consistency due to vested interests, personal vendettas and the whims of judges.

Cardiff's recent record of what were considered to be corrective punishments would have made the Devil blush. Minor offences led to almost permanent occupancy of the stocks at the Guild Hall and the pillory. The whipping post was always busy and attracted many spectators. Frequently there were examples of punishment that were mind-reeling. Ann Harris, a Cardiff girl, for the theft of four shillings, was whipped on her bare back from the County Gaol in St Mary Street to the West Gate and back. Two colliers were whipped along the same course for stealing two bottles worth sixpence. In the gaol, manacles, iron foot-shackles and thumb screws were still in use. The gallows at Cardiff gaol had been busy for centuries and was known as 'The Drop'. For twenty years until 1788 the Great Sessions were held in Cowbridge because of the unsatisfactory conditions of the courts and penal centres in Cardiff.

During this time hangings were carried out on the gallows at Stalling Down. By now, though, trials and executions were held in Cardiff once more. To make the stout gibbet erected at Waun Ddyfal (Little Heath), timber was taken from the Great Oak of Canton which had been uprooted when the turnpike to Cowbridge was built.

Madam Price felt it wise to seek the counsel of her friend Dr Yorath ap Rhys before deciding what to do about Catharine's plight. He repeated to her what he had told the unresponsive group at the Plymouth Arms and she was pleased that she could now disassociate Catharine in her mind from the world of 'common' thieves. Her former maid obviously belonged to a tiny minority who stole small items compulsively. Just one thing didn't seem to ring true until the doctor explained the reason for it.

'Iorri,' she said, 'I was told that Catharine had lost her mind completely, but when I visited her in the gaol she not only knew me but she also eloquently defended Henry James. She was very anxious to take the blame for what had happened.

There is no doubt that *she* is now the stronger of this puzzling pair'.

'Ah, yes,' said the doctor, 'according to the papers I have read on the illness, sufferers in the advanced stages go through personality changes. When they speak they can move suddenly from relative oblivion to perfectly rational recall of people and events. From darkness to light if you wish. The good news is that both she and her man have found God again.'

The doctor's remarks set Madam Price thinking and she kept repeating to herself as the days went on: 'Darkness to Light. Indeed, Darkness to Light.'

She would have to wait a while before seeing Catharine again for there was the matter of the trial of the three at the Cardiff Assize Court. Although the hearings were delayed the Great Sessions at last were just days away.

Usually at trials of cases which had aroused much public interest the business would be over fairly quickly. Minds were made up before a criminal entered the dock. Strangely in this case although opinion was overwhelmingly in favour of severe punishment there was no desire to reach a quick conclusion. Bizarrely, both the public and the law officers seemed to want a prolongation of the case to draw from it every last ounce of scandal and raw vindictiveness.

The reason for the case being so newsworthy wasn't immediately clear; after all, there had been countless trials of much higher profile offenders in dock for more serious crimes. It might have been the fact that cumulatively the haul of these thieves was enormous, purloined over a long period of time. Furthermore there was a romantic element to the tale. A handsome rogue, a lovely wench and a 'woman of the night' travelling the country and evading capture for so long made a good basis for an adventure story. The added factor of a local connection with their final act, however misunderstood, taking place where justices met, made the saga an irresistible one.

Raglan Sal was first to appear before the court and she put up a spirited argument claiming she had been performing an important service for others throughout her professional life and accordingly pleaded for leniency. She also asked for clemency for her two friends. Sal said that during her eventful life she had had the misfortune to meet many from the dregs of society and was therefore qualified to identify the difference between good and bad people. Her two colleagues were not simply good persons, they were the finest human beings she had ever known. Judge Hardinge waved her out of the court saying, 'Woman, don't waste my time.'

Catharine was brought into the dock wearing that celestial smile again. When the judge asked her if she had anything to say, her answer was, *'Duw, Cariad yw.'* (God is Love).

'Silence, woman!' said the judge. 'You must not offend this court of the Crown!'

Justice Hardinge's angry reaction was not because she chose to quote a verse from the Bible. It was because she did so in Welsh.

'Do you understand English,' he continued.

'Yes,' said Catharine.

'Where did you learn it?'

'At Plas Tyllgoed.'

'English, damn it woman.' said the judge. 'Don't you know the difference? And do you know the difference between right and wrong?'

'Yes.'

'Where did you learn that?'

'At Plas Tyllgoed.'

The judge was now very irritated and said that if the defendant could not enlarge on any of the points being discussed there was no point in continuing.

'Do you accept that you stole items which were the property of others.'

'Yes, small things.'

'Why did you do it?' said the judge.

'I couldn't stop myself,' said Catharine in a matter-of-fact way.

'Were you forced into stealing by another defendant, namely Henry James?'

'No, it was my evil influence that made *him* steal things. He did it for me and if I hadn't been there he wouldn't have done it.'

'Take her away, before I lose my temper,' said the judge. Catharine was duly escorted out of the chamber. She was heard repeating what had become her favourite phrase: *'Duw, Cariad yw.'*

Then it was the turn of Henry James. He stood in the dock physically unrecognisable from his former self. His head hairless, his chin beardless, he seemed emasculated. However, there was nothing feeble about him once he started to speak. He asked the judge if he may make a statement. Hardinge, at once taken with Henry's articulateness and intrigued by what was an unprecedented request, said, 'Very well, man, carry on.'

Henry took a deep breath and launched himself into a passionate condemnation of the justice system.

'I put it to you, sirs, that the so-called crimes of my female colleagues are so trivial you offend the dignity of the legal system by bringing them to trial at all. Do what you will with me, sirs, but think about the gross injustice you are bringing to bear upon two young women possessed of natural kindness. If there are mathematicians among you, think of this unbalanced equation. On one side see the good they have done; on the other see the bad that is being done to *them* and you have nothing less than an abysmal injustice. You might carry on and repeat like talking parrots what you regard as justifiable charges against them. But when did you last question your *own* behaviour? When did you last dispense goodness of any kind? Who are you indeed to hide behind the good book shouting to the world the eighth commandment? Thou shalt not steal! . . . Thou shalt not steal! Well what is stealing? Is taking some trifle so small its absence will never be noticed to be compared with theft of land or the distraint of chattels to which the incurably blind eyes of the gentry are invariably turned? You cannot see that your own wealth comes from theft on a grand scale: the wholesale theft of human flesh. Is the removal of an African from his family not theft? You might understand if you had ever been stolen yourselves, personally. If you had ever been taken by a press gang . . . that is, if you had ever been stolen by the biggest thief of all – the state. If you believe in justice, sirs, let these women go free. If you believe in love for your fellow beings – neighbours or otherwise, sirs, let these women go free. If you believe in the greatest virtue of all, mercy, let these women go free. I admit sirs that I am personally no longer a churchman but I ask you in the name of the greatest authority of all . . . sirs, if you believe in Jesus, let these women go free.'

Judge Hardinge said loudly, 'Take him away from here!'

The next day magistrates, justices of peace, together with the Constable and the Sheriff, met Judge Hardinge to hear his decision with regard to punishment.

He duly announced that the three were to be hanged by the neck until they were dead.

Due to a quirk of quasi-religious court procedure it would be a while before the executions could be carried out. Unequivocal confessions had be obtained from those whose life on earth was about to come to an end. This was not only to satisfy temporal considerations such as confirmation of guilt, but also to cleanse the souls of those about to depart for the next world.

In the event, Raglan Sal's capital sentence was commuted to transportation to New South Wales on the ship *Royal Admiral*. When this unexpected development was reported to Catharine and Henry, they both rejoiced.

Madam Price and her son, John, were allowed to make private visits to the prison over the ensuing week, thus avoiding the 'spectacle for ghouls'. They managed to spend some time with the two prisoners who were allowed to be together for periods. Madam Price felt moved by the obvious bond that existed between Catharine Griffith and Henry James. She wondered what her late husband would have made of it all. John was fascinated by Henry's philosophy and was astonished to find that they were in agreement on many matters. He did not accept that common thievery could be morally acceptable but was, nonetheless, impressed with Henry's claim that several aspects of respectable business were serious forms of stealing.

Catharine's request to have a clergyman come to see her was granted. The Rev. Garmon Rees of Llanilltern and Rhys Rowland of Taihirion both volunteered to visit but the prison authorities insisted on the Vicar of Cardiff the Rev. Molyneux Lowder being the sole cleric to attend. The attention he gave both prisoners was exemplary and reports of his visits have survived in the records:

> *'For the first fortnight I visited them twice a day, and they seemed to pray with fervency, but I could plainly perceive that there was something upon their spirits which must be made known before they could be brought to that temper of mind which would enable them to die in peace.*
>
> *Catharine looked upon Henry with the most tender fondness, but without the least measure of levity. She would weep over him and declare that she was more anxious on his account than on her own, for she was the cause of his ruin.*

*On 25 September the High Sheriff informed me of Sarah
Phillips' reprieve and I acquainted her fellow criminals with
it also . . . they showed not the least dissatisfaction at their
not receiving the same favour.'*

Catharine's confession was read to her on 5th October in the
presence of two witnesses, P. Jenkins, Cornet 16th Dragoons,
and William Stone. She affixed her mark *x* of acceptance.

It appeared that whilst the couple had confessed to most of
the thefts and burglaries, it was felt there must be more, so the
vicar persisted with his spiritual healing. Not in the least put off
by Catharine's frequent reversion to her childhood voice, the
Vicar kept tenaciously to drawing from her every detail she
could recall from her adventure.

*'Upon remonstrating with Catharine on the utter impos-
sibility of her being happy if she went out of the world with
a lie in her mouth, she burst into tears and assured me she
would not affect any concealment, but without reserve honestly
confess every crime she could remember committing; and she
did this with such apparent contrition and real sorrow, that
she left me in no doubt of her sincerity. From this day to
their final separation there was peace between them. Visible
in Catharine's countenance was a composure and a serenity
that proceeded from her eased mind . . . she said she trusted
in the merits of her Saviour now she had truly repented of
her former transgressions. . . . She had requested me to
procure a shroud, as she wished to wear it to the place of
execution. She said she hoped it would be the happiest suit
she had ever put on . . . she gave instructions for some small
alterations in it, with such a coolness and composure as
astonished everyone . . . there was a further request that a
woman then in gaol might attend at the gallows to put their
bodies in the coffins.'*

'On the morning of their execution I attended them early, and found them very composed, and they were remarkably devout during the whole of the service . . . Catharine said that the bitterness of death with her was passed; that a few hours, she trusted, would bring her to perfect happiness . . . Henry too said he hoped God's mercy would extend to him, that, though he had been a vile sinner, God's goodness knew no bounds.

'I returned to them after ten, and prayed with them for about half an hour. The Under-Sheriff came in and, with much tenderness told them he would wait their time. He then asked if their confessions could be depended upon . . . and on their solemnly assuring him that they had confessed everything to me, he left them. I also left so that they may dress themselves for their last journey, but before I went Catharine requested that they might have water to wash their feet, as they did not choose to go with unclean hands or feet into the presence of their God.

'Between eleven and twelve the Under-Sheriff was informed that they were ready . . . Catharine seemed to enter the cart with pleasure, immediately addressing the thronging multitude, and continuing either addressing them, praying, or singing, as they left the County Gaol. Henry said nothing at first but joined in fervently when she prayed or sang.'

A scribe who had been passing through Cardiff stood some distance from the gallows and recorded the scene for the readership of the *London Gazette*.

Angry curses from a furious mob greet the cart as it trundles towards the square. I hear the wagon's timbers creak as it slowly approaches. A cluster of sparks fly from its iron-rimmed wheels as it jolts along the last few yards of its journey.

The crossroads has always been a busy place with vociferous drunks being hurled out of the Queen Anne Arms onto the cobblestones where noisy quoits teams often battle for supremacy and even noisier street vendors call for attention. Occasionally there would be a bare-knuckle fight here between the Cardiff champion and a challenger from the valleys, with the crowd cheering on their favourites to bloody victory. But today there is more clamour than ever. Bewildered chickens are running for their lives and cats are slinking away to the safety of the back lanes. The raucous barking of dogs is competing with the unnerving wails of womenfolk. These sounds are tumultuous now as children skip and scamper before being hoisted onto shoulders, the better to observe the public show for which all present seem impatient. The gibbet which has drawn this uproarious multitude stands silhouetted against a sky now full of gathering clouds. The story of this pair of adventurers who are about to meet their Maker has inspired the imagination of a kingdom. Throughout the land opinion is divided as to the appropriateness of the chosen retribution but those who have gathered here will surely savour the victims' moment of departure – they always do so. The noise subsides and I hear a lone bell tolling from some distant church as a fiddler who has slowly ascended the gallows steps begins to play a woeful lament.

The vehicle finally arrives, its passengers – the young woman and her male associate – sit with their heads bowed. The cleric who has accompanied them is holding a black bible close to his bosom and his eyes are fixed firmly on the heavens above.

The Rev. Lowder continues:

'I was in the cart with them about half an hour, and after their joining me with such devotion in prayer, I asked them if they wished to say anything. Henry said nothing but to acknowledge the justness of his sentence, and to request the

249

*prayers of the surrounding multitude . . . Catharine's reply
was: "I die justly and, I hope, in God." I then took my leave,
so that I can say nothing further of my personal knowledge;
but from the officers attending I learn that she maintained
the same resolution and humble confidence to the end. A
prayer was said in Welsh then she and Henry were tied up –
herself assisting in the placing of the rope, and desiring
in particular that the string around her arms might be
tightened, that she might die the easier. Catharine then sang
a Welsh lament that she had composed for the occasion. She
asked Henry if he felt himself comfortable . . . "Have
confidence," says she, "I know we shall be happy."'*

*'They then joined hands and were presently launched
into eternity . . . and may it be to them a happy eternity.'*

**Paid for bread and wine for administering
the Sacrament to Henry James and
Catharine Griffith, who were executed
7th October, 1791:**   **2s. 4d**

**To cash paid for ropes and other requisites
for the execution of Henry James
and Catharine Griffith**   **15s.0d**

To ditto paid the executioner: **£1.1s.0d**

Total: One pound eighteen shillings and four pence

Amen

*   *   *

Also by the same author . . .

THE
KISSING GATE

Don Llewellyn

£7.99